ANNA & THE AMERICAN PUZZLE

Anna & The American Puzzle

JENNIFER KASMAN

Jennifer Kasman

Library of Congress Control Number: 2020921699
Library of Congress Cataloging-in-Publication Data

Kasman, Jennifer

      Anna & The American Puzzle

      ISBN 978-1-7360600-0-1 (Hardcover)
      ISBN 978-1-7360600-1-8 (Paperback)
      ISBN 978-1-7360600-2-5 (Electronic)

To my sons,

Thank you for showing me the greatest love I have ever
known, changing me on a cellular level and providing me
with purpose greater than I could have ever imagined. I
owe every good thing I may ever be to both of you.

S,

My life has been, and is, full of love because you have
been in every chapter. I love you so much. Thanks for
believing in me.

I recognize that there are divergent views on the use of content warnings. Without expressing an opinion on content warnings, generally, I want to offer one in the event it is helpful to any readers. This book includes content related to sexual assault, identity-based discrimination, and harassment. I encourage you to care for your safety and well-being.

Prologue

At the point I was at, meditating was not an option. It was the way I had to start each day. As a result, I began each summer morning the same way, seated in the soft grass behind my house surrounded by the blue and purple hydrangeas planted around its perimeter, so many of the flowers that they looked like a fuzzy coat draped around my yard. This morning was no different. After spending a few moments allowing my hips to sink into the dewy blades, I slowly closed my eyes and inhaled for breath with my belly as if I was accepting fresh air for the first time. As I started to drift away I noticed, as I often did, how the leaves on the trees around me sounded as they rustled, swaying both together and against each other in the breeze. The wind tickled the tiny hairs on my arms that were still baby soft, as if they had stopped aging while the rest of my body continued its journey through time.

I lost track of time, as I always did, but after a while longer sitting there on this particular day, behind a house I could have never dreamed of calling home during my early life, I re-entered the present with a few slow blinks of my eyes until they were fully open, ready to get moving and seize the day. I walked around to the front of my house, hopped on a bike and rode toward the water's edge. A few of them quickly jumped on the bikes they kept in front of my garage door, pedaling right behind me and chasing my pace, as they did each time I jumped on my bike. I relaxed further with the sight of open road in front of me and pedaled fast towards the horizon, like I had done so many times before, pedaling faster and faster and increasing the resistance until I felt out of breath as I rode.

A little over twenty minutes later, sweaty and out of breath, I reached the wooden fence separating the parking lot from the beach, the same beach I had first visited as a young girl a very long time ago before a series of events and people changed my path forever. I felt the hot pavement through the soles of my thin white Keds as I put a foot down on each side of the bike, propping the bike up in between my legs with my hands still in riding position on the handlebar. I fixed my gaze on the horizon while watching the sun make the top of the water sparkle like flashbulbs from a thousand cameras. I wondered, as I often did, how many of the few people taking in the beach right after sunrise were on "the other side of things" like I was. I caught the glimpse of a stranger as he walked up the path across the sand to leave the beach, an older man with weathered legs and a red baseball cap who gave me a knowing nod as our eyes locked for a quick saturated moment as he passed by me. At this point, I had a strong sense of who was nodding because they knew who I was, and who was nodding because they knew what I knew. But, I also knew enough about this process to know that it was intended to remain a silent dance which meant that I would never truly know if my suspicion about each person was correct and I had to be ok with that uncertainty.

But amidst all of the uncertainty the mystery of humanity creates, there is one thing I know for sure – that given the scars I bear of the many lives that I have lived in my lifetime, there is no one else who could tell this story quite like me.

PART ONE

The Education of a Girl

Chapter One

Spring 2024

I met Maridel for the first time when I was fourteen, a few days before my first school dance at a time in my life when, like most kids at that age, I was truly less than a half-baked brownie of a person. I was also a poor kid who, for some inexplicable reason, was naturally bubbly. When I look back, I recognize that my seemingly "built in" joyful attitude as a child was quite ironic given the economic reality of my life. You see, growing up in America as a kid without *enough* money back then was a lot like permanently living in a basement with only a tiny window well. Each day you woke up knowing it was possible the sun would shine into the basement that day. After all, there was a window, right? Yet, each day would come and go and the basement remained pretty dark. We didn't magically get wealthier. Despite this, I was a kid who still believed, every single day, that I might see sunshine through that basement window, as if I had learned no lesson from its absence every day before. I had no external reason to have hope, but having hope seemed to give me hope. I suppose having hope felt better than the alternative.

If someone told me when I met Maridel that I would wind up living apart from my mother and siblings because of her, I would not have believed you. Poor families generally lived together forever, it became one common way the poor ensured survival in America. In fact, if someone told me when I was younger that my life would take any of the twists and turns it wound up taking, I would not have believed you. But I guess most things in life are unpredictable, right? Like the fact that although we could use the internet and cell phones when I was in my early days of elementary school, I would wind up living in an America where, during the end of elementary school, the internet and cell phones had been banned for use as a form of connection and social communication, social media becoming only a chapter in our *new* American history books for the purpose of reminding us of why there was such a ban.

I distinctly remember the important role the internet and cell phones played in our lives before the ban since, prior to that point, we used the internet and cell phones for almost every task. As a child, I loved playing with apps on my mother's phone, her device a helpful tool when she needed me to be quiet. I remember learning TikTok dances in fifth grade with my friends for the school talent show. I also distinctly remember my utter confusion in sixth grade when my mother told me that the government had banned apps, and google, and all of the rest of it. Much like real estate or other natural resources were divided among the wealthy and powerful throughout history, the ownership of what remained of the internet and cellular communications had been split up between the government and a few government selected companies who offered limited, and heavily restricted, services to citizens.

Despite all of the things that had changed rapidly in America between the time I was born and the point I met Maridel, I can say with certainty that by the time I turned fourteen, there was one thing that had not changed for me at all. Like most girls my age, I had been looking forward to my eighth-grade dance for years, my earliest memory of seeing someone dress up for a dance being when I watched my oldest cousin take pictures at my aunt's house before her eighth-grade dance. It was a city-wide tradition for the eighth-grade public school classes to have a formal dance in June, a few weeks before graduation. Every spring, as I grew up in my neighborhood, there was one Friday night when the restaurants on Montague Street were swarmed with groups of dressed up eighth graders heading to dinner dates, in groups, before the dance.

Every spring, on the Friday night of the dance, I would stare out the front bay window of the pizza place my family went to for dinner every Friday and, as I enjoyed every second of the two salty slices I was allocated from the pie, I would drink in the sight of the soft and shimmering dresses on the girls as they floated up and down the street. Most Friday nights, after we finished dinner, my mother would take us for a walk on the promenade. I loved walking the promenade on the night of the dance, taking in the view of doting parents snapping pictures of their dressed-up children, city skyline in the background, early summer air surrounding the spectacle. I marveled at how the girls looked like adults wearing heels with hair and makeup done, the iridescence of their appearance drawing me in completely.

At the time the date of my eighth-grade dance neared, I had not been to pizza or the promenade in about two years. Like so many others, our family was facing even greater financial difficulties in the time most people now commonly called A.E. (meaning after "the Election," as that election simply became known). Since my mother had to work most Friday nights (which meant I had to babysit my siblings) and could not justify the "splurge" of tipping a server anyway, we stopped going out for pizza on Fridays.

I had prepared for the moment where I would dress up for the dance in my mind for years, hungry for the chance. I couldn't wait for my chance to be one of the girls in the pictures. Since there was no longer "Facebook" to see pictures from the recent dances or fashion magazines to look at for inspiration on how to dress up, I asked one of our neighbors who was a hairdresser to show me some pictures of the "updos" she had done for girls in the neighborhood the year before. I knew she took pictures of her best work and kept them in a binder because I would flip through her binders while she would cut my hair in her makeshift basement salon. She only charged me $10 for a cut, although I knew everyone else in the neighborhood payed $25. I suspected that she took pity on me when she would notice my hair was too long to wear in a manageable ponytail. I played street hockey on our block occasionally with her son, usually when they were down a boy and would reluctantly allow me to play so, in the boy's words, "the teams would at least be even."

Although I remained as enthusiastic as ever about the dance, the anticipation for our dance was far more muted than usual given the reality of the regime we were living under. A number of parents had decided to opt out of letting their daughters go to the dance at all given the Party's most recent edition of the "Feminism for Youth Guidelines for Girls." Our school principal had issued a notice from the Department of Education to our parents stating that the girls clothing would be monitored and those who were not dressed *appropriately* would be dealt with *accordingly*. Despite all of this, I refused to consider that the dance would not be as I had dreamed it would be.

A few days before the dance, my excitement was still evident one slightly humid early summer afternoon, as I tried on my dress for what might have been the millionth time. As I twirled from side to side in my full-length mirror to watch the skirt sway, I saw my mother stand up from her crouched position on the ground behind me after working to fix several nails that had come loose in the floor boards. She gasped slightly when she saw me. I had not tried the dress on for her previously, afraid of her reaction. She cocked her head after freezing for a moment, crossed her arms, and slowly walked up behind me, both of us looking at me in the mirror, me in my new dress and she in her tattered clothing. I could see the wrinkles on her face twitch a bit as she moved her chin around with disapproval, her long black hair tinged with silver pulled back in a low ponytail.

"I am just not sure about this dress, Anna...," my mother said, starting to bite her nails as she eyed me up and down in the mirror, "the last thing this family needs is chatter about you looking too ...," her voice fell off as if she were afraid of the word she would use or unsure of the word to select. I worried when my mother referred to me by my first and middle name because she usually did that when she was angry with me.

"Please, mom," I implored quietly, but with urgency in my voice as I looked at the reflection of her face in the mirror, "I love this dress."

I wanted to wear a black dress with spaghetti straps that I saw in the window of the department store down-town. The nice full chiffon skirt fell an inch or so below my knee with a piped ripple around the bottom. There was an innocent amount of sequins on the bodice, which was a snug sweetheart shape. I loved running my hands down the skirt every few minutes to remind myself that I was wearing the dress. My aunt had helped my mother buy it for me since our budget was too tight to pay for it. From the day we bought the dress home from the store off of layaway, I would open the zipper of the bag it hung in at least three times a night to admire it and inhale the scent of its newness.

"You know you can't wear any make-up right?" my mother confirmed as she continued to frown at me in the mirror. My mother frequently reminded my sister and me of the "make-up ban" contained in the Guide-lines for unmarried women and girls. The primary goal of the Guidelines issued by the Party was to help young un-married women avoid attracting sexual or inappropriate attention. I understood that Guidelines had taken the place of what were previously called executive orders, the decisions the President or Party could make that became binding on citizens when issued. Each time my mother reminded me about the Guidelines, she spoke as if she was relaying new information, although I had always heard about what she mentioned before. My mother would often repeat things that made her anxious, totally oblivious that she was doing it.

I had expressed my disappointment about not being able to wear make-up to the dance to my older cousin Sophie the weekend before, but I knew better than to express it to my mother. Like most people, my mother was terrified of violating the Guidelines. Sophie had responded to my disappointment by telling me that a lack of make-up did not prevent me from standing out since, as she had said to me many times before, I was (in Sophie's words), "naturally gorgeous."

Although Sophie's remarks about my appearance always made me feel embarrassed and sheepish, I knew she was complimenting me from a place of kindness. I considered there was a possibility that I was pretty, but never quite accepted it. I had heard similar compliments from plenty of adults as I grew up, but I still wasn't sure if I was ugly or not. I figured at best there was a 50/50 shot I was pretty and that I should err on the side of caution by assuming I was actually ugly, it was easier to believe that anyway. "So pretty" or "so exotic looking" people would cluck at me or my mother remarking at how unique my blue eyes were, which was unusual given the mix of my mother and father. "The boys will be lining up for her" they would say sometimes and I knew, instinctively, from a young age that I was supposed to be proud at this prediction, although I wasn't sure if I was supposed to feel excited about a line of boys. My mother would insist I say thank you in response to these remarks, so I would robotically thank everyone who offered me such praise.

As my mother continued to ponder my dress, staring at me in the mirror with one hip cocked, arms crossed and her lips pursed, a sudden flash appeared in her eyes as if she had a brilliant idea. She took a few steps outside of my room, picked up the cordless phone from the table in the hallway and started pushing some numbers as she re-entered my room. After a few moments, I heard her begin to speak in the singsong voice she reserved for people she wanted to impress or that occupied positions of authority.

"Hi there. It's Elaine. So sorry to bother you, but Anna is getting ready for the dance and...," she paused listening for a moment, "Yes. They still have the dance and it's this weekend ... right, I'm sure it is a bad idea ... yes, I agree ... well since it wasn't cancelled I figured I would let Anna go and my sister bought her a dress as a graduation gift so you know ... yes, I know ... in any event I wondered if I could ask you a favor. We could use an opinion on her dress. I never got to go to one of these things and we want to make sure she looks appropriate considering ..." she paused to listen again, "Yes. Thank you. Anna and I will be so grateful. We just want to stay out of any trouble."

I watched my mother listen to the person on the other end of the phone for another few moments and I also watched her face turn a bit red and fall, as if my mother sensed that she had bothered the person she was speaking to.

"Sure. We will be here -- thank you so much..." I heard her quietly reply before hanging up the phone.

Chapter Two

"Who was that?" I asked, feeling the hairs on my neck start to stand on edge, already knowing the answer to my question.

"I asked Maridel to help us with an opinion on your dress," my mother replied haughtily without meeting my eyes, "as you know, she is highly connected with the Party and represented New York on the committee that drafted the Guidelines. I want to make sure we are not breaking any rules...especially given how things are these days."

By "how things were these days", I knew she was referring to the fact that a number of women had been imprisoned or otherwise blackballed in their communities for violating the Guidelines, whether they did it to protest the Party or otherwise.

I sat on the edge of my bed for a while after my mother raced out of my room mumbling something about needing to vacuum. The nervous feeling in my stomach growing, I made my way downstairs in my stocking feet and dress where I saw my mother, sweaty, completing one of her quick clean up bursts in our worn and shabby living room. Before I could offer to help, I heard a firm knock on our front door through the screen of the open window in our second floor living room. I would come to learn, in much more detail, that everything Maridel did was firm and relentless. My mother went down the stairs to the first level and opened the front door of our building.

"Thank you so much," my mother said in another one of her "voices," this voice reserved for the moments she felt insecure and sought praise and approval, like a puppy wanting to be pet.

I craned my neck around the banister on the second floor to peek down the staircase toward the threshold, where I saw Maridel towering over my mother.

"Well, of course I am going to respond if someone in my family seeks guidance although this is a busy day for me, as usual, so we will not be able to stay long," Maridel snapped at my mother.

I had no idea why Maridel referred to my mother as family. Although I knew that my mother regularly attended some form of meetings led by Maridel with some other women in our neighborhood, I had never met her in person before, although I had heard about her non-stop from my mother. My mother would constantly inform me how important Maridel was in the Party and how important the meetings that Maridel led, and my mother routinely attended, were. My mother had started attending the meetings not long after my father walked out on us, finding the group through Facebook, back when Facebook still existed.

"Anna, is that you?" Maridel asked in her strong voice peering up at me as she must have noticed me staring down at her. "Your mother has told me so much about you. Come here. Let me see your dress," she commanded.

I stood up from my sideways position peeking over the knob of the banister on the second floor and walked around to the top of the staircase. Maridel walked further towards the bottom of the staircase peering up with a piercing eye. She was tall and lean, but she carried herself as if her bones were thick and heavy. She wore a navy-blue kerchief tightly over her hair and I could see bobby pins sticking out of the kerchief above each of her ears. She wore black cigarette pants and ballet flats with a cream-colored blouse, fully buttoned except for the top button.

"Claire, grab the fabric and machine from the car. She needs a bolero jacket. Black," Maridel barked to a young girl following behind her. The girl wore a long black skirt and white oxford shirt, firmly tucked in with a thin black belt and black flats. I guessed she was in her early twenties, but it was hard to tell because her head was looking down at the floor in dutiful submission. I watched the girl, Claire, scurry back out our front door in response to Maridel's command.

"Claire can get this done quickly. Why don't you and I sit down and discuss how things are going around here while she puts something together for Anna?" Maridel commanded my mother, her voice deep and masculine.

"Of course," my mother replied in solid agreement. I could tell my mother was nervous, but acting dutifully submissive to Maridel, much like the girl Claire was acting.

After Claire returned a few moments later, my mother led them up the flight of rickety brown stairs with filthy carpet from the first-floor foyer to the second-floor apartment we lived in, a duplex that was a combination of the second and third floors. Claire began to set up a sewing machine at the dining room table located in the corner of our living room while my mother motioned for Maridel to sit down on our freshly vacuumed couch. The couch was full of tiny tears that my mother tried to hide with an assortment of dingy throw pillows that were once light blue, but now the color of mud mixed with the sea. I anxiously hoped that Maridel wouldn't move any of the pillows.

Claire motioned for me to stand next to the sewing machine and, a few moments later, I began to feel the gentle pressure of her fingertips as she extended a tape measure across various parts of my chest, arms, and back. The black of the fabric sitting on our table did not match the black of my dress, they were completely different shades of black. I started to swallow profusely to prevent myself from crying at the thought that Claire was going to defile my dress with an ugly jacket, but I knew better than to complain.

"You should try to keep your house a bit cleaner," I heard Maridel say snottily to my mother, "our homes reflect how much control we have of our lives."

I knew she was implying that my mother had little to no control of our lives.

"Yes. I try," my mother replied with shame in her voice, "although it has been hard with my hours ... and the kids ... and doing this all alone." I noticed my mother pause between explanations, as if she knew she had to keep listing different ones until something possibly justified the state of our home for Maridel.

My mother acted as the on-call super for the entire block of row homes that our apartment was located in, all owned by the same wealthy family, and because she did so we were able to rent our place at a significantly reduced rent. My father had picked up the "super" position as a second job a few years before he walked out on us. Thankfully, the landlord had allowed my mother to step into his shoes as a part-time super when she begged to take over the job after he left. My mother was extremely handy. She would tell me it was because she had grown up without much money and they had to figure out ways to fix things around the house, rather than always paying someone to help.

"Well, you are not the first woman to be in this position. You have to pray more. You have to pray for strength and endurance. You need more of that, clearly. And guidance. I think you should pray for guidance as well so *you* can see clearly enough to make the right decisions for the children on your own." Maridel sounded highly annoyed with my mother. I assumed she was referring to the fact that my mother had to invite her over to determine I needed a jacket.

"Yes. I do pray every day," my mother responded quietly.

"Do you pray as a group? As a family? This house requires group strength. Evil got here when your husband left you for another woman. Evil has been here, in this very house, Elaine. Even if you were not the first one to invite evil in, it was here. It will take a tremendous amount of prayer to rid this house of evil residue. You know evil is always trying to find a way in, through a weakness normally," Maridel scolded my mother in an accusatory tone, "...and if your exhaustion results in weakness, you must sleep more and pray more."

Not counting the super position, my mother worked two jobs. There were three of us and as a single parent she had been able to keep us mostly fed, and we got to school on time most days (largely thanks to my assistance laying clothes and breakfast out for my siblings each morning), but there were not many hours left in my mother's days to otherwise pay much attention to us. When my mother was near us, she was so full of stress and so utterly exhausted that it wasn't a very enjoyable experience. She often treated us kids as if we were background fixtures she had to deal with that had been planted in her life by someone else, but not by her.

"Elaine, let's walk around the house and check the windows," Maridel suggested, again speaking to my mother in a tone that did not seem to offer an option to refuse.

My mother looked a bit confused at the suggestion, but stood up to comply nonetheless.

"You can feel evil trying to get in. You can feel it," Maridel said intensely as she led my mother to a window at the corner of our living room by her wrist before standing behind my mother in front of the window. I watched as Maridel grabbed my mother's hands from behind and planted my mother's palms on two window panes, before placing her own hands on top, covering my mother's hands with her own.

"Do you feel that?" Maridel asked my mother in a slightly raspy whisper.

My mother quickly turned her head to look at me with slight concern on her face but, just as quickly, closed her eyes and turned back to face the window they were standing in front of, all signs of concern quickly evaporating into her prayerful submission to Maridel.

"If you focus, you can feel it. I feel it. I am sensitive to his power. I am stronger than him, but I can sense the devil. The devil was here, knocking and trying to find a way in knowing he has found a way into this home before," Maridel said with conviction.

"Ok," my mother replied in a defeated whisper.

"Let's pray here," Maridel said sternly as she grabbed my mother's wrist firmly and pulled her in front of another one of the long living room windows, repeating the same process. Maridel began to recite the Hail Mary prayer while rocking slightly back and forth on her heels behind my mother. After they finished at one window, Maridel would walk my mother to the next window still holding her hands the entire time and they prayed at each window in the living room in the same way. My insides quickly started to burn with fear. I had never been so close to someone suggesting they could feel the devil, much less where I lived. Like most people, we went to church regularly and I was no stranger to messages of good and evil, but hearing Maridel in this moment felt different. I wasn't sure whether to believe what she was saying, or not to, but the possibility of it being true scared me senseless.

When they finished praying in front of all of our living room windows repeating the same prayer they had recited at the first window, they said a few more prayers and talked on the couch as Claire finished sewing the ugliest and worst fitting jacket I had ever worn, even despite the fact that I only wore second hand clothes. The jacket was too wide around my arms and far too tight on my back, completely covering the formerly beautiful shape of the top of my new dress. After I tried on the jacket for Maridel's final approval, Claire quietly packed up her sewing machine and supplies, and my mother motioned for me to walk them out of our apartment with her. We all made our way, me last in line, down the rickety stairs they had just come up a few hours earlier.

As they stepped outside the front door of our brownstone building and onto the stoop, Maridel turned to my mother as we stood in the threshold, firmly placing a hand on my mother's shoulder.

"Remember, we're in this together," Maridel said in a tone that was more scolding than kind or affectionate. I would learn later that Maridel would always say things like this to her "flock" reminding people of the strength of the group and pretending to offer them some comfort, despite the fact that her eyes spoke little other than disgust for people she viewed as weak, which was almost everyone other than Claire.

"I don't have much extra money right now, but I would be happy to pay you for the jacket in installments," my mother offered with her head hanging down.

Maridel looked at the top of my mother's head with a disgusted smirk. I could tell she thought my mother was pathetic. I assumed Maridel probably figured my mother would default on the payments anyway, like we did on almost everything we owed. Nonetheless, I felt a sense of desperate urgency for my mother to look up with some self-respect.

"Consider it a gift for the good of the order," Maridel responded with continued disgust.

My mother looked down at her feet, uttered "thank you" and expressed how grateful she knew I was as well.

"You know you are really going to have to be careful with her," Maridel warned as she turned abruptly to face me, giving my body a once over and then pausing to fix her gaze intently on my face after taking in my breasts, "God has blessed her with quite the appeal," she continued, "it is incumbent upon us to make sure she does not use her blessings in sin."

Maridel beckoned to me to walk towards her. I complied, fear still electrifying my insides. I found myself standing directly in front of Maridel, looking down. Maridel took a deep breath and pressed down hard on my head with both of her hands.

"The force of God is strong and we pray that you will rise to his challenges and abide by what he has chosen for you. You are special to him and your life will hold more meaning than you could ever imagine if you rise to his challenge and command," she bellowed.

And, although I shudder at the thought now when I look back on it, if I am being honest, my fear briefly gave way to a surge of pride when she said these words to me. I remember that in that moment as a fourteen-year old girl, as much as Maridel scared me, having her call me special made me feel good.

Chapter Three

Graduation, June 2028

Four years after the eighth-grade dance, I completed what was left of the system we used to call "high school". There was no formal graduation ceremony scheduled, not only because there was likely no budget for a ceremony, but also because there were so few students graduating. A public high school senior class in New York City would have been comprised of well over one thousand students B.E., but A.E. my class only had a little over a hundred students and a chunk were from another high school that had consolidated with us during junior year.

The United States had been at war on multiple fronts, including at our southern border, since before I entered high school. Healthy children sixteen years of age or older were subject to a draft, an early draft slogan reminding us "if they can drive a car, they can drive a tank." Between the number of kids drafted and the massive numbers of kids who opted into national religious schools using a voucher program that had been expanded A.E., there were not a lot of us "ordinary public school kids" left. Nonetheless, Mrs. Collins, our beloved English teacher and career veteran of our public high school, felt it was important we gather for some type of ceremony.

So, at ten o'clock in the morning on a hot day in early June, at Mrs. Collins's request, we gathered in the school gym for the graduation ceremony she had planned with a few other teachers. Like most of my classmate's parents, my mother could not afford to take time off from work to attend. As a result, our ceremony mainly consisted of a group of students sitting in the gymnasium bleachers, sticky with sweat, in front of Mrs. Collins and three other teachers seated in metal chairs on the gym floor behind a rusty looking folding table. The table was filled with diplomas Mrs. Collins had printed and I had watched her work on rolling and tying shut with yellow curling gift ribbon during our silent reading time in class for the last two weeks.

I had planned to sit next to my best friend, Lowe, at the ceremony, but I ran a little late for it because I had been on the receiving end of another argument with my mother that morning. Anytime my mother came home after working her occasional third job, the overnight shift at a local distribution center, she fought with us kids about not helping out enough around the house. Since I was late, when I got to the ceremony, I quickly slipped into an end seat in the front row of bleachers. I scanned the faces in the crowd behind me until I saw Lowe who gave me a big pouty face and thumbs down as I waved and mouthed "sorry."

As I looked around the hot and dusty gymnasium, daydreaming while Mrs. Collins completed her opening of our ceremony by reading an excerpt from "Oh, the Places You'll Go" by Dr. Seuss, I wandered into my mind's memories of my dad bringing me to games in the same gymnasium when I was in elementary school. There was so much excitement back then with cheerleaders, a concession stand that sold terrible hot dogs (that somehow tasted delicious), and a student DJ playing music during time outs. My high school had been known for its competitive and winning sports teams and there was so much community spirit surrounding the Friday night men's basketball games that a lot of people from the neighborhood would attend regularly, many parents in the neighborhood being alumni of the high school. High school games were cheap fun on a Friday night. Although we never attended a Rainer women's basketball game, I heard they had been champions of their division fifteen years in a row, until a few years A.E. when the sports program was discontinued completely.

The gym was now used for makeshift church services on Sundays, an altar on wheels now located under one of the basketball hoops. Since every citizen was required to attend the national church, various public spaces were converted to places of worship each Sunday to accommodate the large numbers who had to attend. Normally there was a youth meeting after Sunday service with speeches from the local representatives of the Party to the youth in the community. I hated basketball church and youth meetings. It smelled like dirty laundry in the gym which was worsened by the fact that there was no air conditioning. I remember at one time the gym was somewhat cooled for basketball games (like our classrooms or homes used to be cooled with air conditioning as well, even if only with window units) but "luxuries", like air conditioning, now cost too much money for the general population in America to enjoy, a pole hook to open the casement windows at the top of the gym being our best resource to try to get a breeze coming in through the windows to cool us off.

"Anna," Mrs. Collins said my name, loudly, and I was jolted from my reverie. I immediately sat up straighter, noticing a tiny bead of sweat plop down from my forehead into my eyebrow given how quickly I was jolted out of my daydream. Mrs. Collins paused and gave me a knowing look before she continued to speak, having interrupted my daydreams in her classroom all too often.

"Your writing has really impressed me and you are an exceptionally well-rounded student," Mrs. Collins said genuinely.

I quickly gathered that she and the other teachers, who were also standing with index cards in hand, were each taking turns saying something more personal to each student.

I nodded shyly to express my gratitude in response to her compliment. Although I knew that Mrs. Collins's remarks about my academic abilities were as pointless as feathers unattached to a bird given the world we lived in, I still felt grateful for her compliment, particularly since I respected her so much. She often told me how intelligent I was. I loved her writing and literature class more than anything. Despite the fact that it was against the law to speak out or write in ways considered hostile to the Party, I wrote honestly in my essays for Mrs. Collins, as if I had nothing to fear. I knew children were not immune from being punished for breaking the law or being deemed unpatriotic or treasonous, but I trusted her and I knew she destroyed most of our writing after we submitted it anyway, having helped her at the shredder a few times after school at her request. Most of my writing was centered on memories I had of how different my family life was B.E. and A.E., the time A.E. being riddled with fear and fear being, as I described in one essay, "like oxygen for us in that you needed the unseen substance to survive and it entered your body whether you wanted it to or not."

A few moments later, as the teachers continued to speak to each student one by one, the kid next to me elbowed me and handed me a note with my name on it, a slight look of disgust on his face and a sigh as he did so, clearly not wanting to engage with me. I was used to this type of treatment by now after the "Incident." I had become a pariah with most people believing the widely circulated version of the Incident that narrated it was all my fault, and with anyone else who doubted that version of events not wanting to be associated with anyone who had screwed up working for such powerful people, whatever the reason.

I opened the note immediately knowing it was from Lowe given her handwriting on the front. "Want to walk around Dumbo after this stupid thing is over?"

I crumpled the note up into a ball in my hand as quickly as I had opened it. Although my skepticism about the point of being at any type of graduation ceremony at all was undeniable, the last thing I wanted to do was offend Mrs. Collins if she saw me passing notes during the event. Although there was not a lot that was carefree or happy in my day to day life, going to school was the closest thing to a bright spot I had experienced. Since "discretionary" subjects like science, art, and technology had been eliminated from our curriculum, students spent most of our school day in our "homeroom" class which, in my case, meant that I had spent most of my school days in Mrs. Collins's classroom over my four years of high school.

It was well known, in not so hushed whispers, that Mrs. Collins had been living on the edge of trouble for years, daring to teach things in defiance of the Party education guidelines as often as possible, even passing a banned book or two to me and Lowe on occasion. I had also heard from my cousin Sophie that Mrs. Collins also used to organize some of the protests against the Party that Sophie used to attend before doing so became too dangerous. Protests, much like music concerts, had been declared against the law on the grounds of being a danger to citizens because they were potential terrorism and mass shooting targets and increased the risk of a virus spreading after the Cov-19 Pandemic. Protest permits also stopped being issued after the Cov-19 Pandemic, when looting led to violent protests. This fact, combined with the fact that large numbers of people got beat up and gassed or arrested at protests before being imprisoned, eventually resulted in the elimination of protests.

I wasn't sure how Mrs. Collins had not been banned from teaching yet. Somehow, she had even remained our teacher after her use of the words "affirmative action" during one of our classes resulted in her reading an apology script for, among other things, "raising a topic that had been appropriately eliminated from academic discussion and literature as being against our American values of meritocracy and true equal rights." We all knew our classrooms were constantly surveilled, like most public spaces in America, using audio, video, and facial recognition thanks to a technology company that had sold its mined photos and technology to the government years earlier. Despite this fact, Mrs. Collins managed to creatively slip in bits of history that we were certainly not supposed to be learning about here and there during her lectures. I wasn't sure what motivated her to tell truth to us, but it felt like she was trying to protect us by trying to do so.

A few minutes later as I continued to behave as if I was paying attention to the graduation ceremony, the kid sitting next to me elbowed me with another note, and the same look of disgust. I quickly opened the note assuming it was also from Lowe only to quickly realize it was not from her at all.

"You are a disgusting SLUT. You are not even pretty."

I clamped my hand down on the note feeling the familiar lurch of a lump rise in my throat and sadness race through my veins but, as was standard for me now, no tears came. I was numb, completely used to this sort of thing, with similar events having interrupted many moments of my life since the Incident. I had already analyzed several times over whether being referred to as unattractive slut was worse than being called a slut. I had accepted that I was both, and after being called both names enough times, the tears stopped.

I shoved the note in the pocket of my jean shorts, feeling the familiar hole at the bottom of the pocket that was growing by the day while our principal began to close the ceremony with a speech about how bright our futures were. A few minutes later we were asked to line up and walk one by one in front of the table where the teachers were poised to hand us our diplomas. Lowe motioned for me to meet her at the end of the line.

As I approached the diploma table, Mrs. Collins turned to me holding my diploma with both hands, one stacked in front of the other, as if she was giving me something more important than it was.

"I'm proud of you, Anna," she said softly. I nodded, suddenly feeling a link in my armor of numbness come slightly undone.

"Thank you," I muttered and paused for a moment to look into the wide, wise, and tired eyes of the woman whose kindness and care for me felt like a foreign object in my life that I desperately needed, but was never quite comfortable enough to fully accept or think I deserved.

"You don't need to thank me. It has been my honor to teach you. And I think you can do a lot of great things. I truly believe that. I don't know how everything will work out but I know you have everything you need inside of you."

I started to swallow the lump that formed in my throat, suddenly quite intensely aware of the reality that I was no longer a student, and a wave of loneliness washed over me, dense and inky. I had the urge to say thank you to Mrs. Collins, but it was too hard to get the words out. So I just shrugged my shoulders a few times while continuing to nod yes in confirmation of something, although I wasn't sure what.

Mrs. Collins gently patted my arm one last time, holding the posture for a drawn-out moment, before I looked towards the exit where I saw Lowe waving for me to come join her. I took one last breath and gave Mrs. Collins a final nod before walking towards the exit, the room around me feeling more distant and stranger by the second. It had been hard to find one instant of my last year of high school not soaked in the memory of the Incident that had happened the prior summer, but at that moment as I walked out of school, for the first time in a long time I wasn't thinking about the prior summer. The only thing I felt was the odd sensation of being suddenly unattached from a place that I had inhabited for so long.

Chapter Four

The Incident, Summer 2027

The end of my junior year had started off simply enough. Like most kids my age, by the time the hot days of the last month of school had arrived in June, I was ready for junior year to end and summer to begin. Even though summer did not mean a carefree existence for me given how much I had to work at a summer job to earn money, I craved the liberated vibe that only existed in summer air.

Lowe and I both applied for full time hours at the event planning company we had worked at the prior summer, owned and operated by a family in our neighborhood. Our shifts were scheduled mainly from 5:00am – 5:00pm, six days a week, with some later hours depending on the event times and, if we were lucky, some evening overtime hours. I did not look forward to my shoes smelling terrible from wearing them for so many hours each day, a cheap pair from the discount store that did not have proper soles for such long days on my feet, but were all I could afford that complied with the company dress code. I knew from my experience the prior summer buying the same cheap shoes from the same discount store that it would likely only be a matter of days before I had to leave the shoes outside of the front door when I came home from work given the stench my sweat soaked into the cheap foam soles and vinyl would produce each time I slipped them off.

Despite the fact that I was no stranger to work, having started odd jobs here and there around the age of eleven to help my family buy groceries and to buy clothes for myself, I did not look forward to the feeling of utter exhaustion after each work day at the event company, particularly after outdoor events where I often got a sunburn. I also did not enjoy some of the heavy lifting we had to do, despite the fact that I was not a stranger to manual labor on account of my compulsory school work for FEMA. Given the regularity of severe storms and weather events across the U.S., and the lack of resources FEMA had to continue to pay for and manage cleanup from so many recurring natural disasters, many citizens (and particularly public high school students) were assigned to provide remote support services for FEMA when our cities or towns suffered storm damage. A category 3 hurricane a month earlier had ripped off half of a sports complex on the Pier that was frequently used as a meeting and convention site and our senior class had spent almost a month cleaning up heavy debris, even on the days it rained. As a result, I had sufficient experience in using my body to get things from point A to point B.

Despite the things I dreaded about my summer job, I did look forward to spending time with Lowe every day and to my paycheck every Friday. Although my mother would not let me buy things she considered "junk" like art supplies or my favorite Dr. Pepper Lip Smacker, and I had to pitch in most my paychecks to help our family with necessities, I planned to sneak in a movie or two with Lowe using my earnings.

On the last day of junior year, I ran home after we were dismissed from school hopeful that I would not have too many chores to complete so I could enjoy my half day "off" before work began the next morning. When I entered our apartment I saw our neighbor, Mrs. Rhodes, sitting at the dining room table in the corner of our living room with my mother, each woman with coffee cups and a bowl of ice cubes in front of them. They would not "pay over four dollars a cup" for iced coffee at the coffee shop "when a container of Maxwell House cost the same thing and would last weeks," they would often say. I knew the real reason they made iced coffee at home was because they couldn't afford coffee shop coffee every day anymore. So, as they had done on so many other days at our table, I found them in the middle of sitting and chatting, adding the cubes to their glasses of home brew, one by one, so they wouldn't "overwater the flavor too quickly."

"Sit down, Anna," my mother said as I peeled my book bag off of my sticky back.

I hugged Mrs. Rhodes affectionately before plopping down in a chair across from my mother. I adored Mrs. Rhodes. She lived a few doors down from us in the end brownstone of the row of brownstones, turned into multifamily apartments, that lined our street. The tiny garden style backyards behind all of the brownstones in our row were connected and surrounded by a massive fence, so our row shared one common backyard. The second floor of each brownstone had a black metal deck off of it, like a large fire escape, with stairs leading down to the garden level. I could walk from the garden behind our brownstone up the metal steps to her second-floor apartment anytime. She always left the door to her kitchen, located right off her deck, unlocked.

Although Mrs. Rhodes was incredibly kind to my mother, I wasn't entirely sure how she truly felt about my mother. They could gossip like any two good neighbors, and seemed to relate based on their work ethic and knowing each other for so long, but I knew that Mrs. Rhodes struggled with some of my mother's extreme anger, particularly towards us kids. My mother's fits of rage being were well known in our neighborhood and hard for us to hide since she would often have fits in public, especially when she was overwhelmed with stress and exhaustion. Mrs. Rhodes would often check in on me after my mother's worst episodes, pretending she needed help with odd jobs around her house and asking my mother if I could come over to help, which was really code for Mrs. Rhodes allowing me to help her prepare food in her kitchen so there was some time for my mother to cool off.

As I sat down at the table, my mother started to speak, but Mrs. Rhodes enthusiastically interrupted her before my mother could get any words out.

"Anna, the family I work for has allowed me to bring along an extra mother's helper to their summer house this year and I was wondering if you wanted to join me?"

Mrs. Rhodes was the primary housekeeper and nanny for a family in a "wealthy" part of the city and had worked with the same family for years, since their first child was born.

Before I could respond, she continued excitedly, "the pay is great, double what you make at the event planning company."

Mrs. Rhodes had been "brainstorming" with me during junior year during dinners at her house about ways

I could work after high school graduation and pursue some sort of part-time education. Her schedule working as a housekeeper was usually five in the morning to three in the afternoon six days a week but, despite her long hours, every evening she would come home and cook large meals that she put on her table at six thirty sharp every weekday evening. A lot of us kids in the neighborhood would go by to eat dinner at her house every day. Most of our parents worked until later in the evening, or were getting ready at that time of day to leave for overnight shifts, and eating at the Rhodes's house was our only option some days.

Mrs. Rhodes knew I was desperate to avoid joining the military, or worse, be forced into some sort of women's program run by the Party after high school ended. Mrs. Rhodes was old friends with Mrs. Collins who routinely told her how much academic potential I had. Even though I knew I probably would never see the inside of a classroom after high school, Mrs. Rhodes told me not to give up on the idea of attaining further education at some point. I knew my best bet after high school would probably be a service job, like Mrs. Rhodes worked at. Any type of non-service job would be difficult for someone like me to come by. Automation handled many of the jobs that the lower class used to work at and, well, kids from my neighborhood didn't exactly become lawyers or doctors (not that doctors got paid much any-more anyway). Joining some form of Party work, the military, or getting a service gig was the only viable option for many young adults.

I turned to look at my mother after hearing the proposal and she nodded in approval, "I think the money is worth it, Anna, and I know you will work hard for Sheila."

I quickly, and not surprisingly, surmised from my mother's look that her enthusiasm about the pay had more to do with her earmarking what I could help our family with by making more money but, at that point, I didn't care. I had always wanted to see the Hamptons. Everyone in the city had heard of the Hamptons, even if they had not been there. Before cable television was restricted, Lowe and I would sneak in old episodes of a reality television show about housewives that lived in New York in Lowe's basement, even though we weren't supposed to watch it. During the summer episodes the show's stars would all stay in homes they owned in the Hamptons and, based on what I had seen on the show, it looked like a gorgeous place full of well-dressed and beautiful people who held parties, sunned on the beach, and ate most of their meals at restaurants. The one thing that never made sense to me was why, with all of those things, the women on the show always seemed to be unhappy and fighting.

"Ok! Sure." I nodded, excitedly. I bit a hangnail for a few seconds before quietly interrupting Mrs. Rhodes a few minutes later as she continued to rattle off logistics and details about the job.

"Are things there like they are here? Do they have the same Party rules and the Guidelines we do?" I asked.

I had heard rumors that there were certain parts of New York, and the rest of the country, that did not have the Party restrictions that we did, like the technology restrictions, food rations and the Guidelines. When I had asked Mrs. Rhodes about it once before, she replied that her non-disclosure agreement prevented her from sharing details about the day to day lifestyle of the family she worked for. She explained to me that if she broke the rules and shared information about the places she worked or people she worked for that she would be "blackballed" from ever getting a job again.

Mrs. Rhodes seemed to hesitate before responding thoughtfully.

"Well, I will say that things there are definitely not the same as things here. But life has changed for them too, A.E. There are different problems now ... different issues they encounter. And the competition and pressure to make it work in their world is even greater now that they have to worry about the depth of their connection with the Party being critical to their individual success. There are very few oligarchs and way more people trying to find their way into the tiers of loyalty under those people. For the most part, life with them in the Hamptons will likely seem a lot easier than day-to-day life for us. But they have their own pressures behind the scenes too, just different pressures."

I wondered if Mrs. Rhodes was offering too much of her compassion to the group of people she was referring to, the wealthy people she worked for. We were the former "middle class", I was told, and America was now a two-class society. You were either very rich or very poor and there was nothing in between. We were very poor. The majority of citizens were very poor too. Sophie used to sarcastically joke that she thought being considered "lower middle class" was bad enough B.E., but she now considered those days the "glory days." My mother would often remark that she found it amusing that so many people that used to be the middle class or upper middle class that used to look down on us, the same people that we used to admire for their lovely lives and feel jealous of, were now basically dirt poor just like us.

My curiosity about what it was like to be rich was only increased by the fact that people like us no longer had a regular view of the wealthy given the restrictions on the internet, which meant that we rarely got a visual glimpse into what life was like for rich people anymore.

At this point, we only heard what life for the wealthy was really like through rumors or an occasional illicit disclosure from someone who worked for them, which was rare for the reasons Mrs. Rhodes had explained to me. My mother told me that the wealthy preferred the lack of internet access for us because social media had almost started a revolution when the majority of citizens, who were struggling, could constantly compare, minute by minute through pictures on the internet that wealthy people would post, just how little they had compared to wealthy people. She would remind me about the many reality shows that would chronicle the lives of rich kids and celebrities, who would often claim to devote their lives to working for the poor and disenfranchised while driving around in Bentleys and putting ice rinks in their California backyards for holiday parties, "the robes of Mother Theresa replaced by thousand-dollar outfits," my mother would say and shake her head when talking to me about it.

We didn't have many print newspapers or magazines to substitute for the internet either since most had gone out of business thanks to the internet well before the nationwide internet restrictions went into place. The few print publications that were left were owned by companies that would not dare challenge the Party. Plus, most journalists did not wish to risk imprisonment or punishment, or their family's financial or physical security, to tell any version of a story that might be considered adverse to the Party. The television channels that weren't blacked out were too expensive for us to afford now and, either way, nothing was on television that would provide us with a glimpse of what having wealth was like anymore. One of the many videos we had to watch at school from the Department of Education taught us why the limits on the internet and television were in the country's best interest, and why things like reality television had been banned completely. During my freshman year of high school, I remember a woman wearing a long skirt and fully buttoned up oxford shirt in one such Department of Education video explaining to our class that years of reality programs had led to a decline in realistic thinking among the population and, in particular, the youth who had no idea what a real American future actually did, and should, hold for them.

Mrs. Rhodes must have noticed some of the skepticism on my face when she responded to me asking about what rules were in place in the Hamptons. She waved her hand at me in response as if to both dispel my skepticism and scold me.

"I trust you, Anna. I know you will work hard. This job requires a great deal of trust and hard work. Working for the families is an honor and privilege and, if we behave that way, they are good to us in return. We leave in two days on July 1st. There will be a lot to do when we get there to get the families settled for the summer. They arrive right before the 4th of July when they host a huge holiday party and then stay until Labor Day other than a week or two in August when they travel to the Vineyard, so prepare to be busy."

"Who are the "families?" I asked, "I thought you only worked for the Maack's."

"The house has ten bedrooms and the Maack's have a lot of friends and "networking" to do so they often invite other family friends to stay with them. The Maack's invited a family they are close friends with to join them at the house for July this summer and, since that family has a house in Martha's Vineyard, the Macck's swap and go visit the Vineyard house in August for a week or so while we stay behind and do a deep cleaning of the Hamptons house.

Laura Maack was the mother of the children Mrs. Rhodes nannied. I had seen Laura Maack's name on posters that Mrs. Rhodes would stuff into envelopes at home, as a favor to Laura Maack, for charity events that Laura often hosted to raise money for a variety of causes. The only time I had seen Laura Maack in the flesh was when she had stopped by our neighborhood one time to drop off a cake for Mrs. Rhodes during Christmas break. She was stunning. I had watched from the front steps of our brownstone as she double-parked her car on the street with the blinkers on while she gingerly walked in her stiletto boots to a waiting Mrs. Rhodes who accepted the white cake box graciously from her front porch. I remember thinking that Laura Maack's clothes looked like they were shellacked on her body, her hair perfectly long, straight, and bouncy all at once. She looked like a doll.

"I need to call Lowe and tell her," I suddenly reported to my mother and Mrs. Rhodes, realizing that breaking the news to Lowe would be like breaking bad news instead of good news. A few minutes later after talking to Lowe on the phone and hearing her say "it's not fair" more times than I could have counted, I hung up and, fairly quickly, the sadness of missing my summer with Lowe was suddenly replaced with utter excitement at the thought of going out east. My family had never been able to afford any travel, apart from an occasional day on Coney Island. I was in disbelief that I would get to see the Hamptons. I ran to my room to begin to pack.

Chapter Five

Two days after Mrs. Rhodes sat at my kitchen table with her iced coffee and a plan, I was packed and waiting in front of the brownstone where the Rhodes family had an apartment while her husband, Peter, gave her a kiss good-bye on their front stoop and her kids hugged her. Kat, her ten-year old daughter and the youngest of her three children, cried the most as Mrs. Rhodes prepared to leave. I considered for a moment, while watching her children say goodbye to her, what a peculiar institution it was to have some mothers work as nannies to help other mothers enjoy the importance of family. I also wondered why so many of the women who worked as nannies were black or brown, like Mrs. Rhodes.

After the Rhodes concluded their good-byes, Mrs. Rhodes motioned for me to hop in the mini-van parked on the street and she settled into the driver side. She didn't hide her tears. I remained quiet out of respect and stared straight ahead. After a few moments, she turned the key in the ignition, took a deep breath and looked over at me while comfortingly patting my left hand a few times.

"We all do what we have to do," she said quietly. I did not look back at the kids waving on the porch as we pulled away because I knew it would make me feel too sad. The Maack's had rented a minivan for Mrs. Rhodes to use for transporting their kids around over the summer that we were driving out east that day. They had also asked her to pack the van full of various grocery items that they could only get in the city and did not wish to live without for a whole summer, like their favorite Tahini dressing for salads and shawarma.

Once we were settled into the drive a bit, Mrs. Rhodes rolled the car windows down and suggested we listen to music. As the trip progressed, I began to feel even more excited and joyful about my adventure and the music seemed to lighten both of us. About two and half hours into the trip, Mrs. Rhodes turned on the AC, turned off the music and rolled the windows up to drown out the roar of the wind.

"Since we are getting close now, let me run through a few things with you that will be easier to talk about now," Mrs. Rhodes suggested.

"Ok," I replied dutifully.

Mrs. Rhodes started in, "So, as a reminder, Kevin and Laura Maack have three children named Jake, Walter, and Sierra. They are nine, seven and four years old. The other family that will be staying with us in the Parr family. Mrs. Parr's first name is Karen and everyone calls Mr. Parr by his last name. The Parr family has three children, Olive, Aiden and Grant. Aiden and Grant are around the ages of Jake and Walter but Olive is much older, she is sixteen. The Parr family adopted Olive when one of Parr's secretaries became unexpectedly pregnant and could not afford to raise a child."

"Does Olive help watch the younger kids too?" I asked.

"No, no, Ana. Olive is essentially one of our employers too," Mrs. Rhodes said somewhat sarcastically before continuing, "Kevin and Parr work together in finance and the elementary aged kids all attend the same private school. Laura and Karen are very close and travel in the same social circles. As for the living arrangements, you will stay in the maid's quarters next to the kitchen and I will stay in a guest room upstairs near the children's wing. Our schedule is pretty much the same every day. We are up by six to prepare lunches for the children for their summer camp. Laura and Karen normally grab something light in the kitchen for breakfast before they head to town to workout and they usually grab lunch in town after they exercise. Kevin and Parr come out every weekend on the bus after they get off work, except that during the first two weeks starting tomorrow the men take off work to vacation and celebrate the July 4th holiday. You and I only have today to get things set up before they all start arriving tomorrow."

"So what do we do during the day when the kids are at camp?" I asked curiously wondering if I should be taking notes.

"Well, to begin with, there is a lot of laundry for ten people. Lots of cleaning and cooking to do. Towels to no end each day as well. Between laundry, cooking and cleaning, your day will fly by and, before you know it, the kids get home from camp at around 4:30 in the afternoon," Mrs. Rhodes replied assuredly.

"Plus," she continued only taking a pause to carefully stop at another red light, "the weekends go by in a blink as well. We go to the beach on Saturday and Sunday to help play with the kids and make sure they enjoy the beach so the adults can socialize and relax."

"What are Kat and the kids doing this summer?" I asked innocently.

Mrs. Rhodes face fell as she replied in a matter of fact tone and it immediately occurred to me that I may have mentioned them too soon after leaving home.

"The kids will be at the bible camp and Susie will pick them up and put dinner on the table for them as a favor to me every night, and keep an eye on them until Peter gets home from work."

I knew it was not that much of a favor for Susie to help Mrs. Rhodes out. Susie was another lifelong neighbor of ours who struggled to make ends meet and Mrs. Rhodes fed her most days too. Susie had been out of work for years and was unmarried. The Party only provided minimal financial assistance, and barely any food stamps, to unmarried individuals given the Party principle that married people were less of a drain on the economy.

"In any event," she continued changing the subject, "there is a lot for us to do. Beyond the day to day routine, like I said, the 4th is a big event. The Maacks host about eight couples and all of their kids for a massive pool party for the holiday and the kids want to attend every night of the carnival that starts the next night. We attend the carnival as well to help with the kids."

A few minutes later, as Mrs. Rhodes continued to share details about our jobs, my eyes prevented me from listening to her as my brain began to take pictures of what I saw. We had pulled into the freshly paved streets of downtown East Hampton, or "the Village" as I would hear it called over the next few weeks, and I turned my entire body towards my car window, which I had rolled back down to see everything more clearly.

As I stuck my head out of my window, chin perched on top of my two hands and elbows resting on the rubber that the window had just disappeared into, our pace slowed to a crawl on Main Street. I saw houses that appeared to stretch as far as an entire block, many white or light gray with shutters and flowers pouring out of each window, often in primary colors like red, blue, or violet. There were white picket fences and bright green lawns everywhere. Everything I saw looked bright, like a picture book, and pure. The air smelled only slightly like salt and mostly like flowers. We passed a pond that separated the sides of Main Street for a stretch and I noticed a single white swan gently swimming the length of the water, as flawless as the water it inhabited. I had never seen a real swan before.

As we inched along further through town, I took in the delicate storefronts and pristine gray sidewalks. There were little black picket fences around the base of each tree that lined the full length of the street. The crosswalks were adorned with bright yellow blinking signs and crossing guards that motioned for traffic to stop when people wished to cross. Things felt peaceful and pretty. The only indication of something resembling my neighborhood reality was a single small sign with an arrow pointing down an alley advertising a military recruitment center. We had recruitment centers all over my neighborhood in Brooklyn, but this was the first one I had seen since we got near the Village. There was a tiny store for everything like ice cream, art, hardware, clothes, sneakers, and groceries.

Mrs. Rhodes interrupted my gawking, "Did you notice the building with the lighthouse on top?" she asked quietly.

I nodded in the affirmative without looking away from my window, chin in the same place.

"That's the library. It's gorgeous inside and so peaceful. I have a card to use for the kids. I think you might love to get some books there too. They have much more selection than the libraries near us. They even loan some things banned from our shelves, since the local homeowners associations pay fees to keep some banned material here for archival purposes," she explained.

I felt so lucky. I couldn't believe I would get to live in this place for a whole summer and I longed at the thought of visiting the library as she described it.

As in awe as I was of the beautiful tree lined highway, the quaint little shops, the swan in the pond, and the mansions, the charge I got from seeing those things was nothing compared to the charge I got from people watching the small groups of human beings walking around town as we drove through the Village. Everyone looked beautiful, confident, and content. The people I saw seemed to stroll around in a somewhat slumber filled and totally relaxed manner of walking. As we paused at a crosswalk, I watched as a group of women crossed in front of our car wearing different varieties of similarly ripped jean shorts, clearly not ripped because of necessity like mine were. They all had flowing tops, shiny sunglasses only rivaled by their glistening skin, and most donned flip flops or sparkly high-top sneakers on their feet. In a way, although each of their ensembles was different, it seemed as though the looks were similar, like they wore a high-end artistic uniform. Another group of women appeared to my right at one point, riding bikes down the sidewalk before pulling into the lot next to a brightly colored gourmet market. They were riding in their bathing suits or cutoff shorts, two of the bikini bottoms were cheeky bottoms like the one Lowe's older sister used to wear, but the Guidelines banned now. Their bikes were pastel in color with wicker baskets on the front. I could see tan lines on one woman in between the top of her bikini bottom and the base of the tank top she wore with a knot tied at her lower back.

"How are they allowed to wear these clothes here?" I asked Mrs. Rhodes puzzled.

"Certain areas ... like this town ... were carved out as private zones and people pay fees and assessments, like taxes, to live in areas that are not subject to as much restriction. Places like Coney Island are public beaches so we have to comply with the Guidelines there, but in some places, like this one, the beaches and streets have been privatized and a number of things not permitted for the rest of us are allowed because of the taxes and assessments people pay in these zip codes," she explained.

"And the beach?" I asked.

Mrs. Rhodes smiled. She likely remembered my disappointment when revised Guidelines had been issued a few years prior that required all girls and women over the age of five to wear full burkinis on public beaches (which my mother used to remark was ironic since burkinis used to be considered some sign of a terrorist religion in certain places). The year I turned thirteen, I had saved up for my first two piece bathing suit, which I never got to wear since the Guidelines were issued right before that summer when the bikini ban and burkini rule went into effect.

"No burkinis, here," she giggled, "although that won't make a difference to me since I wear hospital scrubs to the beach like the other nannies and housekeepers."

"Oh," I felt my face fall as I responded, my disappointment at the notion of wearing scrubs to the beach, clear and apparent.

"I brought you some scrubs too, but I suspect you will be in the water with the kids so I also got you a simple black one piece that should suit you. I will suggest to Laura that a bathing suit will make more sense for you and we will see what she says," Mrs. Rhodes offered.

I lit up with joy.

"I will take a one piece," I giggled with enthusiasm. I hated wearing burkinis to the beach. I was an excellent swimmer thanks to Mrs. Rhodes and wearing a burkini made me feel pounds heavier. The opportunity to take swimming lessons was very rare for kids who didn't have a lot of money, but the head of the swim program at our local indoor pool owed Mrs. Rhodes a few favors and had taught me how to swim one summer, before the pool opened each morning.

Although I was thrilled to hear I might be able to wear a regular swimsuit to the beach, I also felt guilty hearing that Mrs. Rhodes had to wear scrubs to the beach. I considered that it would probably feel quite uncomfortable wearing pants on a sunny beach, even if they were thinner pants like scrubs, particularly given that Mrs. Rhodes was overweight. Much like my mother and the other working women in our neighborhood, Mrs. Rhodes body was plump and round, especially in the stomach area. When she would occasionally wear shorts, you could see veins pop out of her legs in certain areas, like most of the adult women I knew. The features of most women and men in my neighborhood were largely similar. In addition to often carrying too much weight in the stomach and having bodies that showed other signs of hard work, most adults I knew growing up had hair that looked dry and thin. Often times, the women I knew had exceptionally long hair, not being able to afford, nor having the time, to have it cut often. At least the physical similarities allowed people to hand down and swap clothing easily at our semi-annual neighborhood swap meets, which certainly helped my mother save money on clothes.

We finally pulled up to the Maack's house after our slow crawl down Main Street. I let out an audible gasp and Mrs. Rhodes chuckled again as she had at a few of my questions and responses during the ride. Like the large mansions we saw on the way into town, the house we pulled up to was massive. It was colored a light gray blue and the outside was covered in perfectly patterned shingles. The front door was red and matched the red flowers crowded in a flower pot outside of every window. The circular driveway was made of glistening pebbles that crunched under our car as we drove up and made me feel even more excited about my arrival.

"Wow," I uttered plainly.

"I know," Mrs. Rhodes replied, "It is really something isn't it?"

"Do they ... own this?" I asked.

"Yes. Everyone here owns the homes ... well except those of us who come to work for them," she giggled again.

"It's so big," I observed.

"Yes. It is. And it is beautiful on the inside too. It's pristine, and nice, and full of expensive things, Anna. And it will not seem like reality, because it is not our reality," Mrs. Rhodes gently touched my left shoulder and turned me back toward her and away from the car window before continuing in a soft but serious voice.

"Listen, Anna, this level of wealth can be a lot to take in when you see it up close for the first time. I think it is important for you to experience this level of service, but you have to remember to keep your awe of all of this..." Mrs. Rhodes paused to point at the house from inside the car over the dashboard, "...to yourself. We are the help and one of the worst mistakes someone in service can make is to forget that we are just the help. This is a good job and the best thing to do is be overly respectful to the families. This job is very important to me and my family. I trust that you get that and that you will act professionally."

"Yes. I do. I get it," I said suddenly feeling a bit ashamed at my awe.

"Great. Let's get this car unpacked and get to work. The groceries we brought with us need to be put in the refrigerator and freezer right away. Can you handle that while I get some windows open so we get some fresh air circulating in the house?" she asked

I nodded. After I got out of the car, I stood up next to the front passenger door and took one last survey of the entire picture in front of me. It did not feel like reality. I started to unpack the car and did as I was told, pebbles crunching under my feet with each step I took towards the house, reminding me with each step that I was, indeed, in a very different place.

Chapter Six

Two days after we arrived, both families arrived at the Hamptons house. There was so much excitement in the air. Mrs. Rhodes was right that there was a lot of work to do. I could hardly believe how fast my days flew by. There were children running around constantly, sunscreen to apply, bathing suits to wash, sand to sweep as far as the eye could see (mainly near the downstairs shower where the children were required to rinse off after being at the beach). I felt like most of my moments when the children were home were spent shuffling back and forth satisfying requests for snacks and drinks or mediating their disagreements.

I didn't see Laura and Karen much during the day. Over the few days we had been at their house, they would jet off frequently for "sweat sessions" (which is what they called workouts) and lunch in the Village. In the afternoon, they would lay out in the sun by the pool. Similar to my experience growing up, the kids did not get too much face time with their mothers, although in my case it was because of how much my mother had to work. Mrs. Rhodes thanked me at the end of each day and questioned how she did it without my help. I was happy to help her, and despite a lot of hard work, I was enjoying my opportunity to be at the Maack's home. It felt like living in a doll house.

On the weekend we all went to the beach and I played with the kids for hours in the waves and sun while the adults, excluding Mrs. Rhodes, sat on large colorful blankets and entertained any number of visitors who would stop by our regular spot on the beach. Mrs. Rhodes would either stay behind at the house during our beach days with any kids who didn't want to go to the beach or, wearing her scrubs, she would set up her own chair and umbrella next to our regular spot on the beach with the coolers full of snacks and lunch she would serve to everyone.

Laura had agreed with Mrs. Rhodes that it would be best if I wore the swimsuit Mrs. Rhodes had purchased for me so I could play in the water with the kids. The suit fit me perfectly, it was slightly snug with a modest cut on the hips, thin-ish straps, and the back scooped down lower in an oval shape right below my shoulder blades. My breasts had expanded quite a bit during junior year so I had to wear the cups that came with the suit to ensure that my nipples did not show too much.

As usual, I was a bit nervous about my appearance since I had noticed some people stare at me longer than I felt comfortable with when I was at the beach, like Parr who seemed to stare at me longer than the others, offering me an occasional smile. When I asked Mrs. Rhodes if the suit looked alright before we left for the beach one morning, without telling her why I was worried, she laughed before replying, "Anna, you could probably wear a potato sack and still look more stunning than the women wearing $1,500 swimsuits on that beach. You are gorgeous. Good for you. Enjoy it. Plus, between us, you show them a thing or two about natural beauty."

The pool party on the 4th was spectacular. I spent most of my time at the party playing games with the kids and swimming with them in the backyard pool. There was food to no end and we watched the fireworks from Main Beach downtown, playing with sparklers near the ocean while we waited. I had more fun than I ever remembered having on a holiday. The parents seemed very grateful for our help too as they frequently offered thanks, especially Parr who seemed to be the most attentive of the parents. Parr checked in with me often on how the "little people," as he called them, were doing and continuously expressed he had no idea how "I did it." He even told me several times that "I was truly something."

During the week after the 4th, the village held a carnival as a fundraiser for the fire department. I learned that summer that most of the "luxuries" enjoyed by the families staying the Hamptons had to be funded privately given the economic status quo in the country. Apparently, a fire department with updated equipment was a luxury given a continued economic recession, a massive national deficit, and multiple wars. I got to attend the carnival with an unlimited budget to allow the kids to enjoy rides and buy snacks. I loved every second of the experience outside in the cooler summer evening air, the sounds of ride noises and giggling children making me feel joyful, and the scents of cotton candy and popcorn wafting through the air making me feel warm.

At the end of each twelve plus hour day, I would shower and curl up in what Mrs. Rhodes told me was a Jenny Lynd bed in the maid's quarters where I stayed. I wondered if the maid usually lived in such a nice room. The bed was a dark brown wood and the sheets and bedding were crisp and white with a slight satin ribbon along the edges of the top sheet and the border of the duvet cover and pillowcases. Every day, I would make my bed right after I woke up so it would be perfect when I returned to it each night.

The location of the maid's quarters, connected to the kitchen by a narrow hallway that served as a supplemental food pantry, turned out to be pretty amazing as well. The kitchen was my other favorite spot in the house, only second to my bedroom. To begin with, the kitchen was bigger than the entire first floor of our apartment in Brooklyn. Mrs. Rhodes told me the oven was imported from Italy. The countertops, floor, and counters were different shades of white. There were multiple seating areas in the kitchen including ten barstools around the center island, a huge rectangular dining table, and a separate mini living room of sorts with a flat screen television to watch in the corner.

The crisp white palette of the kitchen created the perfect backdrop for a copious amount of colorful fresh fruits and vegetables displayed in various size bowls and glass containers. When we received the first grocery delivery at the house, I couldn't believe how abundant the food supply was. And, although I knew I probably shouldn't, starting on my second or third night staying in the house, I indulged in the habit of wandering into the dimly lit kitchen for a midnight snack. The appeal of all of the food lining the pantry shelves and counters was too seductive for me to resist. At home, we ate a lot of canned and frozen food and our main dishes were mostly chicken thighs and ground beef, because they were cheaper. Fresh fruits and vegetables were limited and too expensive for us to enjoy regularly. The wars, especially the war in Mexico, limited the supply of produce imported. My mother would often shake her head as I got older and things got tougher telling me that she "could not believe there was a black market for fruits and vegetables."

About ten days into our time at the Maack's house, after a second hectic carnival evening and after everyone had gone to bed, I felt particularly hungry while I laid in my dark room and watched the clock hit midnight. I quietly departed my room in my pajamas to grab a snack in the kitchen. I was intently browsing the bowls of fresh fruit near the stove and debating whether the juice of an apple or orange might be nice with a side of potato chips when I heard a voice behind me.

"I would go for the apple."

I turned around as red as the apple I had been admiring, embarrassed to see Parr standing in the kitchen. My stomach dropped. I was immediately certain I was in trouble.

"Oh. Hi. I was just...." I stammered unsure of how to defend myself.

Parr broke into a smile, "No worries over here. I was feeling hungry myself so I guess we had the same idea. Although, I am more of a chip guy," he said motioning to the bag I had placed on the countertop after snagging it from the pantry.

"Right. May I make you a bowl of chips?" I asked, unsure if I should immediately enter servant mode.

"Relax, Anna. Enjoy your chips. And apple. Honestly, whatever you want. You are allowed to eat here," Parr said with a whispered chuckle.

"Thanks. I'm actually not that hungry. I think I am going to head back to bed, I replied turning on my heel and planning to scurry away.

"Now wait. What is this all about? Because I interrupted your snack? You are off the clock, you know. You are helping take care of my children thank you very much. I think you deserve part ownership of my car if you want it given what you are doing to help us," Parr said reassuringly as he put his hand on my shoulder."

I felt slightly uncomfortable, especially with the familiarity with which he patted me, but he seemed like he was trying to be kind so I quickly persuaded myself to relax and smiled back.

"Have some chips with me?" Parr asked and gestured to a bag, "I am starving. I think my portion of salmon for dinner would have been better suited for a small cat," he reported with another whispered chuckle.

"Um. Sure," I replied awkwardly. I reached for the bag of chips and opened it and I saw him motion to the bar stools at the kitchen island. I sat down and delicately took one chip from the bag and started to chew. I felt nervous interacting with him, but he seemed so kind. I also reassured myself with the thought that he had gone out of his way to express gratitude to me over the past few days. I watched as he walked to the kitchen sink and grabbed two paper towels from the roll. He was wearing light gray sweatpants and a light blue v-neck t-shirt. His sweatpants looked thicker and shinier than most sweatpants I had ever seen, I suspected they were expensive. He calmly walked back over to the island bar top where I was seated, put the paper towels out like plates in front of us, sat down next to me, and proceeded to dramatically pour the entire bag of chips in two huge piles in front of each of us. I started to giggle and quickly covered my mouth to avoid waking anyone. I noticed he was giggling silently while beaming from ear to ear.

"So what did you think of the carnival?" Parr asked between bites of chips.

"It was really nice. I had fun," I replied back grabbing more chips from the pile in between bites. As I chewed, I felt equal parts awkward and intrigued by the fact that I was sitting with my boss in my pajamas as if we were pals.

"I saw you giggling on the swings ... I can't ride those things anymore," he said "Getting old. I get too dizzy."

"Yeah. I felt like throwing up after I got off of it. I can't believe people pay to get sick," I replied noticing a slight smile creep up in the corners of my mouth.

When we had arrived at the carnival earlier that evening, we had broken up in groups to better help watch the kids. Laura and Karen had stayed home that night to host a girl's night moving screening in the home theater. Parr had volunteered to be in my group since I was designated responsible for the four boys. Kevin, Laura's husband, planned to take Sierra to the section of the carnival with the kiddie rides and Mrs. Rhodes offered to shadow Olive and her pals. I had noticed that Parr was watching me intensely at some points that night in the same way I had noticed him watch me on the beach several times. I was nervous he stared at me because he was secretly unhappy with how I was handling the kids or didn't trust me, despite the compliments he had been showering me with.

Parr continued, after swallowing another chip and taking a sip of water, "I noticed you thanked the worker when you walked out of every ride," he said softly, "it was pretty awesome to see that. Most people around here don't display so much gratitude."

"Guess I am just polite?" I replied quietly picking up another chip.

"Yes. Polite. Your parents must be very proud," Parr offered.

"Parent. Only my mom. My dad's not around," I replied.

"I am sorry. Did he...Is he...?" Parr started to ask and I immediately sensed he was trying to ask if my father was dead.

"No," I responded quickly with a mouth I noticed was inappropriately full of chips as I spoke, "My dad is not dead. As far as I know. Just left us. Although, I guess you never know these days with the Party where someone might have gone," I replied sarcastically as I wiped some chip grease on the paper towel in front of me.

"Right." Parr replied and I noticed he seemed uncomfortable at my mention of the Party as he shifted his body and cleared his throat in response. I immediately wondered if I had been too honest and regretted my mention of the Party. For me, the reality of Party control over lives like mine was abundantly clear. In fairness to Parr and the others here in the Hamptons, I wasn't entirely clear on how they felt about the Party and people did not seem to talk about the Party as much, or as openly, as they did in my neighborhood.

It seemed that life in the Hamptons for people like the Maack and Parr families, which I suspected was a reflection of their lives outside of vacation, was mostly lived without the imprint of the Party, with the exception of a few things I had noticed in the short time I had been with them. For example, on one hand, I had learned they were buying some things, like certain food items, from the black market like people in my neighborhood did with the primary difference being that the Maack's purchased gobs of black-market food compared to what we could afford at home. On the other hand, when I drove into the Village with Mrs. Rhodes to drop off cycling shoes for Karen and Laura at their spin studio, I didn't get the sense the Party or the Guidelines were part of their reality at all. As I stood in the lobby of the cycling studio where I was instructed to drop off the shoes that day, I watched as people "air kissed" each other as they arrived. I heard a group of three women chatting about their "other" vacations away from the Hamptons and I even heard one guy in the spin studio lobby complain that his only issue with the Hamptons was that there were not enough places to get his shoes shined. In those places I visited, the air was saturated with wealth and there was no mark of life under Party control.

I must have been somewhat deep in reflecting about my potential offense of mentioning the Party when Parr interrupted, "so ... want a little bit of the good stuff? Talking about reality usually makes me want a drink."

I felt my cheeks color with embarrasement. I quickly figured out he was referring to alcohol, "Oh. I don't really drink. I am not 21."

"I know that," he replied in an obvious tone, "but I figure if kids your age can go to war they should be able to enjoy a drink. Plus, I won't tell if you don't. C'mon. We can hang out on the back porch," Parr suggested.

The blood stayed in my cheeks, but then also began to surge through every vein in my body. Part of me wanted to run away. I was terrified of getting into trouble and nervous, but I also didn't want to offend Parr. He seemed genuinely interested in getting to know me.

"Ok," I cautiously agreed.

The house was still quiet. It didn't seem like anyone else was awake. Parr grabbed a bottle of something that I had not noticed before on the counter and slid open the back slider-door to the deck. I followed him out and immediately inhaled the scent of the garden. I heard him whisper "this way" and saw him motioning for me to follow him down the wide stairs built into the hill that sloped down towards the pool. I complied. I remember thinking for a second that he had mentioned sitting on the back porch, which was closer to the house, but I figured he was trying to make sure we did not wake anyone.

I was barefoot since my original plan had only involved the kitchen tile under my feet, the same type of pebbles from the driveway filling the space between stairs hurting the soles of my feet as I slowly made my way down the hill.

The table by the pool had some lit solar candles on it. Other than the glow of the few candles, the only other light provided was from an occasional firefly passing by and the soft lights under the water in each corner of the pool. It was beautiful out back at night. The yard was surrounded by tall trees and silence, apart from the water occasionally turning on to fill the pool a little. Parr sat down at one end of the table and motioned for me to sit next to him, which I did.

"Are you cold?" he asked.

"A little," I replied.

"Problem solved. I will grab an extra sweatshirt from the guest house," he said. He got up and ran into the guesthouse door, which was a few feet from where we were sitting, and quickly returned with an oversized sweatshirt.

"Thank you," I replied pulling the gray sweatshirt over my head.

He handed me a glass full of something, "White wine," he said, "It's good stuff. The least I can do considering how hard you have been working for us. You know, you might be surprised to hear this, but I didn't always feel comfortable having so much help. We did not have help when I grew up. I wasn't born into money like my wife or Laura and Kevin. I guess I got lucky between marrying Karen and being able to become an investment banker, despite my lack of resources. I am not sure I could accomplish all of it now with the way things have changed in the country. Plus, I bet you would never guess this, but I have dyslexia. My point is, that I probably understand a lot more about your life than you realize."

I nodded, smiled with gratitude and sat up a little straighter with more confidence. I remember immediately feeling more comfortable when he mentioned that he wasn't always well off, as if he was a little more like me.

"I am really grateful for the opportunity to work here," I replied genuinely and took a sip of the wine. I didn't normally drink but I figured since I had shared an occasional glass of wine with Lowe when she would steal it from her older sister, I would probably be fine.

As we sat at the table a little longer, Parr continued to rattle on about his upbringing and accomplishments, mentioning how he was proud of figuring out creative ways to make it through law school and his CPA exam even though he wasn't "too smart" in his words. I listened. It seemed very important to him to convey to me how similar we were. After a few more sips of wine and trying to intently listen to what Parr was telling me, it occurred to me that I must have been drinking faster than I figured because I suddenly felt quite dizzy and lightheaded.

"I feel a little like I just got off the swings at the carnival again," I interrupted nervously as Parr was rattling on about his recent charity auction for a meals on wheels type of service.

"Really. Do you drink much at home with your friends? I know I did around your age," Parr asked and I wasn't sure but it felt like his tone was more sarcastic, and less kind, than it had seemed a few minutes earlier, "You have to be careful. You are a really attractive young woman. Boys your age might take advantage of you," he said.

The ease I had felt in the kitchen talking to Parr quickly began to be replaced with a rush of nervous adrenaline.

"I don't drink too much," I replied.

"Any drugs? I know it is normal to experiment," Parr said in a matter of fact tone, "I sure did."

"No," I replied noticing that my voice sounded strange to me. I did not feel like myself and suddenly I desperately wanted to go inside.

"You ever heard of GHB?" he asked.

"I don't think so," I replied but at that point I started to feel really blank ... it was like I started to miss seconds. I went to stand up, but I felt so lightheaded I found myself almost falling and grabbing the table with both hands fiercely.

"Hey. Hey. Shhh... You don't want to wake anyone do you?" he whispered. "You may have had too much already. Let's get you some water," Parr offered as he put his arm around my lower back and started to help me stand up.

I felt grateful for his help and awful that I had let myself get drunk. The last thing I remember *before* things went black for me was standing up with Parr's help. Then I lost time. The next thing I remember *after* things went black for me was waking up on a bed I did not recognize, without my clothes on, feeling incredibly sick to my stomach. I felt fuzzy. My head was throbbing and pulsing. I noticed Parr at the end of the bed pulling his pants on. My stomach flipped. "Where am I?" I thought to myself, but grasping for clarity or speaking felt like too much to muster so I lay there unable to move much.

"Hey," Parr said walking towards my head until he was looking down at me, "You feeling ok?" he asked.

I tried to talk but my mouth felt like cotton. I also felt terrifyingly confused.

"C'mon. Get up. You have to get back to your room," he said firmly, "I will walk you up but you have to be quiet, ok?"

I started to try to get up by placing my elbows under me, but I was struggling to get balance. The next thing I knew, Parr was pulling me up by my shoulders and pulling my shirt over my head. I was like a lump and, as I was trying to gain my composure, I felt a huge whack of pain across my face. As out of it as I was, I knew he had hit me.

"Get it together," he barked in a low and angry tone.

My face hurt so much from his smack and I started to feel tears welling up in my eyes. I knew if I opened my mouth I would start sobbing and I was still so confused. I felt both of my hands, one on top of the other, reach for the cheek that he had just hit. I was grateful my arms were starting to work a little again.

"Ok ... Ok," I repeated fearfully suddenly finding a mild version of my voice.

A second later, Parr shoved me back down on the bed and I felt him pulling my underwear and pants on. My legs were tingling and a little numb, but I could feel the soft cloth of my pajama pants slide onto my legs.

"Let's go," he said, pulling me up by my elbow that was still bent having just supported the palm of my hand that I was using to provide comfort to my aching cheek.

In a second I was upright, somehow, and allowed him to walk me to a door. When we walked outside, I realized we were leaving the guest house. Parr walked me up the same wooden stairs I felt like I had just walked down seconds ago while I leaned heavily on him, his arm around my waist. The pebbles were getting stuck to my feet as I climbed. I wondered how I had lost time. The last thing I remembered was sipping wine at the table. I started to feel the urge to throw up and I tried to lean towards the grass to puke. But, as I turned my head towards the grass next to the steps, Parr ripped me back upright by my hair, and the pain stopped me from vomiting.

"Seriously, Anna. Shut up and be quiet. You don't want to lose your job, do you?" Parr whispered in a threatening tone.

I fearfully and furiously shook my head no, and allowed him to guide me back in the slider door of the main house. All of the lights were off including in the kitchen. Parr walked me into my room and helped me sit down on the bed. After that, he left the room shutting the door behind him. The last thing I remember after that, before I must have passed out cold, is leaning off the side of my bed to throw up, making sure to aim for the floor so as not to destroy the beautiful bedding.

Chapter Seven

I sat up in bed and the stench of my vomit immediately confronted me, making me gag. I must have slept through my alarm because although it was ringing on the table next to me when I sat up, it hadn't woken me up. When I grabbed the clock to shut the alarm off, I noticed it was thirty minutes after I was supposed to wake up. Just as I was trying to collect my thoughts, Mrs. Rhodes barged in to my room and yelped, loudly. One of the children, Jake, ran in behind her and ran back out when she yelled at him to leave. A few minutes later, Laura barged into my room just as Mrs. Rhodes was trying to help me out of bed and to the bathroom, which was thankfully located inside my bedroom. The bathroom had a pocket door and Mrs. Rhodes was trying to use her foot to slide the door open, while holding me up under my armpits ,when Laura barged in.

"Oh my god. What happened?" Laura shouted at Mrs. Rhodes.

"I don't know, ma'am," Mrs. Rhodes replied curtly, "She was late and I came in to check on her and found this."

It sounded to me like Mrs. Rhodes was about to cry. My head felt like a thousand sirens were going off in it. The space between my legs was sore.

"I am going to take the children outside for a while," Laura said as I heard Karen calling Laura's name. I saw Laura leave my room.

"Anna. What happened? What happened?" Mrs. Rhodes cried with desperation as she finished helping me into the bathroom and settled me onto the shower floor.

"I don't know." I started to sob. "I had some wine and I got sick."

"Wine? With who? Where? I don't understand. You went to bed when I did." The confusion in her voice was only rivaled by the confusion inside of my head.

"With Parr," I responded meekly, "he asked me to hang out by the pool with him last night when I went to get a snack and I don't remember how I got so sick."

"What? That doesn't make any sense, Anna. Why would you do that? Why would you be with Parr?"

"Mrs. Rhodes, please come out here right away," I heard Laura shout from outside of my room, "The children are playing on the patio and I need to speak with you right now."

"Ana, I'll be back in a few minutes. Just sit here and don't move, ok?" Mrs. Rhodes instructed.

I nodded and heard the door to my room shut a few minutes later. The water felt good and I looked straight up at the showerhead so the water could hit my face. I was shaking. I felt like I had nothing left on my insides except for air. I was still crouched on the floor of the shower when Mrs. Rhodes walked back in with a towel and knelt down on the bathmat next to the shower.

"Let's try to clean you up, Anna," she said and I could tell she had clearly been crying hard. Her eyes were puffy and her lips and cheeks had the swollen look of someone who had been forced to calm down before a cry was complete. I knew the look well.

Mrs. Rhodes, still on her knees, eased closer in towards me and began to run her fingers through my hair, cleaning the dried puke out of it. I handed her the shampoo that was in the corner on the floor next to me. She gently washed my arms and back and legs without getting too close to my torso. When I was finished being cleaned off, I grabbed her forearm as she helped me stand up. We walked back into my room and she had already laid wet towels all over the floor to clean up the mess my vomit had made.

"Thank you. I am so sorry, Mrs. Rhodes," I whispered.

She did not say anything in response to my apology. I could tell her face was devastated and uncertain. She helped me get dressed and told me to sit in the chair in the corner of the room and sip some water while she changed the bedding. I did as I was told watching her mop and remove the formerly crisp and clean bedding, now stained with my puke and what appeared to be some blood, putting on new pink sheets. Eventually, she motioned for me to come back to bed. I laid down, my head heavy with sadness in contrast to the light fluffy pillow. Mrs. Rhodes pulled the new blanket over me up to my neck, covering my arms, as if she was entombing me in the soft cotton.

At one point, while she continued to wipe down the room, I noticed the house was unusually quiet. "Where is everyone?" I asked, afraid of what she would say but desperately wanting to break the silence.

"Everyone went to the beach for a while except for Karen who went to her sister's place out here for the day," Mrs. Rhodes replied quietly and I noticed a sadness on her face I had never seen before. Mrs. Rhodes helped me sit up again and handed me some Advil and more water. "You should rest now, Anna," she said, "You will need to leave in the morning. I have to phone your mother and tell her what has happened. She is going to be upset Anna, so try to be understanding about that when you get home. It might make things easier on you with her if you are understanding about how all of this might make her feel."

"Ok," I repeated and I realized, as the words came out, that I sounded like I was in a trance. I knew Mrs. Rhodes well enough to know that she wasn't telling me to prioritize my mother's feelings out of principle, but to try to help me manage my mother's likely rage.

Mrs. Rhodes stood up next to my bed and pulled a laundry basket towards the bed from near the bedroom door. She began to furiously fold what looked like a basket of clean towels that we had washed the day before. As she folded, she placed each perfectly folded item on top of the blanket covering me, turning my body into a laundry table. She swiftly placed two clean towels on top of the blanket at the point where it covered my feet and took a long deep breath before continuing to speak to me.

"Ana, Parr told Karen that he could not sleep and went down to hang by the pool and get some air where he found you drunk. He figured you must have gotten into their liquor cabinet. He said you were wobbling and he helped you back into the house because he was afraid you would fall if you went for the stairs by yourself or drown in the pool if he left you down there."

Mrs. Rhodes continued furiously folding and placing towels on my feet. I noticed some of the piles on top of me were getting quite tall and I tried to stay extremely still so they would not topple. I noticed she was breathing heavily in between sentences as a pile of washcloths started to take shape by the fingertips of my left hand.

"He said you threw yourself at him by the pool and he shoved you off. He says he handed you a bottle of water in the kitchen after he walked you upstairs, but you waved him away and disappeared into your room," Mrs. Rhodes continued quietly.

I guess I could have mounted a defense for myself at that point, at least to Mrs. Rhodes, but I didn't. I didn't remember what had happened the night before and I felt horribly guilty that I had made the poor decision to drink wine. I knew I shouldn't have. I was mortified at my condition. Even though I knew in my gut that I was hurt, I decided to ignore my gut at that point, because I figured it would not save me anyway. I turned my head to look out the window, my body still frozen so as not to disturb the piles, and felt the tears well up in my eyes before beginning to sob again.

"Anna. You can't keep crying like that," Mrs. Rhodes softly scolded me. She grabbed the towels off the bed in a few swift motions and I heard them drop back into the basket. I turned my head back towards her as she sat down next to me on the bed. Her shoulders were slumped and her head was down. She put her hand on my shin, closest to her, through the covers.

"Look, Anna. I know you..." her voice trailed off.

At this point, I felt the sobs coming again but I was so desperately trying to stop my sobs from coming out that they would up sounding like muffled hiccups.

"We won't convince them otherwise," she continued softly, "and at this point if the worst that happens is that Karen and Laura send you home ... that is not the worst outcome considering they could call the authorities for theft or something else."

I noticed her voice start to break and hearing her start to cry made muffling my sobs even more challenging.

"I am so sorry, Anna."

Mrs. Rhodes suddenly lifted me up to a seated position and pulled me into her chest in an embrace. We both cried in that position for a few minutes until we heard kids thundering into the kitchen. I laid back down and rolled over on my side facing away from the bedroom door and closed my eyes. I felt her take the pile of washcloths still sitting on my bed, but I did not turn around to look at her again. I heard her go into the bathroom in my room and turn on the sink for a moment. The last thing I heard before I fell asleep was her gently shutting the door to the bedroom.

I slept until the next day. When I woke up, my bags were packed and organized neatly in the corner. I put on the clothes that had been laid out for me on the chair, presumably by Mrs. Rhodes. I must have been deeply asleep because I hadn't even heard her enter my room to pack my things. Eventually, Mrs. Rhodes collected me and told me it was time for her to drive me to the bus stop. When I walked out of my room through the kitchen to the front door, Laura Maack was sitting in the kitchen at the dining table. The house was silent, so I assumed the children were still sleeping. Laura looked at me as I passed through the kitchen, but quickly looked away when our eyes met. I thought about apologizing because it seemed like what I was supposed to do, but the words never came out of my mouth. I continued my slow walk through the kitchen and into the foyer where Mrs. Rhodes was waiting for me with the car keys.

When we got to the bus stop, Mrs. Rhodes lifted my suitcase out of the car and grabbed me right before I stepped onto the back entrance of the bus to give me a hug. It felt like she did not want to let go, but I knew I had to leave, so I pushed her away gruffly as the exhaust from the bottom of the bus blew heat towards the bottom of our legs.

"I know you didn't do anything wrong," Mrs. Rhodes said to me as I turned to walk onto the bus.

I felt a lump in my throat but I was determined not to cry. I took the first step onto the bus.

"Anna, wait," Mrs. Rhodes said.

I turned around on the step with my head still down trying to fight some tears.

"Anna, as difficult as this is...you need to be careful here," Mrs. Rhodes said.

I knew she was right and, given the world we lived in where I was all too aware of the seemingly unlimited power of those with power, I knew I would heed her advice.

Chapter Eight

When the bus arrived in the city, I walked the entire way from the bus stop to our apartment. When I walked in the front door, I was greeted with silence. The apartment was quiet. Everyone was at work and I knew my younger siblings were probably at the bible camp. I knew Mrs. Rhodes had spoken to my mother, but there was no one waiting to meet me at the bus stop. I doubt my mother or sister could have taken off work to meet me anyway.

As soon as I unpacked my bags, I took another shower even though I had already showered again that morning in the Hamptons before leaving for the bus stop. I was immediately reminded by the sight of our shower how much dirtier our shower was than the one I had been using in the Hamptons. After I got dressed, I decided to clean the bathroom since it appeared no one had done a great job cleaning it in my absence. My sister Lizzie was the first to arrive home a few hours later that afternoon. Lizzie appeared in the bathroom doorway as I was putting the cleaning supplies back under the bathroom cabinet.

"Hey," she said quietly, standing with both of her hands on each side of the bathroom doorway as if she were holding it open. I recognized the sweat and sun-burned look she had going on from working outdoors in a New York City summer. Lizzie had just finished her freshman year at Rainer High and had happily taken my job at the event planning company for the summer when I agreed to go out east with Mrs. Rhodes.

"Hey," I replied.

"So. What happened? I mean. I kind of know what happened from mom's fit about it last night but...what actually happened, Anna? Are you ok?" Lizzie asked with as much tenderness as she could muster, which wasn't much since she was one of the more stoic and reserved among us kids.

"I don't know. I don't remember much," I could feel myself starting to cry again as soon as I started to talk about it. Speaking about it felt like digging around in a cut. I had rehearsed how the scene with my mother would go in my mind on the bus over and over before I got home. I practiced, in my head, exactly what I would say to my mother, but I was unprepared for Lizzie. Given my mother's tendency to express her anger and rage in whatever means she felt appropriate, I had considered different strategies I could use that might somewhat manage what I knew would be her angered response. I even thought about throwing myself in my mother's arms for comfort, although we had never been physically affectionate and I imagined the contact would feel awkward for both of us. Lizzie's questions made me feel less prepared and more exposed.

"Well. I am sure you know she is not dealing well with whatever she heard from Mrs. Rhodes," Lizzie warned me.

"Yes. I figured." I said in a perfunctory tone. If nothing else, anticipating my mother's likely rage for a moment seemed to stop the tears from flowing in front of Lizzie. The physical altercations my mother had engaged in with us kids our whole lives when she was angry always had a way of shifting my focus to survival. You couldn't think about crying when you were in survival mode, fending off her physical attacks, which varied in intensity depending on how "extra broke" we were at any given moment.

"Listen, Anna..." Lizzie said gently, "Just take it easy on her. You know if you fight back it is going to be bad for all of us."

On hearing Lizzie's words, I immediately felt the familiar sense of defensive rage towards my mother, which I kept hidden on the inside of my body, roll up from my legs into the base of my stomach. As siblings, our bond was largely forged and only existed as a product and function of how well we dealt with my mother. It was like a war zone every day in our house and we all had different scars from that reality. Every event or occasion in our lives was set on the backdrop of how my mother would receive the information or process something. I waffled back and forth ferociously between hating the way my mother behaved and feeling sorry for her. I knew she had not been the recipient of an easy life and, at times, I felt it was my duty to accept her rage given the sorrow she had been through. But there were also moments, like this one, where the unfairness of not being able to have feelings of my own felt overwhelming, especially when a sibling would remind me that having any feelings could be detrimental to all of us. Each of us children were conditioned for survival, but it manifested in different ways for each of us.

I nodded my agreement with Lizzie and I watched as she left the doorway, heard her shut her bedroom door, likely preparing to hide. When one of us was not in trouble, it was always a good idea to lay low and stay out of the argument. That is, unless you were me and had to step in to defend the younger ones from blows, which I often did.

An hour later, my mother came home. All in all, the next few hours weren't that much worse than other fights except for one thing. Sure that my "careless behavior" in the Hamptons had exposed her to increased risk and possible consequences (*"What kind of mother will they think I am because this happened?"* she had screamed at me several times during the course of our "talk"), my mother did something that would ultimately set my life on a completely different trajectory in a matter of seconds. She called Maridel.

"You are really fortunate that I have continued a friendship with her," my mother said referring to Maridel after she hung up the phone with her, "and you are incredibly lucky that out of all the places in the country you could have been born, you were born here where she is a leader. She has become extremely powerful you know and we are lucky to call her a friend." In the back of my mind, I remember thinking how insane the concept of Maridel being my mother's friend sounded, since I knew my mother had no choice but to play by the rules people like Maridel had helped create. In the years since I first met Maridel before my eighth grade dance, our day to day life under Party rule had changed even more. Given Maridel's appearances on state television and the rallies she held in the city that my mother dragged me to on occasion, I knew she had become a powerful Party leader, her current reach far in excess of what she had attained with her original Facebook group.

My mother continued on, "Maridel has agreed to help me with your situation. I am going to meet with her after church this weekend and she is being kind enough to offer to help fix the mess you got yourself and your family into."

I did not respond to my mother when she told me that Maridel would get involved in my "situation." I just looked out the window in the back of the living room where I was seated on the floor following the session of mayhem with my mother that had preceded her call to Maridel. I partially opened the cheap vinyl shade that covered the window I was sitting near, which my mother had pulled down at the start of our battle. Dusk was just settling in but, as it often did, it already felt like night in my house, the sun casting a gloomy brown light into the living room. I got up and walked outside, sat on the front stoop, and watched the sky until the sun officially disappeared, before heading back inside to go to sleep.

The next morning, I decided to go to work with Lizzie and ask if they would hire me back, despite Lizzie's concern that they might try to shorten her hours if they gave me some hours. I saw Lowe standing near the owner's son, River, biting her nails (like she always did when she was worried) as soon as Lizzie and I arrived at the event company warehouse. The second Lowe saw me, she ran towards me. Lizzie had told Lowe the day before that I was coming home (and why I was coming home based on what Lizzie heard from my mother).

"Oh my god, Anna. I have been so worried about you. I wanted to come by your house last night, but I was afraid your mother would flip out. I know it's not true, what I heard. I will kill the bastard if you want me to. I will," Lowe uttered firmly into my neck as she bear hugged me.

"It's ok. I'm ok," I said stoically into her ear through her slightly sweaty hair that was plastered near my mouth as a result of her embracing me. As touched as I was by Lowe's response, it still felt too raw to talk about anything that had happened. I hadn't slept much the night before and it was taking everything in me not to cry.

Lowe pulled back from our embrace urgently after a few seconds, "What are you going to do? You have to tell someone what really happened, Anna. What happened? I know you would never make a move on someone, much less a grown man who is your boss."

"Stop!" I suddenly screamed at Lowe.

I noticed the look on Lowe's face change to a combination of wounded and afraid at the force of my response. I immediately felt terrible for snapping at her, but my response felt involuntary.

"I'm sorry, Lowe. I didn't mean to yell...I'm just not ready to get into it. I don't want to talk about it."

I noticed that my statement sounded more like a pleading whimper, my voice sounded as wounded and raw as I felt on the inside. Lowe's face changed again and I could see tears of compassion in her eyes. She rubbed my arm gently.

"Wanna work today? Keep your mind off things? I promise not to bring anything up," she said softly, "I brought an extra sandwich in case you showed up today," she nodded and smiled softly at me.

I nodded my head yes in appreciation and took a deep breath. Lowe turned on her heel and walked over to River and began to talk to him but, after a few seconds, it looked like whatever he said in response had angered her. They began to fight until River's dad came over from the front office and intervened. Both River and his dad appeared to be reasoning with Lowe as I watched from afar. Suddenly, my heart felt like it was sinking further into my stomach. I saw Lowe turn around and look at me with horror as if she didn't know what to do next. River and his dad walked aware from Lowe and she walked back over to me.

"They said you can't work here this summer," she whispered, "I tried, Anna. I promise. They won't budge. I told them I would quit, but they reminded me that there were tons of kids waiting for the chance for any summer. You know I really need the money to help my family out."

I nodded in understanding. Lowe embraced me again and then she told me she had to get to work. I saw Lizzie in the distance starting to load chairs onto a truck, but she didn't make eye contact with me. I walked home and went to bed for the rest of the day. As the day wore on, I would wake up in between spells of sleep and stare outside my bedroom window for a while before willing myself back to sleep. Eventually, I woke up in what I could tell was afternoon light and decided to clean the kitchen. My mother didn't approve of us napping during the daytime, so I figured when she came home to a clean kitchen she might not ask me questions about my day or whether the event company had re-hired me.

The next morning, Mrs. Collins called our house and said that she could use help sorting old books and doing odd chores in her classroom over the summer. Mrs. Collins told me that she had already contacted my mother to get her permission the night before and my mother had consented. Mrs. Collins mentioned that she heard my job out east had fallen through. She explained that the work was unpaid, but she thought she could work up a small stipend for me.

So the next day I started my new summer job working for Mrs. Collins. The work allowed me to avoid talking and remain mostly in solitude, and I was incredibly grateful for that. Mrs. Collins didn't push me to talk. She allowed me two one hour breaks each day, one in the morning to read, and one in the afternoon to eat lunch and write. I knew she was being overly generous with the scheduled breaks, but I took advantage of them anyway. I didn't feel like reading or writing, so I just drew doodles or started at the football field from the bleachers I would sit on during each break.

A few weeks later, summer ended. I began, and made it through, my senior year quietly and mechanically. Word had gotten around about my short time out east. Except for Lowe, and Mrs. Collins who seemed to go out of her way to ask me how I was doing every day, people avoided me. I understood why. You were either in the good graces of wealth and power or not and, if you weren't, you wanted to be. No one wanted to be seen consorting with someone who had been kicked out of the inner sanctum of service to the wealthy, no matter what they thought of me or what they suspected the truth really was.

Chapter Nine

June, 2028

On that last day of school following Mrs. Collins attempt to give us a graduation ceremony, like every other day, Lowe and I walked home from school together, stopping at her house first. I hugged Lowe in front of her building when we got to her place. My mother had mentioned to me the night before that she planned to come home early from work so, when I got home from graduation, we could discuss what I planned to do next. I was hoping she might have figured out a way for me to join her at one of her jobs as a starting point. Lowe was going back to work at the event planning company that summer, but the Long family (our neighbors who owned the company) still refused to hire me back despite the fact that I had worked for them since the summer before seventh grade. Apart from work for Mrs. Collins, to date, it appeared I was unemployable in the neighborhood.

When I got home and saw my mother sitting on the stoop of the brownstone with the only suitcase that we owned next to her, I paused in the center of the street in front of my house. Maridel's red Buick was parallel parked in front of our building. I thought about turning and running as fast as I could, but I didn't move. Maridel walked towards me and met me in the spot I was frozen, before touching the back of my shoulder with her right hand.

"Anna. Your mother and I think it is best if you come join one of my programs today," she said plainly, "God has given you many gifts and I think it is time we put them to good use, for higher purposes."

The same "Claire" that had sewn a jacket for me before my eighth grade dance was standing next to the back of Maridel's car and opened a door to the backseat. Despite the years that had passed, Claire looked exactly the same, except that her hair was cut much shorter. I stood still for a moment and looked at my mother with pleading eyes, but she only looked back at me with anger, her arms crossed and biting her bottom lip. I knew I had to comply. I knew I had no where else to go. I walked over to the car and sat down in the backseat. Claire shut the car door. My mother walked the suitcase around to the trunk and then came around to my side of the car. She didn't look at me, but spoke to me through the window, which was only rolled down about a quarter of the way.

"This is for the best. Make sure you work hard and do as they say," my mother said firmly.

I was breathless. I wanted to ask if she had told Lizzie or the others that I was leaving, but I didn't.

Maridel got in the car and started it.

As we pulled away from the only home I had ever known, I guessed where I was heading. I suspected I was being taken to a Christian educational home for young women, but loosely referred to as a CEP, run by the Party. Sometimes, young women would be taken to a CEP as a consequence of breaching the Guidelines. The President had promised to accomplish prison reform and shut a bunch of jails, so CEP's also housed women that would normally wind up in prison for a variety of offenses too. In the years A.E., many young women even voluntarily applied for acceptance to a CEP having no better options, and not enough resources to do much else or ensure food on the table. My mother had mentioned to me once that Maridel had a lot to do with helping some of the women in our neighborhood get a CEP placement since she ran a model CEP program in New York and helped design CEP programs across the country. Some of the advertisements for CEPS made them seem like colleges. My sense was that they were more like upgraded homeless shelters.

During the drive, I racked my brain for anything I knew or had heard about CEP facilities. Although the television commercials made them seem rather pleasant, we had heard rumors to the contrary on occasion. Rather suddenly, my brainstorming was interrupted by the thought that I would not be able to tell Lowe where I had gone. That realization was enough to finally bring tears to my eyes. I hung my head and tried to cry quietly while looking down at my lap so Maridel and Claire wouldn't notice me crying.

We drove for a little over three hours according to the car dashboard clock I checked every so often before pulling up to a large single-family home. The ride had been silent, at least no one had spoken to me. I had noticed signage for Monticello, New York on our way.

"Here we are," Maridel said dryly as she turned the car off, after we had parked.

Claire hopped out and started shuffling toward my side of the car and opened the door for me.

"The red carpet treatment" I thought sarcastically and, although I intended to say the words silently to myself, they escaped my lips and I said them out loud. A second later I was in tremendous pain, crumped against hood of the car above my open car door. Maridel had slapped me across the face, hard.

"You will quickly learn that sarcasm is not the best strategy here," Maridel scolded me

I nodded my agreement quickly and stood up straight from my crumpled position.

Maridel continued in a scolding tone with her arms crossed glaring at me, "Now, go inside because you will need to get a short orientation before dinner and prayer."

I walked up the L shaped sidewalk that led to the front door, which Claire was opening ahead of me. The first thing I noticed as I crossed the threshold was the overwhelming smell of cleaning products, a combination of nauseating lemon and bleach. I could see the living room and part of the dining room from the foyer. The house was simple and clean with white carpet through-out and plastic runners covering large chunks of the car-pet. The furniture appeared outdated, like it was from another decade. A woman who looked slightly familiar to me walked into the foyer wearing a navy pants suit.

"Welcome, Anna," she said politely, "We have been expecting you. Let me show you around. I am Susan, the dean of this CEP. Follow me."

Susan looked familiar to me, but I wasn't sure why. She walked me around the three stories of the house showing me around. It wasn't until we were in the basement chapel that I realized she had worked at the coffee shop around the corner from my house, that is until the coffee shop changed to being run by all robots and one human manager a few years earlier.

"You worked at the coffee place, the coffee shop on Clinton Street, didn't you? I remember your face." I said slightly worried that I shouldn't remind her.

Susan smiled slightly and looked a bit surprised, but did not respond to my question.

"Dinner is at 6:00 every night followed by nightly prayer in the chapel. Lots of food here so eat up," Susan said with a slight rise in her voice at the end. I wondered if she remembered that I used to like the pink cake pops as an occasional treat at the coffee shop, back when we had enough money to buy them.

"Thank you," I replied feeling sheepish at her lack of response to my question, "Where should I go now?" I asked.

"Let's head back to my office so I can review the rules of the house with you and fill you in on your schedule and upcoming classes too," Susan gestured with her arm for me to head up the stairs in front of us.

"Classes?" I asked, slightly hopeful. The mention of school gave me some hope that maybe the CEP would just feel like school, which wouldn't be so bad.

"Yup. You learn more about the Party's work, how to behave at a Party rally, why we have been chosen to do God's work," Susan replied from behind me on the stairs with zero emotion in her voice.

"The rallies that happen in the city?" I asked.

"Listen, you will hear about it all soon enough."

Susan motioned for me to pause for a second on the landing of the stairway we were climbing. She leaned closer to my face.

"My advice for you is to enjoy the fact that Maridel wants you to be her special project for whatever reason. She has specifically requested that you work with her. My guess is you will get out of here more than the rest of us since she is on the road so much," she whispered nodding her head in agreement with her theory before motioning for me to continue up the rest of the stairs.

"Plus," Susan continued to whisper as we climbed, "for people like us, this whole thing is actually our best bet, you know? I mean, where was I really going to go after being a manager at a coffee shop, right?"

I continued to climb the stairs with Susan following behind. I was grateful that she had acknowledged that I correctly recognized her from the coffee shop. I also felt a slight dash of hopeful pride at the fact that Maridel had asked to work with me. I considered that, perhaps, she was going to look after me and things wouldn't be so bad for me at the CEP.

We ended the tour in Susan's office where I was schooled on the policies and procedures of the house. I started to read the long lists of restrictions and rules.

1. *No phones (cell or otherwise), computers etc. and no access to same, anywhere (voluntary or otherwise). This should be an obvious restriction given the regulations and technology bans in place, but we think it worth repeating. In order to have a pure and prayerful heart, you will not spend any part of your life engaging in virtual reality.*

2. *We encourage you to write letters to your family and friends with positive news about your work*

here. All letters are screened before sending and when received to make sure they do not contain details of Party business or criticism before they are mailed. Our work here is confidential and in the interest of national security.

3. *You are provided with a stipend for clothing every six months, which you can use to purchase cloth-ing from the catalog we will provide you. Dresses or skirts should fall below the knee. No revealing tops will be permitted. Consistent with the Guide-lines, no make-up is permitted...*

I was deep in reading about the punishment system for breaking house rules when I heard Susan begin telling me about my daily planned schedule. I paused my reading to pay closer attention to what she was saying.

"Since you will apprentice with Maridel, that means her schedule will be your schedule. Claire has been working with Maridel for years and will continue to do so. Claire will make sure to inform you of your daily itin-erary. Your room has been prepared with all of the items you will need. If for some reason something is missing, you can submit a request for further accommodation. Also, we have a sisterhood retreat in the basement af-ter prayer once a month for the new residents to share their story and meet the existing residents. You will get to know more about the other women here at that time.

If you work hard, follow the rules and stay out of trouble, I think you will find your time here quite enjoyable."

Susan abruptly stood up signaling to me that it was time to leave her office, her face and tone of voice displaying an odd combination of authority and anxiety.

"How long is the program here?" I asked as Susan walked around to the front of her desk towards the doorway of her office, which I noticed for the first time did not have a door.

Susan stopped in her tracks but did not turn around to face me as she replied without missing a beat, This is not a program, Anna. This is life now."

I guessed from the ease and strength of her response that she had been asked that question before. Susan and I both remained unmoved for a few more seconds before she rolled her shoulders back, angled her head slightly higher and left the room just as Claire was walking back in to collect me.

Chapter Ten

Fall, 2031

Three years living in a CEP had passed by in the blink of an eye. Every day that I walked inside the CEP, I still noticed the strong lemon scent of the cleaning products used by the housekeepers right away, as if it was the first day I arrived. I had lost a fair amount of weight. It wasn't for lack of food. The CEP had plenty of food and we could eat as much as we liked. I just never seemed to have much of an appetite.

Most days, like today, I was "on the road" for a rally with Maridel and Claire staying in a motel and sharing a room with Claire. Maridel had asked Claire to quiz me on the background of Maridel's involvement with the Party to make sure I was more prepared for the routine media interviews following the rally that we were scheduled to attend that day. Claire had informed me that although Maridel was continuously pleased with how I physically appeared on camera or on stage with her, she had been unhappy with the content of my responses that appeared on television when Unity Media, a Party controlled broadcasting station, had interviewed me following a rally the prior week. Now that I had travelled with Maridel for a few years, and she continued to show increasing signs of her age, she was gradually expanding the amount of time I spent in front of the camera relaying her "messages."

"Ok. So, if you are asked any question that could lead to a response about Maridel's history with the Party, how will you explain she became committed to the Party?" Claire asked.

"I say..." I began.

"You say happily and with enthusiasm..." Claire interrupted.

I took an exasperated breath and put on my camera face. I was really good at my camera face by now but today I was cranky and I had not warmed up to this practice session idea. Claire was relentless. I was tired.

I took only a slight pause before crisply responding, "I say that years before the election that saved America, Maridel was one of many citizens that sensed our need for a President, like our President. She witnessed that we were in the midst of a moral crisis and that women, in particular, were suffering from a wide variety of moral crimes that were being committed against "true feminism", "family values," and God. So, rather than accept that sin and disaster were the only option, she got active at a grassroots level and she started organizing in her community. She held meetings for her friends and neighbors, and these meetings grew into a movement because of the desperate need for real and positive change in America."

"And, if they do what they are supposed to, they should follow up with a question about the role of men in the movement given that is the theme of our rallies this month. How do you respond to that?" Claire asked, turning her nose up to stare at me through her thick glasses.

"I say that in the beginning of the movement, Party members were mostly women although men have now realized that they have to stand with women more than ever, especially given the witch hunt of "me too" that sought to destroy many good men." I finished my sentence going out of my way to make sure it sounded as bright, committed and clear as I knew I was trained to make it sound.

"Better. Could still use some improvement but I imagine she would be more pleased with that," Claire replied dryly.

"Would she?" I said somewhat sarcastically.

Claire glared at me and she often did.

"Anna, do you know how many girls would rather be traveling with us versus doing any number of things they are forced to do in the CEP, or outside of it? You always seem so ungrateful for this opportunity, it's like nothing makes you happy," Claire said, clearly highly annoyed with me, again.

I had received this lecture from Claire several times before. Claire was so impressed with herself, her position with Maridel and what she was told by Maridel about her potential for leadership in the Party. She certainly bought what Maridel sold. I wondered how she was not more exhausted. Keeping up with the façade required by Maridel was difficult. But, there was no cracking, Claire. On occasion, when I would try to get Claire to respond to me in a human manner by lobbing some sarcasm or a light joke her way, I found she was impenetrable each time.

"We need to go now," Claire commanded, "The rally will begin shortly and we can't be late."

With that, we left the motel room to meet Maridel in the parking lot. For most of our trips, we stayed in low budget motels so, as I was told by Maridel, we would avoid the appearance to our citizens that our aims were pecuniary in nature. Although I sensed that Maridel was somewhat disgusted on occasion with our motel style accommodations, she would often say aloud (as if to also remind and convince herself) that her sacrifices for the Party would pay off in the long run. I sensed Maridel had higher ambitions within the Party, but I wasn't privy to the details of the world she operated in, nor did I understand where that ambition might lead.

I followed Claire out of our room, suitcases in tow, and we piled into Maridel's car and began the short journey from the motel to the stadium where the rally was being held in Pennsylvania. Like always, there was a contingent of security guards waiting to waive us into a secure parking area and escort us into the event. Claire and I travelled with Maridel across the country for rallies, moving from location to location like I understood politicians running for President would campaign before Presidential term limits were abolished, which happened right after the President was elected to a second term. When the President ran for a second term, the results of the election were not in his favor, but he and the Party refused to accept the results claiming that the election had been hacked and imposed military rule until he got a friendly court to agree with him and the Party.

We attended huge rallies in stadiums and large parks, but we also visited smaller leadership groups within the Party. We held smaller town-hall style meetings all over the country too. The small leadership groups we visited might invite us into a church, school or even a leader's home or local community center for what were still called "family meetings," the name given to these small gatherings in the early days of Maridel's franchise and organization, which she started a few years before my mother had joined her Facebook group.

Most rallies had the same agenda. The really I was at on this particular day in Pennsylvania was no different. There was an invocation where we started with a prayer. After the prayer, Maridel approached the podium, as she always did, with her hands in prayer and head bowed. Claire and I were seated in chairs on the back side of the stage, much like altar boys would sit behind a priest, our golden colored chairs under stage lights so bright they made us sweat and prevented us from actually seeing the faces in the crowd, which resultingly appeared only as the dark shadows of a multitude of human heads.

Maridel took a few deep breaths in and out of her nose, noisily and such that the microphone picked up the awful sound, before she began to speak to the crowd.

"Well they said the Future Was Female didn't they?" Maridel began throwing up air quotes with her hands to express her negative view of what she often referred to as the *previously* liberal slogan.

The crowd erupted with applause, as it always did at each rally.

"Well, I'll tell you what. I like the look of this room. Lots and lots of strong women are in this room today and lots of strong men who support those women."

The crowd erupted again with applause. Maridel took a pause to let the applause settle down before continuing, waving her hand around with feigned humility urging everyone to quiet down.

"The future certainly was, and is, female but make no mistake that the future is not false feminism battling against faith-based values. You see feminism was used as a mask for murderous abortions, extramarital sex, the destruction of families and the ignorance of God – our creator. Feminism was used as a reason to destroy good men with the witch trial of the "me too movement," she continued loudly making sure to use her fingers to display air quotes again when she mentioned the me too movement.

"I mean, my friends, feminism allowed mothers in places like Iceland to terminate pregnancies if there was any deformity in a fetus while claiming that genetic screening was actually good! But we saw through the lies."

The crowd erupted in applause again. I had heard this particular speech enough times by this rally that I practically knew it by heart. Despite having sat on so many stages across the country, I still hated sitting on stage each time and always felt out of place doing so. As I sat, I would often silently predict in my head what the next speech line to come out of Maridel's mouth would be, as a game to keep myself occupied and forget everything going on around me.

Maridel had slowly silenced another round of applause before continuing in an even more angry tone of voice.

"Women finally came together to stand for true feminism, for true female values, and to create a better world for our children. The future was female alright, but not the kind of female that was a perversion of what women were put on earth to do and to protect. Before our President was elected, children's suicide was up ... children ... think about that for a moment. Cyber bullying was at an all-time high largely due to an unregulated Internet and commonplace use of cell phones and other devices among children. Divorce rates were off the charts. How many women did you know that struggled through a divorce as a result of a man quitting on his family, often times having an affair with another woman? How many women did you know who basically carried around a file box of papers with them for years during a divorce, having their lives turned upside down. As our young women grew up, if they attended college they normally spent more time binge drinking instead of studying. Despite women making bad choices on college campuses across America, those who called themselves feminists would have you believe that it was always a man's fault when alleged sexual assaults occurred!" Maridel had been pounding her fists on the podium forcefully during this part of her speech and I could tell she was breaking a sweat, as she usually did when she got riled up at a rally.

As the audience burst into continued shouts and cries of agreement in response, I thought about my father walking out on my mother, as I often did at this part of her speech. I knew from my classes at the CEP that Maridel's primary motivation in originally starting her organization was her painful and public divorce, following her husband's affair with a much younger woman. Maridel became increasingly angered over what she felt was a morality crisis in the U.S. and in the midst of joining some online support groups for victims of adultery, she began to hear countless stories of women across the country that, like her, had endured pain and struggle after being abandoned by their husbands. Maridel refused to believe that the only option for retribution was in the expensive and dysfunctional court system, much less in a support group, so she set her sights on how politics and cultural activism might have a greater impact on the issues that enraged her.

Being educated and fairly well off, Maridel was able to quickly organize her concept into local in person meetings and online meetings for people outside of New York City that followed her on social media. Eventually, she started being booked for larger speaking engagements (including at conservative political conferences) and she developed a way to franchise her organization, meeting structure and resources. There were swaths of underemployed or unemployed women who were desperate for a way to work and raise their children at the same time and she would get them to buy into her franchise. The pyramid and franchise of her organization allowed her to earn enough money to eventually form a political action committee, also backed by a wealthy family that was impressed by her substantial and totally devoted following.

I watched as Maridel pulled the microphone out of the podium holder before the last part of her speech so that she could walk around the front of the stage. She paused in the front center of the stage with her arms crossed, starting to speak again in a more quiet tone of voice, seemingly sympathizing with the audience.

"So, if you are ever in doubt about why we are on this mission and why we must support the Party, remember, our young people were in a world where the entire view of appropriate feminine behavior was skewed. School shootings seemed to be a regular occurrence, and yet some of these same phony feminists were telling us we should not have guns on hand to defend ourselves. Predators and terrorists could operate on what they say was a "free and open internet." Think about that! People actually thought we would be safer with a free and open internet, while those who planned to do harm were exploiting it for their evil purposes. We were living in virtual reality, not God's reality. Things had gone too far. We, the true brave in the home of the brave, wondered ... is it an accident that an apple appears in the Garden of Eden and on the front of the electronics and devices that were destroying our moral fiber? No! It was not an accident! It was God warning us! God used that apple to ask us ... Will you reject the apple of temptation? So we did. We resisted. And I want to thank you for your courage and commitment. The movement requires that we do the work every day. And you are not alone! A larger family in the Party is here for you!."

"A larger family!" the crowd shouted in response. Most people who attended rallies knew the responses to shout, like how people memorized the mass at church.

"True feminism!" Maridel shouted, as she put her right fist up in the air.

"True feminism," the crowd chanted in response. The responses always sounded like thunder to me and would often make me jolt on the inside, although I knew better than to move an inch from the force of it all. I was trained, among other things, that I was to stay calm and collected at all times.

After shaking a few hands of attendees in front of the stage with Maridel, we walked backstage and I completed two or three interviews in front of a Party backdrop, including one for the youth news program on Unity Media. Maridel seemed more pleased with my performance than she had the week before, nodding her head from behind the camera as I gave the last interview.

On our way out of town in Maridel's car that day, I listened to Maridel as she praised herself about the success of yet another rally. I could tell she got pretty high from the experience. Claire and I both offered some positive feedback because, in my case, I knew I had to and, in Claire's case, she wanted to.

Maridel chuckled incredulously as she drove with one hand and pulled a few bobby pins out of her hair with the other hand while continuing to praise herself, "and the crowds they just get bigger every time. I am just overwhelmed with the support we have. You know, when I started this movement I knew it would work because it required people in pain and those who were angry to buy in. And it was so clear to me that I had a world stocked with potential customers for that reason. It was my sense for business that turned this into something. There is such a tremendous market for those in pain and suffering. My customers are the wounded and the wounded are pretty much everyone," she finished her sentence bitterly, finally putting her other hand on the wheel.

I looked out the car window as Maridel continued praising herself to Claire for a while. I was grateful that the rally had taken place, and concluded, earlier in the day so we didn't have to stay over again in the motel. Since Maridel drank a lot most evenings, she had taught me how to drive her car over a series of weekends, so I could drive us home from rallies when she was either too tipsy or hungover to do it. I hated driving because it made me feel even more trapped to have control of a vehicle and zero ability to determine where it would go. Grateful to be alone in the backseat, I placed my head against the window and listened to the raindrops that had started to fall, wishing for a storm to drown out the voices from the front.

PART TWO

The Family

Chapter Eleven

Fall, 2031

Laurel meticulously followed the morning routine she had created for herself every day. First, she would pour her cup of tea from the tray her assistant always placed on her desk right before she arrived at the office. After that, she would turn her chair to face the floor to ceiling glass windows lining the entire perimeter of her office and begin to look at the Manhattan skyline. Normally, she would raise both of her hands up for a few moments, palms facing the city, to remind herself of all the power she had over the place. She would spend about an hour after that sitting in her oversized leather office chair, sipping her tea and internally musing about the significance of her role in saving the United States of America. She had read years earlier that it was important for successful leaders to engage in reflection or meditation each morning, so she made sure to do it. She figured that since she was the puppeteer who pulled the strings in the most powerful country in the world, she should do everything she could to stay focused at the highest level.

Laurel hated everything about New York City before the Party took control of it, its sheer identity being, in her view, the opposite of the good Christian values she was raised with. She had visited Manhattan a handful of times B.E. and witnessed firsthand the moral and literal filth disguised as "artistry" or "diversity." For a few years A.E., Laurel had been based in Washington, D.C., where the initial surge of activity was when the President won. But when the second phase of the Party's movement for control began in those "resistance" states that were tougher to gain control of, Laurel decided her presence would make a greater impact in New York City, the ultimate troublemaker of a city. At least now she could tolerate New York City more since it had been so significantly altered by the Party Guidelines, the changes a constant and pleasant reminder to Laurel of just how much she had accomplished.

Before the Party gained control of New York, women that dressed like Laurel would have stuck out like a sore thumb on the streets of places like Manhattan, where the "freaks" (as Laurel referred to them) used to roam. These days, thanks to the Guidelines, far more women that dressed like Laurel roamed the streets of Manhattan, religious women resembling more of a pioneer woman given the ankle length skirts and conservative blouses they wore every day. Laurel had mousy brown hair that fell below her shoulder blades and she always wore her hair half up with a slight poof at the top, her thick bangs slightly curled under where they fell at her eyebrow. She wore the same thick dark red glasses (she had several matching pair in case she misplaced them) and the same red lipstick every day. She had a bright white smile thanks to her father who encouraged her to have veneers put on after braces did not properly straighten her teeth. Her breasts were fake, a college graduation gift from her mother, and she had already endured two surgeries to further improve the appearance of her fake breasts over the course of her lifetime.

On this particular Tuesday morning, Laurel smiled as she finished the last sips of her tea while repeating the last of ten repetitions of her self-designed mantra several times "the Lord and Laurel own this city now … the Lord and Laurel own this city now…" Mid-mantra, Laurel's assistant knocked on her office door to inform Laurel that her driver was waiting in front of the office building to take her to the Unity Media broadcasting station. Unity Media had been founded by the President and his family, with Laurel's support and financing.

"You know better than to knock before exactly 9:55am," Laurel screamed.

"I'm so sorry," her assistant whimpered, "I see now that I am a minute or two early ..."

"Can you tell that I am ANNOYED?" Laurel barked, glaring at her assistant. "Don't let it happen again. This is what I pay you for."

Laurel grabbed her bag and brushed past her shaken assistant before heading to the elevator. After hopping into the SUV waiting in front of her office building and speeding through the usual city gridlock in her self-funded motorcade, thanks to demanding that her driver use the blue and red sirens she had insisted be installed on the car, Laurel arrived at the Unity Media television studio. She was immediately treated like royalty, as usual, being briskly ushered into her dressing room by an intern who had waited outside the guest entrance to greet her by the velvet carpet and stanchions that Laurel required the station place outside the entrance anytime she arrived there.

Laurel briefly inspected her dressing room after she entered it to make sure her list of demands had been complied with. She found her favorite items stocked in ample supply including cocoa butter lotion, gardenias, sparking water, expensive almonds and her favorite Zestar apples. She never used any of the items that she asked be stocked in her dressing room, but it was critical to her that they were available just in case she wanted them.

"We will be ready for you in 10, Ms. North," another intern popped in to the dressing room to announce.

"Wonderful. Please time my last powder and lipstick coat accordingly. I always need a little extra for the cameras," Laurel barked at the hair and make-up person cowering in the corner of her dressing room.

A few minutes later, final coat of make-up having been applied, Laurel was led to a bright white living room scene in front of a blue backdrop with the current Party slogan written in large white letters.

"Ms. North, Good Morning," Elizabeth Carlson, a morning anchor for Unity, said through a huge smile extending a hand, "we are so honored, as always, to have you here with us again."

Although Laurel did not trust Elizabeth completely (since she used to work for a liberal news station when they were still allowed to operate) and was a recent hire at Unity on account of her good looks, Laurel was fairly confident that the cushy salary and free boob job that was a part of the Unity hiring package had persuaded Elizabeth she was finally on the right side of the universe and would keep her "political views" in line. Plus, the benefits of a hiring a former liberal reporter often out-weighed any risk since it reminded the viewers that everyone, even liberal reporters, eventually saw the "light" and came around to supporting the Party ways.

"Always my pleasure," Laurel replied in a serious and somber tone of voice to avoid seeming too excited to appear on television again. In truth, Laurel loved being on television as much as she loved the attention she got from speaking in front of large crowds and representing the Party publicly in any capacity. Being so deeply connected to the President and his victory had its perks, and her role and involvement should have come as a surprise to no one since, as she would often remind everyone, she was the woman who had made it all happen by funding the underdog candidate for President and sparking the Party movement.

Laurel plopped down into one of the white armchairs on set and smoothed her navy blue ankle length skirt out perfectly over her lap and legs, her ankles crossed and knees tilted slightly to the side, the posture she always took when speaking publicly to mimic how the women in the British royal family sat on camera. Laurel blotted her lips a few times and took a measured breath, relaxing into her largest grin as a man behind the camera in front of her signaled the start of the show, counting from five to one with his fingers in silence before pointing at Elizabeth to indicate they were live.

"Good Morning and welcome to this morning's Unity live segment, The North Family, history and mission," Elizabeth began loudly, "I am thrilled to have Laurel North with us again, a great friend of the show and Unity Media. Today, on the sixth anniversary of her father's passing, Laurel will share some intimate details with us about her personal life and her legendary father, the late Steven North, gone from this earth, but his legacy very much still with us."

"Thank you for having me," Laurel replied making sure to intentionally soften her tone to her most humble voice, "My father was the greatest to me and, I believe, the greatest to so many people. He was one of the greatest Americans that ever lived and I am thrilled to have the chance to share more with you and the American people about his life's work to save our country."

"Indeed Steven North was instrumental in forcing change in American politics beginning with the election that saved America, but I want to go back even further, Laurel, to your memories of him growing up and how he raised you. What did you learn from him early on and what things did you notice about him that contributed to his ultimate success and to your success? Can you take us back to what life was like for you, Laurel, growing up as the daughter of an American billionaire and the man, we now say, laid the groundwork for the revolution that saved our country?" Elizabeth asked stoically.

As usual, Laurel had insisted that Elizabeth ask a series of open-ended questions that Laurel had prepared and provided to Elizabeth in advance so Laurel could control the narrative in her responses. Laurel was highly experienced in sharing her family's "story" learning the talking points early on in her life, which was common for any billionaire and their children. The narrative of "the family" was as important as anything they actually accomplished.

Before responding to the question, Laurel rocked slightly back and forth three times while nodding her head in the affirmative, "I'd be happy to share some of that, Elizabeth. My father raised us in an ordinary town in the Midwest, the heart of America, where we did not have to lock our front door at night until Daddy's profile grew and then our security team made sure we did," Laurel chortled.

After an awkward pause Elizabeth quickly realized she was supposed to laugh too, and forced a chuckle in response.

Laurel pretended not to notice Elizabeth's slow response before continuing in a slightly defensive tone of voice, "there was not too much to do in our little town and some might think that would make us small minded but there was a shopping mall, a bowling alley and a movie theater, which allowed us to be cosmopolitan enough I suppose. Saturday was for college sports. Sunday was for church. It was a simple and wholesome life and, of course, we were well-known given Daddy's work and profile."

Of course, Laurel did not mention that, in reality, although everyone in town knew who Steven North was, most people in town simply knew her as one of "Steven's kids" and rarely called her by name. After all, her father was a legend, a titan of the real estate and agriculture industries but she was simply one of "Steven's kids" or "Steven's daughter" or his "youngest". Steven North owned a national portfolio of commercial real estate which included office buildings, malls and apartment units, and he also owned massive amount of farmland. Although his real estate holdings yielded a significant fortune, it was his development of a tech concept that revolutionized the American agriculture and food production industry by turning farming into a fully robotic process that caused the North family wealth to skyrocket.

Some magazines said Steven North was worth eight billion dollars. Laurel knew he was worth much less, but the truth about their actual wealth didn't really matter since the rich always exaggerated their wealth for the magazines that ranked wealth. One strategy families like hers used was to count "intangible value" as part of their wealth (kind of like, what the value of your name and reputation was in your own view). People respected Steven because he was rich but, more importantly, because he had come from a hard-working start and led a faith-based life. Steven started work as an executive at a relatively young age for his family farming company, often repeating to Laurel and her siblings his words of wisdom, "Being rich is not enough to truly succeed, you have to know how to manipulate the soil."

"And your father made his fortune in real estate, is that right?" Elizabeth asked.

"Well it certainly began that way. He was a big thinker and on top of inheriting large tracts of land he also purchased property people said would never turn into anything. But those people were wrong because my father had a vision and turned those plots of land into some of the largest real estate developments in the country. Between that and his tech developments, I can just say that we were just lucky that God intended for him to lead and prosper. As you know, it is no accident that the people God wants to hold wealth do so. It is certainly no accident," Laurel concluded assuredly.

"Well I think there are a lot of God-fearing Christians who would agree with you about that, Laurel. Did you realize just how unique, powerful, and important your father was when you were a child or was your day to day life fairly ordinary?" Elizabeth asked.

"I would say we were always taught to put God first and, in that sense, no matter how life changed, God remained a constant. Abiding by God was our priority no matter what took place externally," Laurel replied intentionally making sure to arrange her hands delicately in her lap as she replied.

In reality, Laurel did not mention that she had been remarkably rejected and lonely most of her life, despite her family wealth, so describing a wholesome faith-based life was better than making up stories about a dream childhood she never had. From the outside, it would have appeared that growing up one of Steven's kids was not so bad. Laurel was treated like a princess in town, no one ever told her no, and she was fairly insulated from any negative comments about her family. Her parents made sure she had a tight group of pre-selected wealthy friends, most of whom were children of people they did business with, which also ensured her selected pals would suck up to her as needed. She spent her summers on expensive vacations and attended high dollar sleep away camps. She attended a private school reserved for the fourteen to twenty kids per class who could afford it. She always had a room full of toys and technology, including the latest and best things, as well as her own art collection and more designer label clothes than any child could ever wear.

But most of Laurel's weekend nights as a teenager were spent alone in the "hangout den" that her parents had let her design in a room adjacent to her bedroom with a flat screen television, surround sound speakers, arcade games, and a full mirrored wall with a ballet bar that she never used. Laurel would often sit in her hangout den, looking out her window listening to music, stewing with her anger over her loneliness that seemed to grow by the day as she grew from a child into a young woman. Despite the nose job her parents got her at fifteen years old and expensive clothes, Laurel knew she was not exceptionally attractive. No matter how many changes she made to herself or her den, thinking each time that her life would change and become full of friends and dates with boys, it never ended up the way she envisioned it (apart from the occasional sleepover she would host that other girls were forced to attend by their parents).

Laurel felt like she watched so many other girls "sprout" and develop a feminine beauty that she never developed, and her palpable hate and rage towards these other girls grew over time. Sometimes, her anger was so overwhelming that she would find herself scrunching her face up in anger with the inside of her bottom lip touching her top teeth, especially when she saw boys in her class (and even male teachers) fawn over "pretty" girls at school and on television. She was sure most of them were unintelligent and could not believe that girls could so easily get attention for what she considered to be the wrong reasons. She considered most of them were likely sluts (or acted like a slut). After all, since they did not possess her pedigree, wealth, and connections – why else would they get so much more attention if not for using their sex appeal to get it?

"Well we can all agree that putting God first is a good way to live, for sure," Elizabeth replied seriously to Laurel's prior response before asking, "and how did politics start to fit in this picture for you?"

Elizabeth crossed her legs placing her elbow on one of her knees right after she asked this question, using her hand to prop up her chin and stare at Laurel to show her intense interest in Laurel's response. Laurel had reminded Elizabeth in her pre-interview notes to use body language to convey her enthusiasm for Laurel's responses, and she had suggested Elizabeth use this gesture. Laurel noticed Elizabeth's moves seemed a bit too forced and delayed. This annoyed Laurel significantly, but she knew better than to get distracted on live television and quickly resolved in her mind that she would deal with Elizabeth later.

"I studied government and economics as an undergrad and finished law school at the top of my class. I was fortunate to gain a true understanding of the reality of our government system and I didn't like what I saw, Elizabeth. Neither did my father. Our country had stopped putting God first and the government was being used in a perverted manner. What was called feminism was really a movement to destroy good people and violate Christian values. My father had long been raising funds through the church and various non-profit organizations we created to get people in office that would fight for righteous and just causes. Following law school, I joined him in that mission. You can say it is my life's work. We saw that the best path to save our country from the horrors we were witnessing was to get our folks, the people who understood how much trouble we faced, into office to save us," Laurel replied confidently before continuing, her voice rising slightly with certitude, "ultimately, separating church and state makes no more sense than separating ourselves from God. We accomplished great change and put America back on the path to security and prosperity. God wanted things to transform. I am really just God's messenger. The Party is simply God's collection of messengers."

Chapter Twelve

Fall, 2032

Maridel told me that I would need to pack more than usual for "convention week" since we would be in Washington, D.C. for a full seven days. Most of our "family meeting" trips were just two to three days and I was pondering how to roll up more blouses without wrinkling them when my roommate, Veronica, walked in.

"I am so jealous you get to go to the convention. I wish I could go. How did you get the money gig as Maridel's little pet anyway?" Veronica whispered knowing she would get in trouble if anyone in leadership, or one of the other girls from the CEP who liked to snitch, heard her talking in such a casual manner.

"What a gig. I am so so lucky," I whispered sarcastically smiling at Veronica. "I actually have no idea why I got so lucky but why do you want to go to the convention so bad?"

Veronica was already at the CEP when I arrived and it took a few weeks before we understood that we could speak freely and trust each other. One night, I heard her whimpering in her sleep and asked her if she was ok. We whispered for hours that night and told each other about where we had come from. Veronica and her family had been a little bit better off than kids like me. Instead of working from a young age while going to school, her parents had actually set up her pretty well to focus on education, but their efforts wound up being pointless since higher education eventually stopped being a viable path to any kind of job for anyone that wasn't the small uber rich class in America.

Since we were roommates, it was easy to talk openly with each other, mostly in the still of the night in hushed whispers. Although we were monitored on video throughout every common area in the CEP, the decision was made to not wire any tech into our rooms to eliminate any possibility that we could reverse engineer some kind of access to the outside world using it. For this reason, Veronica and I actually enjoyed some privacy in our bedroom. We told each other everything about our past, families, and backgrounds. Veronica's mother had worked in fashion in New York before she lost her job. I loved hearing her stories about fashion week and the people she met. Having Veronica as a friend in the CEP made things a bit easier to bear.

"Well, to begin with, you are going to get to stay at a five-star hotel and I have been in those hotels before before and, let me tell you, it is the best. Plus, you are going to get to meet all of these famous sickos in power that have made our lives so glorious. Maybe you will even meet the President!" Veronica laughed and softly tossed a pillow at me.

"I'll tell him you say hello," I said through a snarky smile sarcastically, before changing to a more serious tone, "Listen, V. Please behave while I am gone ok. I don't want to get back and learn that my roommate was taken away to some crazy camp or chained up in the basement for a few days to learn a lesson."

"I promise to be here when you return. Nowhere else to go anyway," Veronica confirmed with a sigh.

A few minutes later as I continued to pack, we heard a knock on our bedroom door.

"Yes," I replied to the knock because "Come in" would sound far too permissive. All of us at the CEP were mindful to use the right words to reflect our subservience.

The door opened and Claire entered the room, "We are leaving in twenty minutes," she instructed me snottily, "As you know, Maridel does not like to make a lot of stops on the drive, so I suggest you get to the kitchen for a light meal before we leave.

"Of course. Yes. Thank you," I replied obediently.

"Leave your bags outside the door and I will make sure they get to the car," Claire finished as she turned on her heel and left our room.

The door shut and Veronica stood up.

"Well, let me give you a hug before you go," I said.

We embraced. I grabbed my bag to roll it out into the hallway.

"Listen," Veronica said quietly right before I opened the bedroom door, "Be careful. Be smart."

I twisted back to face her with my hand still on the doorknob preparing to open it.

"I will."

I made my way downstairs to the kitchen after leaving my suitcase outside of my bedroom door as Claire had instructed. I opted to order pasta from our short order cook. I hadn't slept great and hoped that a heavy carb meal would make me pass out on the long car ride.

I gobbled my food down and hopped in the car waiting for me out front twenty minutes later. My plan worked and, a few hours later, I woke up in Maridel's car as we were pulling into the cobblestone circular driveway in front of the hotel in Washington, D.C. I was slightly mad at myself for not being awake during the trip so I could have seen some of the Washington, D.C. monuments and landmarks that I had only seen pictures of in books, but not being forced to engage at all with Maridel and Claire by sleeping was worth missing the sights. After Maridel put the car in park, three men in uniform opened our car doors. I stepped out of the car and two more men in uniforms rushed over to collect our bags from the trunk. I waited for Maridel to take the lead and followed her through the double front doors of the hotel, held open for us by two other men in uniform.

As I walked into the lobby of the hotel, I slowly felt the low bun my hair was arranged in reach the top of my back, my neck skin folding, as I looked up and around the interior of the lobby in awe, butterflies multiplying in my stomach. Taking in my first sight of the hotel was like observing another universe in slow motion, and my eyes were drinking in the picture of everything around me with thirst and fury. The lobby was two stories tall, dark and succulent. It had black and silver walls with plush furniture perfectly staged in every location. I allowed my fingertips to graze the back of a velvet chair within reach and felt the hair on my arms stand at a tension as a result. A bright glass installation that looked like a million octopus tentacles hung from the ceiling, and the way the red, orange, and gray glass colors swirled throughout it made me wonder how the colors ever stood alone. I felt the tops of my legs burn with interest as I inhaled the sultry clean and salty smell of the hotel.

As my chin eventually found its way back to its natural position while Maridel was at the desk checking in, I slowly observed various women and men in beautiful clothing casually strolling around, greeting each other and shaking hands or patting each other on the shoulder, just short of a full hug. The people I saw milling about seemed calm, relaxed and firmly confident all at once. There was a sign on an easel by the front desk advertising the convention, with lists of various meeting titles and corresponding ballroom assignments. I quickly sensed that this convention was a much bigger deal than I had realized. My observations were interrupted by Maridel barking at me.

"Stop gawking," Maridel commanded. She had finished speaking to the desk clerk and approached me. I hadn't noticed because of how immersed I was in taking in my surroundings.

"I apologize," I replied mechanically.

Maridel began to describe how nicely received she was at the front of the hotel with VIP treatment. As I heard her express how glad she was that she was finally being truly recognized by the Party, I scanned the room in boredom and caught the eyes of a man I had seen walking around the lobby and shaking hands with a few people moments earlier during my gawking. He was wearing a gray suit and he stood out more than others in the lobby, the pop of his shiny shoes and the sheen of his hair adding a certain gloss to his appearance. I watched him smiling from ear to ear while speaking to a few people who approached him, his hands authoritatively on his hips. In the few moments I spied on him, he exuded power while holding court in the hotel lobby.

Suddenly, as I was watching this man, he must have noticed me staring and turned to look right back at me. I immediately turned my head and looked down, embarrassed for spying on him. Even though I kept my head down for a few minutes, I had the odd sensation that he might be watching me as I started to follow Maridel through the lobby to the elevators. When we stopped at a table with a glass container of ice water sprinkled with cucumbers, and I waited for Maridel to pour and drink three tiny cups of water, I quickly took a glance back behind me to where I had seen the man standing. Sure enough, he was staring right back at me while continuing to talk to a small group of people whose backs were to me. He smiled when our eyes met. I quickly turned my head back around and did not return the smile.

While riding on the elevator I was elated to learn I had my own room. Although most days Maridel was out of sight once the 5:00 hour came in the evening, I was thrilled for the added privacy of having my own room. As we walked towards the elevators, I could not imagine what the hotel rooms would look like given how opulent the lobby was. I wondered if my room would also have one of the shiny silver buckets of fresh flowers strewn about on every console and coffee table I passed in the lobby.

"Do you have a schedule for me?" I asked Maridel quietly as the elevator stopped on the floor she and Claire were staying on.

"Yes. Claire will drop it by your room later today. For now, just make sure you meet us in the lobby near the front desk at 7:00 for dinner. We are one of the few Party units invited to dine at the dinner hosted by Laurel North this evening and, without going into details that you would not understand anyway, you should know that this will be one of the most important honors of our time here, and likely your life. Laurel is one of the most powerful and influential contributors to our movement."

"Yes. Thank you." I replied quietly, head hanging down in its usual posture as they got off of the elevator and the doors shut.

I continued on the elevator to the ninth floor. As I stepped off of the elevator, and started to move down the hallway looking for my room number using the signs on the wall, I could feel how much thicker and opulent the carpet under my feet was compared to anything I had stepped foot on before. I had to pull hard on my suitcase to roll it down the hall since the thickness of the carpet was like quicksand to the wheels on the bottom of the case. The men in uniforms that greeted us had taken Maridel and Claire's luggage, but she had informed them that I had to carry my own. When I got to my room, I noticed that even the door handles were coordinated with the shiny light fixtures installed on the hallway walls. Every element of the hotel worked in concert to create endless eye candy and a feeling of calm isolation.

When I opened the door to my room, my eyes immediately took in sheer white drapes with sunlight cascading through them. The ceilings were tall enough that I had to look up to see the tops of the windows. The lights in the room were low and there was a soft music playing from within the room (which I would learn over the course of the week was always turned on every time the room was made up). I pulled my suitcase inside and wandered into the room, eventually passing the large king bed which I brushed with my fingertips to feel the linens. We only stayed at motels on road trips with Maridel and my family had never even been able to afford a hotel at all, anywhere. The only other time I had been so taken in by my surroundings was during the summer in East Hampton. For a second, the memory of the linens on the beds in East Hampton that summer entered my mind. I briefly shuddered at the memory, like I normally did when something reminded me of that summer. I quickly closed my eyes and took a breath, pushing the thought out of my mind far away where I kept the other memories, like I had trained myself to do.

Rather suddenly, I thought of Lizzie and how much she would love the hotel. It had been years since I had spoken to anyone in my family and after a while, the letter responses from Lizzie got less frequent. My mother never bothered to write except on a few holidays where she would express how glad she was that I was given the opportunity to be in such a structured and positive environment (and I sensed her letters were more for show than anything else). I wasn't allowed to write to Lowe since writing letters to relatives was our only writing privilege in the CEP. I eyed the pen and paper on the nightstand and wondered for a second if I could get away with a real letter to someone while I was here. I had wondered the same thing at every motel we stayed at while on the road with Maridel, but just as quickly as the thought entered my mind, I reminded myself that the risk was not worth it. As I was often reminded by those around me, I had a lot to lose if I blew the opportunity to be in a CEP, since chances for success did not come along often or easily for girls "like me." It wasn't hard for people to convince me that this was true so, like every other time I had considered trying to write, I didn't pick up the pen.

Chapter Thirteen

There were sure as hell a lot of things they did not teach you in law school about the real world, Elliott thought to himself anxiously as he stared at himself, naked, in the mirror at 5:30 in the morning after finishing his shower. He turned away from gazing at himself in the mirror every few seconds to sip his green juice that was perched on the granite countertop of his closet island. Like every other weekday, Elliott woke up this morning while it was still dark out. During his morning shower, he would mentally go from "zero to sixty" in a matter of seconds as the shower water hit his body, his mind racing with the list of things he would need to accomplish that day at work. The only mode Elliott knew was "short of breath with stress" mode given how much he was responsible for at the White House and the pace of his job each day. When push came to shove, if a ball was dropped at the White House, it was Elliott's head that would be chopped off by Laurel. Being the President's chief of staff and psychologically babysitting the President while serving the many masters that put the

President in office, including Laurel North, was far from an easy task.

Elliott always took some time to stare at himself in the mirror each morning before he got dressed because it did bring him some comfort to see that, despite the incredible stress he was under, his regular workouts and strict diet had prevented his body from tanking in the same way that his doctor constantly told him his blood pressure was tanking. After getting dressed in his enormous walk in closet, selecting a light blue shirt and gray suit from his color coded wardrobe, Elliott pecked his wife on the forehead on his way out of the bedroom as she slept. He whispered in her ear how hot she was, as he did each morning, and relished in her satisfied smile as she offered him a slight mumble of appreciation without opening her eyes.

Although Elliott had any number of trophy wife options before getting married, he felt like he had really lucked out meeting his wife, Robyn, because she was willing to spend so much time working for charitable organizations, which made him look good. Plus, she was somewhat reasonable by comparison to her friends since many of them opted into even more shopping, fitness, and dining than she did. Not that her $40,000 monthly shopping bills and expenses were pleasant to see (or pay), but he knew it could be worse. When he had suggested to Robyn once, while she had been in the middle of managing a second renovation to upgrade the swimming pool and tennis court only three years after their last upgrade, she had laughed at him and asked if the country club or private school tuition for the kids were next "to go."

After one final pat on his Robyn's behind, Elliott quickly dashed down one side of the double staircase of his Potomac, Maryland mansion, realizing that he might be a few minutes late for his meeting with Laurel. He immediately cringed at the thought of listening to Laurel whine about him being late in the annoying flirty way she always spoke to him. Elliott was not dumb and knew that Laurel wanted more from him than just the political errands she tasked him with. Keeping her happy and avoiding fulfilling her deepest desires, while keeping his job and maintaining his power, was nothing less than a herculean task. A short commute later that was only unreasonably extended given the number of cars on the Clara Barton Parkway, slightly sweaty from all of the cursing he had spewed at other drivers, Elliott approached the door to his office. He immediately noticed Laurel sitting behind his desk typing on his computer, her suitcase annoyingly blocking the doorway. For a moment, it dawned on him that she must have actually been able to get his password to log on to his computer. The extent of her power was alarming, but he knew better than to say or do anything in the moment other than to force a smile.

"Oh hi there, B. Good morning," Laurel smiled too brightly as she greeted him in a syrupy tone.

"Well ... look who decided to visit us from the big city," Elliott replied rolling her suitcase out of the way and into a corner, noticing that Laurel had left a tote bag open on his chair with a black lacy bra half out of the bag at the corner. The "accidental" clothing leak looked staged and he must have stared at it a bit too long because Laurel quickly interrupted his gaze.

"Oh dear. I hope you don't mind I was sorting a few things in here after I arrived. I came straight from the airport and have to head straight to a meeting on the Hill before I check into the hotel, so I figured you wouldn't mind if I left some things in here for the day, B."

Elliott had no idea why she insisted on calling him B. He had never asked her to or said it was ok with him.

"Laurel, Do I ever mind anything with you? Honestly, the way you talk sometimes makes me worry that I haven't properly conveyed how grateful I am for you. You know I couldn't live without you," Elliott said as he turned around and plopped into one of the guest chairs in front of his desk, watching as Laurel's face lit up, "So, what business does my visitor from New York bring me this morning?"

"Well," Laurel began more cautiously, "I'm afraid I have a big one for you and I suppose we need to strategize about how to handle it before the convention meetings begin."

"Are there ever small things you have for me?" Elliott asked jokingly, already feeling his chest tighten further with stress.

"Maridel," Laurel replied, "It's about Maridel. I think we have reached the point where her services are no longer useful to us. It's time we replace her and she move on to other ... opportunities."

"Maridel?" Elliott asked feining shock, "as in our family meeting/town hall television star formerly of Facebook fame?"

Elliott had known this conversation with Laurel about Maridel was coming for a while, but he knew better than to act anything other than surprised when Laurel announced one of her major decisions. Maridel had begun to lobby for more of a decision-making role in the White House over the past several months given, in Maridel's words, "her devout following and role in the President's success." Laurel always found a way to end anyone who even came close to the ballpark of her power domain, particularly when that person claimed any credit for what Laurel felt she was solely responsible for achieving. In terms of an invitation to a seat at the White House power table, you were either invited by Laurel or not, and there was no other way to get an invitation. If you dared to ask for an invitation, it was usually a sign for Laurel that it was time for you to go.

"Yes, that Maridel," Laurel said sounding annoyed, "although, with how much less and less she is appearing on television, I am not sure we can really call her our television star anymore. And that's part of the point. It's time. Her services have been helpful, but it's time for her to move on. End of story. I've decided. And you know I always have this way of knowing what is best when it comes to these things," Laurel said matter-of-factly.

As with every other prior "termination" Elliott had helped Laurel with, the thought was not lost on him that these people who had essentially devoted their entire life to the Party and were abruptly cut loose when their "shelf life" expired really had no other "opportunities" to move on to. The cycle was a constant reminder that he had to make sure he was never next.

"Got it," Elliott replied dutifully, "I'll put my best soldier on it. You have spent some time with my deputy Harper, right? She is doing really great work for someone who has only been around a year or so and she could benefit from the experience seeing this one through to the end. In fact, since she has often relayed media talking points to Maridel over the past year, their prior relationship should serve to provide some groundwork for the conversation."

"Right, Harper." Laurel replied flatly, with an edge in her voice all too familiar to Elliott.

Elliott knew when Laurel felt threatened or jealous. There was a specific way Laurel acted whenever Elliott mentioned another female staffer in any sort of positive way. Elliott felt strongly that the women who worked in the White House had to maintain a certain aesthetic so good looks and an attractive figure were conditions of hiring, particularly given the President's "love" of women. Beyond the morale boost Elliott felt everyone got from being surrounded by attractive people at work, the President was like a cat to a ball of yarn when it came to engaging with attractive female staffers, so "hiring hot" also helped Elliott manage the President. Laurel seemed to eventually be bothered by anyone Elliott hired.

"I totally defer to you, of course, on Harper being involved. I only care if you are happy," Elliott replied in an intentionally flirtatious tone hoping to calm Laurel down.

His approach worked, as it usually did, and a second later Elliott saw the color rising in Laurel's cheeks as she sat up straighter and replaced her frown with a bright while smile through her lipstick drenched lips. He never understood why someone who blushed so easily walked around in clown red lipstick all day.

"You are the best, B. Thanks for always considering my input. I suppose I don't care who does it, as long as it gets done. Let's just make sure the process goes smoothly. I don't want any mess to clean up. Ok?" Laurel said.

Elliott nodded in response, the stress knot that permanently resided in his stomach growing. How the hell he was going to fire Maridel without her fighting back was beyond him, given her profile in the Party. It would likely require some highly creative thinking, to say the least. Since Elliott had been suspecting this conversation about Maridel was coming, he had the foresight to begin some "research" on Maridel a few months earlier. Elliott's research partner was one of the best in the business and always seemed to find information that helped persuade people to capitulate to his demands and, in the case of someone he needed to remove from employment, accept a reasonable severance package. The trouble with blackmail at the upper echelons of Party leadership was that people at Maridel's level had information the Party would not want disclosed too, so blackmail and threats at a high level was a more intense and complex process. He knew it would be better for Harper to have the blood on her hands if things got messy with Maridel, so his plan of lining up at least one potential buffer seemed to be on track.

"Well, I better get going. My meeting starts soon," Laurel stood up from behind Elliott's desk and walked over to her baggage in the corner, "It may be a good idea for us to meet again later and talk some more about your plan with this Maridel thing. Are you free if I need you?"

Elliott did everything he could to prevent his face from revealing his disgust at the thought of being forced to met with Laurel again as he stood up to walk her out of his office.

"You know I am always free if you need me, doll, but I do need to get over to the hotel for some last minute convention planning and I want to shake hands with the visitors from Germany given their substantial invest-ment in the Party recently. Raincheck me?" Bryan asked, sweetly.

Laurel nodded her agreement, clearly disappointed. Elliott noticed the skepticism in her eyes. It did not take much for Laurel to become paranoid when she did not feel enough of "the love" from him. He quickly walked over to where she was standing and gently eased the edge of her lacy bra back into her carry-on bag, effort-lessly, before zipping up her case, taking care to do it slowly so she noticed. As he picked up her bag off the chair, he noticed she was blushing again and panting slightly. He knew he had succeeded in distracting her.

"Call me later. Let me know how the Hill goes," Elliott offered as he handed Laurel her coat and bag.

"Yes," Laurel said breathlessly, "I will." And with a pat on her back from Elliott, Laurel walked out of his office.

Chapter Fourteen

I was doodling on the note pad I found next to the huge bed in my hotel room while sitting in the empty bathtub, dry and fully clothed, my pen and paper propped up on my kneecaps which served as my easel. The bathroom was beautiful and made of floor to ceiling cream colored marble with a soft white fuzzy bath mat rolled up on the back of the tub, and a tray full of bath products adorning one side of it. There were fluffy white towels on every hook and stacked perfectly in tightly wound rolls in the open cabinets under sink. Most shockingly to me, there was a television flush inside the bathroom mirror that was playing the Unity Media station at a low volume. I must have examined the mirror for at least twenty minutes trying to figure out how the television was a part of the glass of the mirror while I opened every bottle of the bath products on the counter to inhale the scent of each one before I retreated to the tub. As I worked on doodling a daisy with the heavy blue pen that had been stationed next to the note pad, the phone rang and startled me so much that

I practically leapt out of the tub in one motion. There was a phone next to the toilet. I slid across the bathroom floor after hopping out of the tub to answer the call.

"Hello?"

"Would you enjoy turndown service this evening?" I heard a man's whiny voice ask.

"Turndown service?"

"Yes. Would you enjoy it this evening?"

"I am not sure. What is that? I might need to ask ...." Awkwardly I realized I had never needed to refer to Maridel and Claire in public before to someone who didn't necessarily know who they were. As I was deciding how I should describe them..."teacher...leader...boss...", the annoyed man interrupted my thought process.

"May I suggest you accept it and you can reconsider your decision tomorrow if you don't enjoy it," he said curtly, before hanging up abruptly.

I hung up the phone and wandered out of the bathroom and into the walk-in closet to finish unpacking. As I emptied my suitcase, my mind immediately started to inventory the clothing I had brought along with me. I thought of the way people in the lobby had been dressed and recoiled at the thought of wearing my clothes around that crowd. The clothes I had from the CEP were still nicer than anything I ever had at home in terms of the quality and brands, but they mostly made me look like a dowdy grandmother as opposed to a person who apparently stayed at a five star hotel. I had brought along skirts in every color which came down slightly past my knee (in accordance with house rules), several blouses, a few silk scarfs (which Claire often told me to wear around my neck), low pumps in black, tan, and gray, some cashmere sweaters and belts with plenty of panty-hose, and a few headbands.

I was considering some of the outfits Veronica would create for fun as we would hang out in our room. Of course, Veronica would never leave our room in the "looks" (as she called them) that she would throw to-gether. To avoid getting caught, she would usually rip them off as quickly as she had thrown them on, after taking a glance at herself in the mirror and doing a spin on the imaginary runway she would walk down in be-tween the twin beds in our room. I figured I should dress up a bit more than I usually did given how important Maridel stressed the dinner was, so I started to play with the clothes I had, laying them out on the bed and match-ing different pieces together to see how they looked.

At 6:45pm I was stationed in the lobby. I had selected a navy colored skirt to wear that was just slightly too snug, the same one Veronica told me looked more like a "pencil skirt" and had asked me how I got permission to order given how "non-CEP" it looked on me. I had not received permission to order it, but had claimed it when another girl had been kicked out of the CEP and we were told we could raid her closet to take her clothes. I wore navy pumps and instead of opting for the normal dark gray blouse I wore with navy skirts, I opted for a light cream colored blouse that I tucked in tight, instead of tucking in and blousing it out like I normally did. I had also folded one of the cream colored scarves with a midnight blue and cream floral print into a thin rectangular band and fastened it around my waist like a belt.

My figure was still long and even leaner given the weight I had lost since living in the CEP. I pulled my hair half up instead of completely in a full bun. I could not stop smiling at how much more "real" I looked when I examined myself in the full-length mirror on the back of my hotel room door. For the first time in a long time, I felt pretty. My hair had remained the golden blond it had always been and it smelled good from the products I had used in the hotel shower. I had successfully manipulated the hairdryer from the bathroom with my brush to blow my hair into soft waves, like Lowe used to do for me when we had an occasional sleepover. I was seated on a plump and plush red chair looking at the elevator when I saw Maridel and Claire get off of it. For a moment, I hoped that the fact Maridel was dressed up more than normal in a shiny long skirt and cap sleeved blouse with a bow at the collarbone meant that I had made the right decision about my clothes. Any confidence I had in my decision instantly evaporated the moment I stood up and Maridel saw me, her eyebrows and lips falling into a disgusted scowl.

Maridel walked towards me until she was standing right in front of me, close enough that I could smell her breath.

"Exactly what are you wearing?" she growled, without even the hint of an actual question in her voice.

"I assumed I had to dress up for dinner," I replied quietly.

"If anyone would be required to dress up, Anna, it would not be you. You are a background fixture. You are here for the sole purpose of being my assistant and responding to the things I need and ask you to do. This evening, your sole job is to field questions from people who want to meet me and remembering who they are, since I clearly can't be expected to greet everyone who wishes to meet me at these events. As I explained to you when you arrived at the CEP, you are an extra arm for me. Your voice is sometimes required but irrelevant. It is your job to manage my details and the second you forget that you will be replaced." Maridel was speaking to me in one of the most cutting voices I had ever heard her use. I was no stranger to her speaking harshly to me, so I knew I was in serious trouble.

I was immediately filled with fear and remorse.

"I am so sorry," I stammered, "I did not mean to offend you. May I excuse myself to change into something more suitable?" I spoke as I looking down at my feet in shame.

Maridel continued to snarl at me, her voice rising with anger as she continued to reprimand me.

"No. You may not. We will be late if we wait for you to do that and at least your skirt covers your knees. We will discuss this later. I told you years ago how important it is that you don't use your blessings for sin, Anna. As you well know, sin includes desire and disobedience and it also includes drawing attention to yourself and craving attention, especially for the wrong reasons."

"Yes, mamm," I replied quietly, my head still down and my hands trembling by this point.

We were specifically and intensely trained in our classes at the CEP to avoid attracting physical attention at all costs and that any such attention should only be bestowed on us by a husband following marriage. Maridel turned on her heel to walk into the ballroom where the dinner party was being held and motioned for me to follow her. I almost ran into her as she paused one last time on our way into the ballroom to turn back at me, her anger while speaking causing spit from her mouth to hit my forehead as she issued one final warning to me.

"And please remember, Anna, as we meet people if you speak, people assume it is because I am letting you speak for training purposes. It is your job to make it clear that I do the work and you only speak when, and because, I let you do so for practice."

I nodded my understanding before continuing to follow her into the ballroom.

The scene in the ballroom we entered was abruptly in sharp contrast to the scene I had just experienced with Maridel in the lobby. The room felt fully of excitement. There was soft music playing and food displayed ornately on round tables around the perimeter. Most people were huddled in groups talking and greeting each other in animated tones, drinks in hand, the hum of voices louder than the music. Waiters in starchy black and white uniforms were making their way around the room offering glasses of champagne and wine from large trays. We were immediately presented with such a tray and Maridel eagerly accepted a tall glass of champagne. I noticed what appeared to be a raspberry floating in the top. I watched as she took a long and swift drink from the glass and then followed her as she began to wander the room. As we walked around, she barked at us quietly with the reminder for us to take mental notes as we greeted people so we could remember the details of the conversations she might forget. I observed that although we were walking around the room, no one came over to us right away, despite how crowded it was.

As we neared a table with the largest shrimp I had ever seen piled on top of what appeared to be a crab's leggy body parts, a man jumped in front of us.

"Maridel, Am I right?" the man said.

I suddenly realized it was the same man who had stared at me in the lobby.

"I don't think we have met before but I have heard a lot about you even from far away here in good ole Washington," he exclaimed.

"Mr. Deen, it is an absolute pleasure," Maridel said in a grandiose tone, "I am sure you have not had too much time to hear about me given the importance of your daily duties."

"Oh. Don't be modest, Mari," he replied.

I noticed Maridel cringe at his unapproved abbreviation of her name.

"We may have fine leaders that enjoy their moments at the pulpit, but everyone including the President knows how critical your work is to the Party's movement," he said placing his hand on her shoulder as he spoke. She seemed uncomfortable with the contact. Maridel took another large swig from her glass, finishing what was left of the champagne in a single sip.

"Well. Thank you for your words of encouragement. I'm sure you mean *our* movement, not just the Party's movement," Maridel replied with an annoyed edge in her voice, "after all, it was me who..."

The man cut Maridel off abruptly, "and who do you have with you this evening? I am so sorry for being rude," he said extending his hand to me, "I should have introduced myself sooner. Elliott Deen, Chief of Staff to the President of the United States."

My mouth must have been hanging open a bit because he quickly followed up with an intoxicating smile and, in a low voice, said to me, "Don't worry I am not as fancy as my title sounds."

I immediately shut my mouth and extended my hand to shake his. He smelled like fresh linen even from afar, and his hands felt strong and soft.

"Believe me. No apology necessary," Maridel replied, tartly, to Elliott, "This is just my assistant, Anna. I have also brought along my associate, Claire," Maridel said proudly placing her hand on Claire's shoulder. I noticed Elliott look intently at the placement of Maridel's hand before giving her a look I could not interpret.

"I assume with the recent surge and strength of the youth movement within the Party and our focus on the next generation of leaders you must have considered it wise to bring along some of our strongest Party youth members. The President would love to see this. Good instincts, Mari," Elliott replied with equal tartness.

Maridel began to back track a bit seeming embarrassed at her uncontrolled dismissal of me, quickly taking her hand off of Claire.

"Well, of course," Maridel stammered a bit, "but you see ... Anna is not really working directly with the youth yet, she is still training with me, mainly at my rallies."

"Well. I have seen Anna on television at your rallies quite a bit lately. This week will be a good opportunity to get Anna involved in some youth training seminars

I should think. As you know, this is a critical time for this movement, particularly with respect to the youth, to make sure we keep things under control. You know, Anna, you may not realize how fortunate you are to be learning from such a master. Maridel's legacy and imprint on the Party's past is clear. I have been routinely informed at the highest levels of how instrumental she was in the early days of the Party rising to power," Elliott informed me glowingly.

"I'd like to think our work in the early days continues to ring true today," Maridel replied sounding more and more annoyed at the suggestion that she was more relevant in the past.

"I will tell you what. Why don't I learn more about what you are up to over dinner? I will have my seat moved to your table. The President asked me to get as much ground level operations intelligence as possible this week. I would love nothing more than to hear from you how work in the field is progressing," Elliott suggested.

"Well, I would be honored to provide information for you to report back to Pennsylvania Avenue," Maridel replied, appearing to thaw slightly at the mention of the President.

"Great. I look forward to hearing more over dinner," Elliott said looking at me with smiling eyes as he replied to Maridel. I watched Maridel flag down a waiter carrying more champagne. Elliott winked at me before walking away. It felt like his arrival and departure from where we were standing was nothing short of a force of nature.

After another hour or so of smiling and nodding at the few people that came over to meet or greet Maridel, we finally entered an adjacent room for dinner. The room was no less opulent than everything else I had seen at the hotel. The lighting was low and I noticed a podium at the center of the room. The tables were set with crystal clean glasses and dinnerware placed perfectly in front of low lush centerpieces made up of overflowing red, white, and blue flowers. It occurred to me that if this was what the mysterious life of Party leadership was like, it did not seem that bad. Just being in the room listening to a harp player, seeing the vast amount of food, and feeling the energy in the room actually felt like more fun than I remembered having in a long time, or ever. It felt important.

Chapter Fifteen

We followed Maridel to our table after she picked up a card with her name and our table number on it. Maridel sat down at our table first, Claire sat down next to her, and I sat down next to Claire. My eyes were drawn to the soft rolls stationed in the center of the table next to tiny silver trays of butter that were cut in the shape of pineapples with a pineapple pattern imprinted on them. I was starving, but I knew better than to touch anything or eat until Maridel started to eat. My gaze on the dinner rolls was only broken because I heard Elliott's voice suddenly from behind my chair.

"We meet again," I heard Elliott say. The hair on the back of my neck rose for some reason. "I hope you won't mind if Harper Broderick joins us. Harper was enthusiastic about the opportunity to speak with you too, Maridel."

The woman standing behind Claire's chair was stunning. She had long and glossy dark straight hair and thick black glasses. She was wearing a black pantsuit that looked like it was cut just for her, a light gold fitted blouse and tall black heels. I noticed the diamond watch on her left wrist and a delicate gold necklace close to her throat as she slightly moved and extended her hand around the corner of Claire's chair towards Maridel to shake her hand.

"It is nice to put a face to the name, Maridel. I assumed you received the messages from my assistant, Peyton, today trying to set up a face to face for us this week," Harper said with a slight edge in her voice.

Maridel grimaced in response.

"Of course. Unfortunately, my schedule has been a bit more hectic than usual today, so I haven't been able to respond yet," Maridel replied darkly. I could tell that, for whatever reason, Maridel did not seem interested in getting to know Harper, nor was she enthusiastic about her presence. Despite the fact that Harper had extended her hand from a standing position, Maridel did not stand up to extend her hand in response but, instead, quickly shook Harper's hand from her seated position in an almost dismissive manner.

Harper seemed to respond to Maridel's seated handshake with a knowing smile, walked past her chair and confidentially took a seat next to Maridel, on the side unoccupied by Claire who, despite what I was sure were Claire's best efforts to avoid doing so, was staring a little too long at Harper. It was hard not to stare at Harper. She was beautiful and exuded a seductive confidence and grace. A few seconds later, as I continued to stare at Harper who offered me a slight closed lipped smile as she was placing her napkin on her lap, I heard Elliott's voice on my left. He had apparently seated himself next to me, on the side unoccupied by Claire. The elbow of his suit jacket grazed my arm as I noticed that he slightly moved his chair closer to me.

"Are you having fun?" Elliott asked.

I froze for a second unsure of how to respond. I briefly nodded my head in the affirmative.

"You know, I doubt your fearless leader will be paying much attention to you right now given the conversation Harper is having with her. And, for the record, your fearless leader is not in charge of me or what I want to do, so I hope you will indulge me in some casual dinner conversation this evening, Anna. For example, you might tell me this is the most boring event you have ever been to. Personally, I would rather be at home relaxing."

I was beyond nervous. On one hand, I knew there was zero chance Maridel would have ever sanctioned me casually speaking to Elliott, or any man for that matter. On the other hand, it was clear Elliott Deen was important and I knew I couldn't be rude. I quickly glanced over at Maridel and observed that she and Claire were immersed in what Harper was saying.

I turned my head slightly towards Elliott trying not to make direct eye contact.

"Seems like a lot of food?" I questioned. It was the first thing that came to mind but when I said it out loud, it did sound like a silly thing to say.

Elliott reached for a roll and offered it to me. I started at his hand holding the roll for a second, unsure of what to do. He nodded and pushed his hand further towards me, motioning for me to take it. I gently took the roll from his hands, tingling a bit with nervous energy when I did so because my fingers brushed his for a second. Elliott swiftly reached for a second roll and started to apply butter to it for himself. I glanced back towards Maridel again. She was still immersed in her conversation with Harper and had even angled her chair towards Harper, with her back to me. I noticed her pointing her finger at Harper while she was talking.

I began to cautiously eat the roll. I was nervous to eat in front of Elliott for some reason, but I was also starving and couldn't resist doing so.

"Have you ever been to a party like this before?" Elliott asked me.

"Nope," I replied quietly scanning the few other people who had settled into our table. The others had politely offered Elliott and Maridel brief hellos and handshakes when they had arrived at our table a few minutes earlier, mentioning that they worked for Unity Media. Like Maridel, they seemed immersed in their own conversation and were not paying attention to me or Elliott, possibly aided by the fact that Elliott seemed to dismiss them pretty quickly in an annoyed manner after they greeted him.

"Most of the social events we attend when we go on the road are much smaller," I continued, taking a sip of water from the glass in front of me with ice cubes melted so thin that I was forced to swallow a few small remnants of the cubes. "Usually they are hosted by someone in their home, nothing fancy."

"Got it. Well, lucky you for not having to be subjected to these things before," Elliott continued, "I remember in the early days of my career thinking that these professional social events were incredible, like mini weddings where we discussed business and strategy and got to eat and drink whatever we wanted, but after a while they wear on you. These things become less fun and more routine and obligatory, and how many buttered rolls does one need to eat at a decorated table with people from work right?"

I felt slightly embarrassed for a moment because I was in the middle of downing my second buttered roll when he said it. I shrugged my shoulders in response. I had no idea how many buttered rolls someone needed to eat, but I sure loved the rolls I was enjoying.

"I've watched a bunch of your coverage, at the rallies. I had my assistant pull some of the tapes of it for me after I figured out who you were, you know after we saw each other in the lobby," Elliott was smiling as he mentioned the lobby.

I squirmed at his mention of the lobby. It appeared Elliott was enjoying that I was squirming, his smile growing bigger.

"Your good, Anna. It seems like you have found a calling going in front of the cameras. You are so..." he paused as if to consider his words carefully, "genuine and innocent, but clear and assertive at the same time. Do you enjoy your work?" Elliott asked.

Although for most of the conversation I had been starting straight ahead while responding to Elliott for fear of seeming too engaged or angering Maridel by violating protocol, his question caused me to abruptly turn and stare at him directly in the face. I was shocked not only because he admitted to watching me on tape in advance of meeting me, but also because he referred to my CEP duties as "my work".

"My work?" I said, noticing I sounded a little too sarcastic. I quickly corrected my tone to a dry one before continuing, "I'm sorry, what I mean to say is that I am very fortunate to live in the CEP and being Maridel's assistant is a privilege. You know, Maridel is really just letting me do this kind of stuff for training."

"Right," Elliott paused again to take a sip of water, and it looked like he was smiling slightly, "uh huh. You know, if I didn't know any better, I would say you almost started to respond honestly to that question at first. Am I making you feel comfortable?" Elliott asked with a flirtatious smirk before leaning to whisper into my left ear as if we were longtime intimate friends sharing secrets, "I think I might like the honest Anna even more."

The conversation with Elliott had me quite distracted and I felt myself getting even more flustered while grabbing a third dinner roll. It didn't help that he was incredibly good looking and exuded some kind of energy that made me feel like I was in the presence of power.

Elliott continued, "Look, I probably shouldn't put you on the spot. I know there are rules you have to follow. I am just interested in hearing a little more about what life is really like for you. You seem fascinating to me. And, for what it's worth, based on what I have seen on tape and learned about Maridel and you today, I think you are becoming more than Maridel's messenger. And you should know that with some of the challenges the Party faces to keep American youth persuaded of the greatness of Party principles, there is a lot more you can do along with others your age to keep us on track."

Hearing Elliott call me fascinating caused a surge of adrenaline to rush through me. While I sat immersed in the feeling for a second, servers began to place a the most beautiful salad I had ever seen in front of us with carrots on top cut into the shape of some kind of flower. I stared at my salad for a second before turning back towards him to respond.

"Honestly, I'm probably not as fascinating as you think. I would rather hear about how you got to be your ... job ... or role ... or whatever you call it ..."

"How I got to be the raging success I am today?" Elliott said in a jokingly drawn out low voice like an announcer.

I quietly giggled, "Yes. I guess that is what I mean."

"Well. I'll tell you," Elliott continued, "I got here because of a great education, a lot of hard work, some law school and I guess being in the right place at the right time with the right people. I guess the Party would tell you that I am one of those people who God considered worthy for success."

'Is that what you think?" I asked.

Elliott smiled, "You are curious, aren't you? Well, Anna, I will be honest with you as long as it stays between us, as friends." I nodded my head in agreement, blushing at the mention of us being friends.

"I think what those of us who reach the top have in common is luck. Luck, Anna. Luck as to who we are born, who we meet and when we meet them, where we meet them and who they know at that time, what the people we meet need at the time we meet them and what we can provide at that time. Just think about it. A brief second or a single encounter can change a person's entire path. One slight change in the history of the steps any one of us takes in our life, and the outcome of where we end up could be totally different. We like to think we are in control by making decisions that point us in a certain direction, but the truth is that very little that truly impacts us in the long run was ever in our total control at the time the plot points of our life take shape. Luck.

Fate. Whatever you call it. That is what I really think," Elliott replied matter-of-factly.

I found myself hooked on his words and stared back at him intently. It might have been my imagination, but I felt like he knew I was eager for him to say more.

"I'm used to power, Anna," Elliott continued, "I have a lot of it and I use it. I control more things now than I ever could have imagined. But even with my power and status, I know there is still a lot that continues to be determined by luck. There are so many things outside of my control that could change how much power I have, that could change my status."

"It sounds a little sad when you describe it like that," I replied softly.

Elliott seemed to relish in how intently I was listening to him. I could tell he liked how interested I was in him and the things he was saying.

"Or, maybe it's not sad. I depends on whether luck leads to better things. Either way, people like me get used to living on the wing of luck, on the edge every day, knowing we might fall off the wing at any second. The ride can still be pretty great in the meantime."

I felt my face soften.

"Well, if the ride is like this party, it sure looks pretty great from the outside," I replied sincerely.

His eyes sparkled looking back at me. I took a delicious bite of salad and found myself relaxing, not even aware of anyone else in the room at that particular moment. Elliott proceeded to ask me if I might like him to point out some of the "major players" (as he called them) who were in the room. I agreed and he started to quietly point out various senators, business leaders, Party leaders, media celebrities, and foreign dignitaries. I didn't know who most of the people were, but I listened intently, totally impressed at the significance of the titles and descriptions of people he provided. It was certainty enough to make me feel insecure, like I was undeserving of being in the same room. He seemed so happy to be quietly teaching me from our table about who was in the room. When he pointed out Laurel North, the same woman Maridel had mentioned to me when we arrived, I noticed that she seemed to have an annoyed looked on her face when she saw Elliott pointing to her table and giving her a little wave. As he concluded telling me who was in the room, the servers placed a plate of steak and chicken in front of me smothered in a creamy sauce. I noticed the two stalks of broccoli were crossed in an x, perfectly, on top of what appeared to be some kind of potato with a puffy top.

"Tell me about yourself. Where did you grow up?" Elliott asked gently as he started to slice his steak.

"In the city...Brooklyn," I replied taking another sip of the icy cold water.

"I love how people from New York often say "the city" first as if it is the only city in the country," Elliott said chuckling.

"Isn't it?" I replied and I noticed that I sounded slightly flirtatious. Elliott quietly chuckled. He seemed to enjoy my response more than I expected.

"Well there are a lot of people in this room who would disagree with you and I think even more who would consider the city to mean Washington, D.C.," Elliott said tossing his tie over his shoulder before he took a bite of the steak from his plate. I wasn't sure why but the motion he made with his tie made him seem even more powerful, every motion he made being swift, confident, and intentional.

"Do you have any family?" he asked me.

"Yes. I am the oldest of four kids," I confirmed.

"That must have been tough, especially these days. Lots of mouths to feed," Elliott quietly responded.

I nodded, "We started work pretty early in my family for that reason. I think I was about twelve when I started really working major hours," I replied.

"Hard work runs laps around the rest of us who paid for degrees in some cases. You seem pretty well spoken. Did you get to take any college classes?" he asked.

"No. But my high school teachers were great and one of my teachers would give me the old AP syllabus in a bunch of subjects, so I read a lot and I guess I was lucky in that sense. I used to read books like people drink water," I replied with more confidence in my voice than I had heard in a long time.

Elliott nodded as he continued to eat his dinner plate, tie unmoved from its protected perch on his broad and muscular shoulder that bulged slightly through the taut fabric of his dress shirt. He had dispensed with his jacket and placed in on the back of his chair.

My eyes wandered to the podium at the front of the room.

"Do you give a speech tonight?" I asked gesturing to the podium.

"No. No," Elliott chuckled, "It is nice of you to think I am that influential, but that honor will be reserved for the President and some Party leaders. I am more of a behind the scenes guy. I run things. I fix things. I get things done out of sight, mostly. Do you know much about what I do?" Elliott asked me.

"Not really. I would like to," I responded.

Elliott looked at me and smiled in response. I was completely drawn to him. He knew it and I could tell he liked that I was.

"Well, I don't know about your teachers and the AP syllabus being lucky for you, but I think meeting me today might be lucky for you," I heard Elliott say as whatever sauce drizzled on the bite of steak I was eating made my cheeks pucker a little. My face flushed and I felt the butterflies in my stomach also rush every direction they could through my body, up my esophagus and into my neck, behind my ears and into my lower belly and the tops of my thighs.

I started to gently cut my dinner into smaller pieces, suddenly much more aware of how I appeared with every move that I made. I wanted him to like how I moved. I found myself further straighten my spine and relaxed my shoulders at the same time. As I continued to place tiny forkfuls of warm dinner into my mouth, listening to the hum and buzz of the ballroom, I liked the way I felt and, quite alarmingly, I was enjoying the way it seemed I made Elliott feel too. Rather instantly, I started to crave more of whatever it was that I was feeling.

Chapter Sixteen

I slept so well in the hotel room on that first night of convention week. I mean, I slept like I have never slept in my life. And I took the longest shower I had ever taken the next morning. I felt like I never wanted to step out from under the massive showerhead stationed in the middle of the shower ceiling. I even figured out that the buttons I pushed on the shower wall made water spray out of the walls too.

The night before had ended stressfully, despite how much I enjoyed myself during dinner with Elliott. Right as dessert was served, Maridel had abrubptly stood up and instructed Claire and me that we were leaving before dessert. I could tell she was drunk and upset. I stood up quickly in response only to have Elliott touch my arm and motion for me to sit back down. He suggested to Maridel sternly that she also sit back down and stay until the end of the event, so as not to offend the President or him. It almost seemed like he was intending to issue a threat to her. I noticed Harper start to eat the dark chocolate cake in front of her as if she did not have a care in the world.

Seeing Elliott tell Maridel what to do and feeling him touch me drove me crazy in a good way. It felt like he was protecting me. Maridel had obeyed Elliott's suggestion, a look of shock on her face as she sat back down and motioned for Claire to do the same. Maridel had barely uttered two words to Claire or me on the elevator ride up after the event ended, in fact they did not even look at me. Claire looked like she might cry and the last I saw of them was their backs as they stormed off of the elevator towards their rooms.

I was laying out my clothes the next morning preparing to revert back to my standard manner of dressing, in a bit of a depressed fog at the thought of seeing Maridel, when the phone rang. I jumped again -- still not used to the phone ringing.

"Hello?" I answered.

"Anna, Hi. It's Peyton, Harper Broderick's assistant," a young woman responded.

"Hello," I replied.

"Harper wanted me to tell you that she has arranged with Maridel for you to attend the youth leadership meetings and training at the convention today. We have someone on the way up to give you a full schedule. Elliott Deen also sends his regards and wants you to know that he is thrilled you will be participating today," she relayed in a matter-of-fact tone.

"Yes. Ok. Um. Thank you?" I replied thanking her in the form of a question and feeling totally confused. I hung up the phone and plopped down in a seated position on the bed. I caught a glimpse of myself in the mirror on the wall at the foot of the bed and I noticed myself smiling, a tiny smile. For some reason, the thought of Elliott made my body feel warm and flush again.

"Lucky," I thought quietly to myself.

Rather suddenly, with a burst of energy, I ran to my closet and pulled out every article of clothing I had. I knew I would be breaking the "rules" (again), but this time I felt more confident about doing it. After all, Elliott had not made any negative remarks about my outfit the night before being too inappropriate. I settled on a dark tan skirt. I put on black pumps to keep things simple and a black cardigan that ended right where the high waist of the skirt began. I decided the buttoned cardigan would adequately replace a blouse, even though I usually wore the cardigan on top of a button-down shirt. I noticed in the mirror that the cardigan clung to my breasts a little more than I expected, but figured I could always cross my arms in an emergency to hide my figure.

At that moment, a knock on my door interrupted my examination of my outfit. I ran over to the door and answered, still slightly breathless from getting ready in a hurry. A man with an earpiece running down one side of his face handed me a folder, "your schedule and information for the rest of the week," he said. On the top was a small sealed card with my name on it. I took the folder, shut the door, and tore open the sealed card.

"Don't be nervous. I know you are.
You are going to learn so much today.
You are going to be a natural. I've got you covered."
- B

My heart lurched and I found myself smiling again. I put on a thin black ribbon as a headband and wore my hair down for what felt like the first time in ages. I grabbed my room key and the folder and practically jogged out of my room and to the elevator.

I started to scan the contents of the folder on elevator ride. The agenda in the folder (entitled Youth & Young Adult Mission Schedule) showed that I was supposed to be in the Crystal Room at 9:00 am for Introductory Remarks. As the elevator doors opened to the lobby, I suddenly started to panic, about everything. I had not checked in with Maridel about the change of plans, despite the fact that Peyton suggested Maridel had approved everything. I was wearing an unapproved outfit and I was a CEP girl on my way to a business meeting in a ballroom. I walked off the elevator, in what might have looked like a trance to anyone passing by and made my way towards the center of the lobby where I had seen the ballroom directory the day before. I thought about turning back to my room to change, but then I remembered Elliott's card and it gave me a burst of confidence.

"Don't be nervous," I said to myself, silently.

As I entered the Crystal ballroom, I saw rows and rows of chairs lined up in an orderly fashion. I was immediately relieved that the other people (who all appeared to span near my age) were dressed in a fairly modern, although conservative, style and plenty of women had their hair down. I wandered over to the coffee table and filled a cup with steaming black coffee from a fancy silver urn and quickly grabbed a pastry from the next table. I made my way to one of the empty tall tables with white linens, keeping my head down while eating to avoid eye contact with anyone. I felt like a total imposter being in the room, far too terrified to risk meeting anyone or look up as if I belonged in the room.

A few minutes later I heard a voice over speakers that penetrated the entire room.

"Good Morning. Welcome. Please be seated for introductory remarks."

Everyone in the room started to file into the seats
and so I followed. A few seconds after everyone was settled into seats, filling all of the chairs, a middle-aged
man who looked to be in his late forties approached the
podium as the room erupted in applause.

"Good Morning. Good Morning. For those who don't
know me I am Ryan Smith ... head of the Youth and
Young Adult Division of the Unity Party. I am so happy
to be here with you today and I love the energy of this
room. Am I right?" he said enthusiastically as he briefly
joined in on the clapping that had engulfed the room.

"My friends, we have so much to cover this week
and we appreciate your commitment to the Party and
the fact that you are attending this convention week to
strengthen your bond with the Party, to plan for your
future as our next generation of leaders, to commit to
the work that is never done, and to improve your skills
and capabilities to better do your work. Before we begin,
I always think it is helpful to provide a history lesson
of sorts, a reminder of some of the economic challenges
that led to our work becoming necessary in the first
place. Other speakers you will hear from this week will
remind you of other reasons our work became necessary

to save our beloved country, like the level of immorality we faced as a nation before the Party won the White House. And you will learn how we started at the most democratic level, building our Party in so many church halls and local meetings."

The room erupted in applause again with tiny murmurs of agreement and encouragement directed towards Ryan and what he had said. After a few moments, he motioned for the applause to stop.

"Look folks, I have spent the better part of my career focused on growing the economy, creating jobs, and building wealth which trickles down to our citizens. And prior to 2016 when the Party finally won the White House, my friends, wealth, talent, and success were under assault. Basically, blessings from God were under assault. Those of us who generate wealth in this country were selected by God to lead and prosper. If God didn't want those of us who attain wealth to have it, he wouldn't have given it to us, but some citizens had an agenda to take our blessings from us."

I noticed many of the heads in front of me nodding in agreement.

Ryan moved from behind the podium and started to walk down the aisle while continuing to speak, "I mean, I'll tell you folks, it was bad before the Party made things right. If certain people could have come charging at the wealthy with pitchforks prior to our President taking office, they honestly would have. And when you are successful one day, and you will be successful my friends because you made it here after all, will it feel fair to you that someone comes charging at you to take what you have been blessed with? We thought the burden of succeeding in business and being drivers of the economy without any appreciation from so many American people was tough enough, but things got way tougher than we ever imagined. At the time the Party had to take control of our country, most Americans did not understand just how hard we leaders worked, just how much we leaders had to handle, just how much brains, creativity, ingenuity, and sacrifice we leaders had to make to maintain our businesses and lives (which again allowed benefits to trickle down to so many). Few of the average worker said thank you, Mr. CEO, because I know you do more than I do to create our American economy and jobs which trickles down to me. People didn't get it!"

Ryan took a pause and had clearly entranced a captivated audience before continuing.

"So we got organized, we developed a strategy, and we executed our strategy. Just like good business people do. And we are going to do those three things here this week with you, the future leaders of our country. If you are here, it means God has chosen you to be here. God has selected you to inherit the resources of our beautiful nation and lead others. We want you to take the concepts we impart to you this week home and recommit yourself more than ever to the critical work and mission of our Party and God. We know that he has something special in store for you."

The room erupted in more applause. The enthusiasm of the crowd, in response to hearing what Ryan had to say, was evident. I found myself slowly clapping, uncertain if I should be clapping or not. I had never really heard something along the lines of what Ryan Smith was describing, the struggles of the wealthy described like he had just summarized to the crowd. It was a curious thing to consider.

During my first small group session, our leader was an older woman who introduced herself as Ruth, a former Vice President of Marketing for a major American retail company. Well-dressed and well-spoken, Ruth kicked off the session by describing her background and randomly selecting a few people in our group, not including me, to introduce themselves and describe where they were from. The group members who responded had come from all over the U.S., and even some other countries.

Ruth asked us to join hands and pray after the selected introductions, and reminded us to take lots of notes during our classes at the convention. I took the cap off of the pen that was on the table in front of my chair next to a notebook emblazoned with the Party logo as Ruth began her lecture to us.

"So, like any good business or marketing endeavor, one of the earliest things our Party had to do was identify our potential customers. Anytime you try to persuade others of a mission or want people to take action in response to your goals, you have to know your audience, right? So, we know now that all citizens fall into what the Party calls CC's or citizen categories. We built these CC descriptions largely based on all of the data that social media helped us mine years ago and surveillance helps us mine today. If you understand the type of person someone is within the CC's, you have a far greater chance of using a corresponding method of persuasion to help them support the Party and understand their role in society. Remember, we are helping people here. A stronger country means everyone has a greater chance of success, prosperity and security. Not everyone can be at the top. It's not possible in a strong economy and secure country. People at the bottom need to understand that by being at the bottom, and embracing that reality, they help create a stronger and safer America."

I noticed people nodding in agreement.

Ruth continued, "So let's turn to the fifth page of the handout and let's go through the list, "LRT. Low Resource Target. We start here because this citizen is both the most common and the most attainable to persuade to take on a given role to support the Party. This group might have formerly been referred to as "poor" but in our world, we simply view them as having minimal or low resources by design and we want to convey to them how their life can have purpose despite that reality. LRT's need to know that their commitment to the Party and work for the Party can provide meaning to a life that may never be fortunate to experience significant, or any, financial wealth."

Hearing Ruth describe the LRT made me think of my mother and the way she would describe her early meetings with Maridel's group. Although I was young when my mother started attending meetings, I knew enough to know that my mother felt like she was a part of something bigger than herself. I learned in the handout and the session with Ruth that there weren't just LRT's. The Party had codes for all types of people. Everyone fell into buckets. There was data and surveillance to backup how each person would be most likely to act. It was interesting to see the power of data and computers used for Party purposes, particularly since those things were so out of reach to most of us in daily life. There was also a category for PR's, prosperity reflectors, those people whose sole job was to disseminate images of their life and success to convey what being "chosen" by God to succeed looked like.

I took a lot of notes during the lectures I attended. I paid close attention. There was some part of me, in a visceral sense, that struggled to accept some of the information that was being conveyed to us at the convention. Perhaps I struggled most accepting the concept that the wealthy had suffered before the Party won the White House, my skepticism about this concept remaining steady from the time I heard Ryan Smith mention it through every other lecture I attended that included the concept, which was most of them. Nonetheless, I tried to keep an open mind each time I started to feel uncomfortable listening to speakers describe things in a manner that was so diametrically opposed to my personal experience. After all, since they were clearly in charge, I considered that they might understand something about how the world worked that I did not.

Chapter Seventeen

Although I had not seen Elliott during my meetings and training at convention week, he had checked in with me at the end of each day by calling my room. Although he had his own home nearby, he explained to me that he had opted to stay at the hotel during the convention given his rigorous daily schedule and the amount of entertaining he had to engage in. Plus, he could get over to the White House a bit easier in between convention events by staying in town.

On the third night he called me, Elliott told me that his call to me was the best part of his day. I, of course, was bubbling over with things to share with him about what I learned each day, confident in my ability to be candid with my new friend. Elliott stroked my ego in every way possible, continuing to remark how bright I was, that I was a natural at taking in the information, telling me how much potential I had to do more. It felt good to flex my brain again. I hadn't done so since high school classes with Mrs. Collins. It felt good to be called smart. Elliott told me I was special, and hearing it allowed me to hope that I might be. After all, since he had power and importance, I figured the things he said carried more weight and meaning. And so, rather quickly, the flattery began to seep through my skin.

I was totally perplexed by the fact that Maridel had essentially disappeared from my line of sight. I had been instructed by Peyton not to contact Maridel and to only call Peyton if I needed anything, 24/7. When I asked Elliott about Maridel and when I would meet her to go back to the CEP, he told me that Maridel was aware I had a busy schedule and that Peyton would arrange all of the logistics and be in touch with me about it.

Other than Ruth's class, I attended seminars on psychology, Party history, Party principles, legal updates themed the "law and order" sessions, and emerging issues. Everyone in my group was very friendly and kind. Only one girl asked me if I was from a CEP. When I confirmed I was, she responded with "I figured" coupled with a kind and knowing nod. Most of the women wore suits or, in the case of what I assumed were the more religious women, a minority wore long skirts and button-down tops, much like Claire's regular clothing. Peyton had been nice enough to have a few dress suits delivered to my room on the second day of convention week.

Of all of the classes I took, my favorites by far were the speaking and hosting classes. During these classes, we each got a chance to read from a teleprompter and sit for mock interviews where we were peppered with questions about the Party's beliefs. Given my experience on the road with Maridel, the subject matter came naturally to me, with the major difference at the convention being that we also had wardrobe coaching, hair and makeup, and tried on the nicest clothes I had ever touched or seen in my life. We taped a series of demo reels trying out different forms of communication and interview formats.

The last demo reel taping on Friday, which was the last day of convention week, was only for those of us who had "passed" the prior rounds of screen tests. I noticed Elliott and Harper walk into the back of the room during my taping. Although they were too far in the back for me to speak to Elliott, he gave me a thumbs-up at one point during my mock on-camera interview. That night, after we had finished our end of convention ceremony, I sat in my room, still in full hair and makeup, wearing a somewhat fitted black suit dress. I loved the way I looked in the mirror. I felt wondered how long I would be able to keep the fake lashes on once I saw Maridel. I assumed I would be reunited with her the next day since the convention was ending. My hair smelled sweet from the hairspray in it. The thought of rejoining Maridel the next morning made me feel desperate and depressed.

When I called Petyon to confirm when I was supposed to leave and rejoin Maridel, she only told me that plans were in the "works" and to sit tight until I heard from her. As I started to pack, wondering if I was supposed to leave the new clothes behind, my phone rang. It was Elliott.

"It's me," he said casually with a familiar tone and the hair on my neck stood up with excitement. "You free for dinner?"

"I'm supposed to be at a closing dinner with my training group," I replied.

"No worries. You can miss that. Trust me, I know people," he said assuring me.

"Um ... ok, if you're sure it's ok, I'd love that," I replied, my excitement to see him apparent.

"Great. Hang tight and someone will be by to pick you up and bring you to dinner."

A few minutes later, Elliott's assistant, who briefly introduced himself as Sam, knocked on my door to escort me to Elliott's room. We took the elevator to the 11th floor and Sam led me down the hallway gesturing for me to be quiet by placing a finger over his lips. Sam opened a hotel suite door at the very end of the hall, the only double doors I saw in the entire hallway. Sam told me plainly to have a nice evening, shut the door behind me, and left. I was alone in a dark long foyer hallway. I started to walk down the hall towards the dim light at the end of it, almost tiptoeing, not sure of whether I was just supposed to wait in the hallway, the excitement I had felt on the phone a few minutes earlier replaced with nerves.

At the end of the hallway, I entered a room that looked more like it was part of a home than a hotel room, a living room with low and warm lighting. At the far end of it, there was a large open double doorway to a dining room where I could see a table covered with food. Elliott was sitting at a desk in the far corner of the living room near the dining room, leaning back in a chair in front of the desk. He was on the phone. He motioned for me to be quiet by putting his index finger in the "shh" position over his smiling lips. I gave him the thumbs up and continued to tiptoe over to one of the two plush light-yellow couches in the gilded room and sat down on one.

"Yes, Laurel. Of course. I understand. I will convey that to the President. Yes. I know that is how you feel. Understood," Elliott paused on the phone, "Me? Tonight? I can't, doll. You know any other night I would meet up but I am not feeling 100% and I really think I need some rest. You understand don't you? I feel like you knew I wasn't feeling well this morning. You always sense things before I do," Elliott paused again, "Thank you. Yes. Speak tomorrow."

Elliott hung up the phone and took a huge deep breath that sounded more like an exasperated sigh, "The work is never done," he mused in a somewhat snarky low singsong voice.

"I'm sorry you are not feeling well," I offered.

"Don't be silly. I feel fine. I just said that to get out of something," Elliott replied leaning back in the chair with his arms on each armrest and staring at me with a smile. The silence caused me to fidget a little in my scat.

"Are you hungry?" he asked not moving from his posture and continuing to stare at me.

"Starving," I confirmed.

"I ordered for us," he said in a commanding tone. He was so confident in everything he said and did. It was disarming.

I walked into the dining room behind him. I sat down at the large mahogany table and, although I felt more self-conscious at the thought of him watching me eat than I had on the first night, I was honestly hungry and couldn't wait to dig in.

"I made sure to get extra bread," he motioned towards the center of the table, "since you ate the entire bread-basket the first night we met."

I started to laugh. And not just a polite giggle like I was used to doing with restraint, but a full beaming belly laugh. It felt great to really laugh. Elliott started laughing too.

Elliott had ordered Indian food in from his favorite restaurant in D.C., which he claimed had the best Indian food on the planet (and he confirmed to me that he had travelled much of the planet with the President so he could say that for sure). As we began to eat, I was sur-prised at how casual and natural it felt to hang out and talk with Elliott. I had never tried anything like the food in front of me before. The tastes were strong and a bit overwhelming to me, but Elliott guided me through each dish and he seemed to tremendously enjoying teaching me about what each item was while describing the var-ious countries he had experience eating in. We talked a bit more about what is was like for me to grow up in Brooklyn too.

"How have you liked the sessions this week? Have you made friends? Hopefully no one that would make me jealous," Elliott asked in what was noticeably a lower voice. His remark made me flush.

"I met a lot of really nice people. I mean... I am so glad I got to go," I replied, and I meant it. Attending the classes and using my brain in a productive way, not to mention staying at the hotel all week, had felt great.

After we finished eating and had some post-dinner tea, Elliott stood up from the table and started to walk back into to the living room as he continued to speak to me. I got up and followed him. He sat on a couch and I sat down in one of the golden armchairs across from him.

"I don't know how to thank you for what you did this week, letting me attend the sessions. I am so grateful. I don't even know why you agreed to allow me to go, but everything you did ... with Maridel and everything...I just really appreciate it," I said genuinely.

Elliott smiled.

"Don't beat up on yourself too much, Anna. You have a lot of potential. You are very intelligent and unique."

"Not sure about that, but again, thank you, really." I said humbly as I continuously played with my fingers in my lap.

"You know you are gorgeous, right? I mean, you are not like everybody else. And that fact that you are so well-spoken is remarkable considering where you grew up, and what you endured. I mean the fact that you got the education you did given your circumstances is rare. On camera and off, you're clear and warm. People connect with you easily. The feedback from your group leaders this week was that you have tremendous potential. You walk into a room and your energy is different. It changes the room. And what's best is that you don't even realize this about yourself. So there is innocence about you, Anna. And it is an innocence that many people are drawn to. You're perfect."

I was blushing, not sure of what to say in response. The room felt heavy.

"Come over here," Elliott said and motioned for me to come over to the couch where he was sitting.

I obeyed. I got up and walked over to where he was and sat down next to him, facing sideways and looking at his face. He stared at me for a moment and then cupped my face in his hands, leaned in and kissed me. Not a hard or desperate kiss, but a deep and gentle kiss. At first, only with his lips, but then with his tongue while he moved his hands behind my head and into my hair. When he finished, he pulled back just enough so that our foreheads were practically touching.

"How would you like to come work with me in Washington?" Elliott asked, breathlessly.

Far too overwhelmed to speak, my lips still wet from his kiss and spices lingering in my mouth, I simply nodded yes.

Chapter Eighteen

I think most people who have not visited the White House before do not realize that, when you are inside of it, the White House actually feels quite small and quaint. At least, it did to me. None of the rooms felt as grand as I expected, although they all looked exactly the same as they had in the pictures of the White House I had seen on television or in school books as a child, oddly unchanged in appearance despite the years that had passed. Despite the dated look of the quaint spaces, on the day I started my first day of work at the White House and received a tour, the energy in the building was nothing short of electric.

Elliott arranged for me to move into an apartment in a part of Washington, D.C. called Foggy Bottom with three other White Hosue staffers. My roommates were all very nice and much further along in their time working for the administration, so they were great guides for me. The day I left the convention hotel with Petyon in a black SUV, I only had my clothes from the CEP and the few outfits Peyton had sent to my room during convention Week. That was it. I had no other possessions. Peyton had called me in my hotel room the morning after I had dinner with Elliott in his room and informed me that she would be in charge of getting me "settled and sorted" in Washington, D.C. Peyton was also the one who explained the details of my "arrangement" to me. I was hired to be one of several assistants to Harper Broderick, the woman who had sat next to Maridel at the dinner on the first night of the convention. Harper was the Director of Communications for the White House. I didn't ask what happened to Maridel or Claire, and they never reached out to me. My heart ached at the thought of Veronica being disappointed that I did not return to the CEP.

About a week after Peyton dropped me off at my new apartment in Foggy Bottom, I found myself reporting to Peyton's desk at 8:00 am on my first day of work after being picked up and driven in an SUV, with my roommates, to the White House. The seven days prior to my first day of work had been quite hectic, to put it mildly. I was given tours of my apartment, my building, local places to eat and shop for groceries. I was shuttled to a clothing store and spent hours trying things on to build a new wardrobe with a personal shopper. I had a doctor's appointment with an internist and a gynecologist, the later starting me on birth control pills. I met with a psychologist who had to perform an intake interview with me before I could start work at the White House, that appointment mainly consisting of me repeating my life story and the psychologist taking notes without much to say in return. And, I had more orientation meetings than I could count, where lots of rules that applied to all White House staffers were explained to me in detail.

Not unlike when I was at the convention, I was given a detailed schedule each day of where I was required to be, and at what time, with the only difference being that I now had a device called a "Relay" that allowed me to communicate with certain people like Peyton, my building director, or my "driver" at any time. I learned that our building only housed White House interns and assistants and that, for security purposes, we lived in the same secure location. Each day, I had a morning and evening check in with the building director, who explained she was like a college resident assistant (I had no idea what that meant). I had a curfew to abide by. Although I was allowed to be out in the neighborhood, it had to be at designated locations and only with a "buddy" and the director knowing where I would be. I didn't really need to shop for too much since there was a cafeteria with twenty-four hour food available in our building and at the White House, and all of our personal necessities and clothes could be ordered by sending a Relay message to our "shopper." It was explained to me that all of this was for national security purposes.

On my first day, I found myself feeling both nervous and excited as I was ushered to Peyton's office. I also found myself looking around hoping to see Elliott. I had not spoken to him once since I left the convention hotel, but he did have flowers delivered to my apartment wishing me good luck on my first day. I sat in a brown leather chair that was tufted with bronze nails in a sitting area outside of Peyton's office, fidgeting a bit with anticipation when she interrupted me picking a little bit of lint off my skirt.

"Anna. Morning. I hope you are settling into life in Washington ok," Peyton began coolly. She motioned for me to follow her into her office. When I entered, I noticed that there was a door with Harper's name on it behind Peyton's desk.

I sat down in a chair in front of Peyton's desk as she sat down behind it. The desk was covered with papers and I noticed her office was a total disorganized mess. In addition to the desk being covered with piles of books and papers, there were extra suits, jackets, and sweaters draped everywhere and various boxes and bags of gifts I would learn later various people often sent to her as a sign of gratitude. For whatever reason, she rarely opened these gifts and didn't have time to throw them away. She must have noticed me looking around at the mess.

218 ~ JENNIFER KASMAN

"It's a little messy in here right? I always intend to get around to cleaning it, but I'm just too slammed. In any case, it is how my office has been for years and I know where everything is."

I nodded my understanding with a smile before quickly changing the subject. I certainly didn't want to make her feel bad for the state of her office, although I was judging it.

"Yes," I replied enthusiastically, "in response to your question, I am settling in great. I love my apartment and everyone has been so nice. Thank you so much."

Peyton always seemed clinical in her tone with me and I noticed that she had cringed a bit at my response. I had noticed a number of the staffers that I had met so far seemed to behave in the same manner, always serious, cool, and muted.

"Great. Glad to hear it," Peyton replied, "Listen, Anna, you have a lot to learn and it is partially my job to bring you along. I will try to be patient but you will see that things get very hectic around here very fast. Make sure you pay attention to everything so you can learn as much as you can just by observing day to day operations. You will learn the most by copying how other people you work for handle things."

"Of course. Thanks again!" I replied, enthusiastically.

The bubbly nature of my response appeared to continue to annoy Peyton. I watched her grimace after I expressed my gratitude, so I made sure to ask my next question gingerly.

"I wondered, Peyton, am I allowed ... is it ok if I let my family known I am here? Or my friend, Veronica, at the CEP, or anyone from my old neighborhood?"

"Unfortunately, no," Peyton replied, dryly, "I'm afraid not. I think we could arrange for you to send some letters to check in at some point down the road but the thing is, Anna, you have been selected for this role when any number of other people would have given anything for this job. And, as you probably noticed with the volume of non-disclosure agreements you signed, it is absolutely critical to the Family that you are loyal, fully committed to your work for the Party and the President and in a complete zone of confidence and trust. After all the work we do here is fairly high level, Anna. It would not make much sense to allow everyone at your level or my level to just go home to our family or make outside friends as if we live some ordinary life working in some ordinary job. This is classified work – at the highest level. The safety and security of the citizens of our country depend on your discretion."

I supposed that made sense, after all this was the White House. I nodded my head in understanding although my face must have displayed some disappointment.

Peyton seemed to notice my reaction before replying in the closest thing to a kind tone I had heard from her yet.

"Listen, Anna. If anyone knows that this process requires an adjustment it is me. Like you, I did not come from tremendous resources either. I was also fortunate to be recruited for a job here by being in the right place at the right time. Here's the deal. If you are loyal and respect the patronage being shown to you, the Family will take care of you – they will take care of everything. These people pick up phones and move mountains. It is pretty great being on that kind of team. The quid pro quo for this type of protection and status is confidentiality and your absolute loyalty to the Family."

I nodded my understanding again feeling a bit comforted by her "relating to me," although I was puzzled as to why she kept referring to a Family. Wasn't I working for the President, indirectly? Elliott had also used the term "the Family" with me a few times as well. I wasn't sure if it was the President's family she was referring to or something else, because she had not mentioned the President by name once when talking about "the Family." I thought better than to confirm with her in that moment given how annoyed she seemed.

The next few days of work at the White House quickly turned into weeks, and weeks turned into months, and months turned into years as I sunk further and further into my hectic and all-consuming work. Being an assistant to Harper was no easy task. Harper expected me to keep notes in every meeting so I could regurgitate anything that was said in any meeting or on any call immediately at her request. Harper told me during the first meeting I attended with her that if she ever saw me without a notepad and pen in my hand, I would be fired on the spot.

I became a shadow to a handful of people including Harper, Peyton and, at times when he could include me, Elliott. It was both surprising and understandable how watching three of them operate on calls and in high level meetings melted into my brain. I quickly became able to talk the talk, keep the notes, and even understand most of the substance of what was going on around me. My brain was never bored and my body was never in one place for more than an hour at a time, quickly transitioning from topic to topic, meeting to meeting, person to person. I was exhausted but totally stimulated in a way I had no idea was possible.

Being around so much power was "intoxicating" and the buzz I got from receiving praise for doing good work became "addictive." The culture of the entire place was so full of people seeking advancement that we all reached for total perfection in our work. Between the competitive and intense vibes between staffers, and the fear of losing our jobs if we were not the absolute best at what we did, it was easy to understand why most of us worked around the clock.

And then, of course, there was the high all of us White House staffers got from being part of a power structure. If anyone got in the way of the goal of any meeting or mission, we could destroy them. Elliott would often say "how cute" when someone tried to mount resistance to what the Family wanted. He would tell me to watch how quickly they changed their tone and became, what he would call, "card carrying members of the Family" when he would remind them who they were challenging, or how much power the Family had, or how "unhappy" the Family would be with an outcome that wasn't to their liking. I was most captivated by watching how the women I worked for operated, mostly Harper and Peyton. They seemed to have a similar vibe, unemotional, cool, and collected at all times --- no drama, no strong opinions and always in line with each other. For whatever reason, the men we worked with seemed to have more latitude to display big emotions, but among the female leaders a more reserved power was valued and appreciated.

During our huddles and meetings, we were always reminded that we were "the best of the best minds in the country," here for a reason that "God had commanded." We were constantly reminded in our team meetings that we were different, that we were special, and that we held power for a reason. It was inspiring and made me want to work doubly hard to do the best job I could possibly do. Feeling nothing but fortunate at my luck to end up working in the White House, I set out to succeed with a rabid hunger. Being around the others gave me the sense that my identity could be like theirs, instead of the one I had in the past. I didn't even have time to think of my past if I wanted to. It seemed to make sense to me, that I might be special. After all, why would I be working at the White House if I wasn't? There was certainly no lack of other kids from poverty they could pick from. I figured there was a chance that all the prior realities of my life were a cosmic accident and this "level" is where I was really meant to be.

I quickly learned over the course of the next few days, weeks, and months as I sunk into my daily routine and lots of hard work that "the Family" was the North family and, specifically, Laurel North at its helm, working on behalf of her mother, who was still living (unlike her famous father), her siblings, and some of her nieces and nephews. We were working for the President's administration, but our mission was to work at the direction of the North family. So, although we would talk about the "Party" and the "President" in various contexts, hearing the term "Family" as the ultimate decision makers guiding our work was far more common. We heard from Laurel North frequently and invasively. It was expressed more often than I could count that the President would not be President without the North family.

As much as I came to love my job, I equally loved the nights where I got excused from returning to my building, with my director's permission after she received instruction from the "highest levels" that I had an overnight event, when Elliott's driver would take me to a hotel room in town to meet with Elliott. We would only eat dinner in his room and not at a restaurant, to avoid being seen. I did not so much crave Elliott's company or the wine he would buy for me to drink, as much as I craved the sense of how I made him feel when we spent time together. Being with Elliott felt like being even closer to power. Before Elliott left the hotel to go back to his family each time we met, we would lay in bed and he would share his stress with me, about work and his financial pressures at home. It was during those conversations that I learned the most about "the Family" and Laurel North. It seemed there was no limit to their power.

I also learned from Elliott, and from observing the way things were handled at work by Harper on many occasions, that the President was a detail that had to be managed in our day, much like any other item on our schedule. Although the President could certainly play an effective role publicly when the North family needed him to, our direction and goals were always those set by Laurel. It was Laurel who suggested to Elliott that I start to film different public service type announcements on video each week relaying different messages about the Party and its principles for, what I was told, was use by the Department of Education. Some of my scripts required that I explain the good that would come from impending policy changes or legislation. My photo was taken often as well in different clothes and settings for what I was told were generic public service announcements.

Three years into my time working at the White House, I felt as if I was on top of the world and counted my blessings often in silent prayer for being "chosen." My life was busy and happy, despite the stress of my job. In fact, the stress started to feel like a part of how happy should feel because it meant, for most of us working at the White House, that we were valued and relied on. As the holiday season of 2035 approached, on the same night as the White House holiday party, Peyton informed me that Harper needed to meet with me urgently. A little before 6:00, dressed up for the party in a crushed dark green velvet top and black skirt that I hoped Elliott would love (even though since he would be in attendance with his wife we couldn't talk to each other too much at the event). I walked into Harper's office wondering if I was getting promoted again.

"Hi, Anna. Sit down, please." Harper began.

I sat down in one of the arm chairs positioned at a slight angle in front of her desk.

"Anna, I need to talk to you about a few things and they are substantial. I want you to keep in mind when you hear these things that this is a natural evolution for you. These changes mean you are growing and your role here is becoming even more critical," Harper said in her usually cool, serious and composed voice.

On hearing her describe the topic as substantial, I smiled figuring I was right to suspect I was being promoted again.

"First, we need to further expand our efforts with the youth in the country. Laurel North has decided it would be best for you to film a lot of new content and video for Phase I of our new targeted approach to the country's youth, and we are going to need to send you out to a few different studios and locations to film, so we have you working with the best technology and professionals.

"Ok," I replied. "What are the other phases?" I asked, assuming telling me about the other phases were the other "things" Harper had to tell me.

Harper looked at me and, although I wasn't sure, for a second she looked sad.

"The other phases are not public information for you, or most other people, at this point. The other thing I want to mention to you is that..." she paused for what felt like hours of suspense, but was probably only a few seconds.

"Anna, the Party leadership thinks it is time for you to be married. We think a marriage will further your image nicely as you move forward into the next stage of your career," Harper said, bluntly.

We sat for a moment in silence. I felt as though someone had slapped me across the face. What did she mean married? How exactly would that happen? My face felt flushed and I looked down at my lap to contemplate how I should respond. I thought about Elliott and suddenly got a sinking feeling in my stomach.

"Anna, The situation with Elliott is too public," Harper said plainly, "it is not in the best interest of either one of you that it continues. I am sure you expected this day would come at some point. The decision that your..."

I noticed she paused again, seemingly careful to consider her next words before she continued.

"your ... relationship ... with Elliott ... well, it has been decided at the highest levels that it has to end," she finished.

I couldn't speak. I knew I was about to cry, and I knew Harper did not consider emotion appropriate behavior in the workplace, so I just tried to keep breathing to avoid letting the emotions flow out of me. I also felt embarrassed. I didn't realize our secret relationship was public information.

"We have arranged for you to meet someone that we think is a great fit for you. His name is James York. He works in finance for the Family, he is invaluable, and is going to be promoted to be CFO for the Party. Chances are you have never met because his office is in the other executive building, but I think you two will hit it off," Harper said flatly.

At this point, fully aware of risking Harper's scorn, I could not stop the tears from starting to flow out of my eyes as I felt fury start to creep in. I may have accepted a life of limited freedom, but I worked hard and found myself instantly incredulous at the idea that I could be forced to marry against my will.

Harper continued firmly without a pinprick of emotion, completely ignoring my tears.

"Anna, James is kind and a really good man. You have nothing to worry about. This is a great transition point in your life and image. Marriage will be a wonderful thing for you and, as you know, marriage is a very important Party principle. Your value to the Party will only increase as a result of this. You know from working here long enough that the Family arranges all kinds of things for the people that work for them. Plus, you should know, this plan has Elliott's full support."

"What?" I whispered, feeling even more sick to my stomach.

"We think a spring wedding will run great in the papers in the regions that your service announcements are used in. As for James, you will be introduced to him tonight at the Christmas party."

By this point, my nose was running all over my face and I was using the crushed velvet of my dark green sleeve to wipe it away, not concerned in the slightest about the sopping wet mess I was creating on my perfect party outfit with my tears and the mascara coming off

230 ~ JENNIFER KASMAN

my face with each wipe. I had no idea what she meant by the wedding running "great in the papers" but I was too upset to ask.

"I will give you a minute to collect yourself," Harper said quietly as she stood up and began to exit her office. Before she left her office, she put a hand on my shoulder from behind my chair, for an instant before withdrawing it quickly.

"There is a mirror on the inside of my closet door, Anna, so you can clean up before you leave the room. I have some make up remover in my top drawer. Take your time. I will see you at the party."

I heard the door shut behind me.

Chapter Nineteen

Fall, 2038

"Can we stay home today?" I asked James as he continued to sip his coffee standing up while reading the newspaper, folded over tightly so he could manage reading, drinking, and standing simultaneously.

"You ask me that every day as if, one day, I will give you a different answer," James replied, turning to smile at me while I stared at him.

"I know," I sighed, "I keep waiting for the day I will get a different answer. Still no?"

"Still no," he said walking to the kitchen chair I was perched on and kissing me on my forehead, "plus you just took off for your birthday, wasn't that enough of a break?" he continued sarcastically. I had just turned twenty-nine a few days earlier.

"Are you hungry? I could make you something before we leave?" I offered.

"No, dear. My wife the Lead Special Communications Assistant to the President is not my cook," he said in an exaggerated tone as he did most mornings.

"I will grab a banana," James confirmed.

"Ok." I smiled, "Does this whole woman in power thing still turn you on? Do you think you would still love me if I was less a power player type of wife and more of a pregnant type of wife?" I asked. I walked over and stood in front of him after I asked, as he put his coffee cup in the huge white farmer's sink in our kitchen.

He looked at me with the sad look he got the few times the subject of children came up. James had been told that he would never be able to have children because he had taken a version of a vaccine that turned out to be a brand that caused make infertility. This fact, combined with our twenty-two year age difference, were just two of the reasons we did not expect to have children. It was also the reason why I wasn't so concerned when I missed a few birth control pills here and there. I was still required to take daily birth control as rule, being a White House staffer.

"Well," I continued while running my hands from his stomach to his chest and landing with them around his neck, "would you still look at me the same way?"

I could tell I was upsetting James because he started to remove my hands from around his neck.

"Why this morning, Anna?" he said gently. "Did you have a dream about it again?" I often had dreams where James and I had two children.

"No," I said more forcefully and putting my arms right back around his neck where they had been, "I need to know, James. I want to know because ... I am."

James froze his stare on me. We stood in silence for a few minutes, I flexed my arms tighter around his neck and I felt tears in the corners of my eyes.

"You are ... what?" he whispered. The look on his face was equal parts shocked, worried, and angry. The sense of him being angry frightened me a little.

"I'm pregnant." I whispered, suddenly unsure that my news was going to go over as well as I had hoped.

James did not move.

"I'm serious," I said and I started to cry because it was clear that the news was less welcome than I expected. "I went to the doctor, I had a test, it is official, about 8 weeks along at this point. I was worried I had cancer because of how tired and crappy I have been feeling lately and it turns out it is not cancer, but it is a baby."

James pulled away from me and slammed a hand down on the counter. I could tell he was entering panic mode.

"But, how ... the vaccine I took. I'm not supposed to be able to. They are going to be so upset, Anna. They don't think I can have children either and they kept you on the pill to make double sure that we would not have children. They have to approve these things, especially given that you film public media for them."

James seemed an equal mix of furious and terrified.

I started to anger. I knew the "they" he was referring to was the Family.

"Are you seriously worried about what they will think about me being pregnant?" I asked heatedly, "We're married. It happens. They don't own us, James. I work for them, but this is our life. So what if they introduced us! So what if they have their hand in everything! At some point, it is not about them. This is about us. This should be a miracle, not a curse," I was shouting by this point, hurt and disappointed at his reaction.

James grabbed me in a tender and forceful hug while I tried to wiggle away in anger, before I finally gave into his embrace and started to cry. Eventually, he pulled back from our embrace and placed his hands on each my shoulders, looking at me directly in the eyes.

"Anna, Look," James began softly this time, "You have made me happier than I imagined possible. I'm sorry if I upset you. I'm just shocked. I'm just shocked, Anna and the thought of us creating a baby," his voice started to break and I could tell he was more afraid than I realized earlier.

I nodded my understanding.

"It's complicated with these people. If I can't protect you, I don't know what I will do. And, Anna, they could not have been clearer with me that their plans for you did not include children, at least not unless and until we adopted when they decided the time was right," James finished, gently squeezing my shoulders.

I nodded again. I knew he was truly afraid of the consequences of my news and it moved me to hear that, despite his fear, he was most worried about protecting me. Although it had taken about a year for me to start to develop feelings for James after we were married, I wound up falling deeply in love with him. James never pushed me for anything after we were married. We started off as awkward strangers, me devastated at being forced to marry a stranger and him gentle with me and apologetic about the situation. We lived together as friends first and somehow, as we did the things that friends do like eat and shop together, and exercise together, and talk, I started to really like him. He treated me with respect. He always wanted to hear my thoughts, and I had a lot of thoughts to share about everything. We shared the stories of our lives with each other in great detail. We had both come from poverty and were poached for Party work. He doted on me in every way imaginable, like making me chocolate chip cookies that were slightly under-baked so the middle was a bit soggy like I preferred. He never pressed me for any physical contact. It was me that wound up eventually making the first move by kissing him one day on a park bench as we sat and talked for hours after a five mile run, watching the sunset. James was my first true love.

James continued to express his concern as he rubbed my arms gently.

"No matter how worried I am about how they are going to react, I'm sure you shouldn't be getting this upset. It can't be good for you or ..."

I noticed his eyes get glossy as he looked down and touched my stomach. He ran out of words at that point and just stood there like that for a second until he finally kissed me tenderly on the forehead. Whether I wanted to admit it or not, I knew our lives were complicated by who we were to the people we worked for. I knew James was right to be concerned. In fact, Harper had also told me several times, including before I married James, that the Family did not plan for me to conceive.

"Anna, people like us aren't allowed to "make moves" without approval since we support the people we do. We just have to be careful. You and I...we...need to make sure we stay safe and in the good graces of people that could do a lot to make or break our lives."

James cupped my left cheek in one hand and ran his fingers over my hair on the other side of my face. I moved in and buried myself in his chest and felt his blue tie, silky, against the side of my nose. We stayed like that for a while before he pulled away from me, kissed me, told me he loved me, and asked me not to announce anything at work until he had a chance to speak to Harper. I nodded my head quietly in agreement at his suggestion. I knew there were rules we all had to play by. I understood the boundaries of our life, despite the fact that we had more resources than I ever could have dreamed of having as a child. We were the service class, even though our clothes were nicer and we lived in a beautiful

238 ~ JENNIFER KASMAN

house. The trappings and trimmings of our entire existence were only at the mercy and discretion of our masters who paid and employed us. I immediately felt guilty
for springing the news on him as if we were some "normal" couple.

As James suspected, the news of our impending arrival did not go over great at the White House, but James
knew when to wield a tiny but of his power and, with the
help of Harper who he told me owed him a few favors,
we were eventually back in the good graces of the Family after apologizing to Laurel North directly. James had
explained on our "apology call" to Laurel North that he
was as shocked as she, Harper, and others were to learn
that I was pregnant. Laurel called me careless for not taking my pill properly, but said she would try to figure out
ways that my pregnancy might be an asset to my communications work, because she had no choice.

It was still hard for me to believe sometimes, despite
my full awareness of her power, that Laurel North cared
so much about the minutiae of the inner workings of
the White House. When I asked Harper about this fact
once and expressed my confusion about how someone
as powerful as Laurel North had time to insert herself
in our personal lives, Harper reminded me that the Party
was Laurel's baby and that Laurel had other motivations
given the massive power struggle within the North family. Since Laurel did not have any children, and her sib-

lings did, there was pressure for Laurel to reduce her share of the empire and she fought, intensely, to maintain her power.

I was further reminded of Laurel's involvement in everything that took place at 1600 Pennsylvania Avenue on the day I was summoned for a call with Harper and Laurel, right before I was scheduled to have labor induced at the hospital.

"Anna, I do hope you are feeling well," Laurel began the call that day in her shrill and nasal voice after Petyon patched her into Harper's speaker phone, "Listen, Harper and I just thought it would be helpful to make sure we were all on the same page with respect to your impending leave. I think there may have been some miscommunication about the plan going forward since Harper mentioned you were planning to take off a few months."

I looked at Harper for help since we were sitting in the same room while on the call. Harper shrugged her shoulders and motioned for me to respond. My stomach was so huge, and I was so uncomfortable by this point, that I was sitting halfway on my side in a desk chair and had to move a little to get the breath for a proper voice to respond to Laurel.

"Well, yes. I had planned...," I paused to correct myself knowing my tone and use of the word planned would suggest I had far too much autonomy for Laurel's liking. "I had hoped to take twelve weeks of leave to get the baby set up in a routine and recover."

"Right. Well, we need to negotiate a bit because that will not work for us," Laurel replied flatly.

I had no idea who the "us" was that she was referring to because it worked fine for the us that included me and my soon to be expanded family. I looked at Harper again who was just starting forward at the phone, cool and collected, as always, her face completely unemotional.

"What will work for you?" I asked somewhat pointedly, barely successful at hiding the fury I felt pouring out of my cells.

"Well, here's the thing, Anna," Laurel continued in a condescending sing song voice, talking to me as if I was stupid. "As you know, part of our *equal rights for one then equal rights for all* campaign has been the elimination of special circumstances for anyone specific to gender or race etc. So, the public relations impact of you taking three months off from work after baby is not the best for us since we don't give dads that right do we? And, listen, I am going to assume that you simply did

not realize that your request for such a huge accommodation would not be best for the people you serve. Anna,
you know that I have always told you that the "secret
sauce" of our inner sanctum of leadership requires trust
and confidence that we know what is best for both you
and our higher purposes. I am thinking that the most I
can part with you for is four weeks, and I suppose I will
just need to figure out a way to manage the difficulty
thrust on the entire staff by granting you the latitude of
four weeks off."

I was stunned. I felt blood rush to my head and my
body started to tingle with anger. I also knew that I
couldn't challenge Laurel so I didn't respond except to
say, "I see," a few minutes after Laurel finished speaking.

After we hung up the call, Harper suggested I grab an
early lunch, which may have been because I was heavy
breathing in the chair across from her desk and she
knew I would need a break. I called James and gave him
a quick summary of the call, but knew better than to ex
press my true feelings about the four weeks of maternity
leave I had been granted since we were always recorded
on the phones within the White House. James could tell
I was upset and reminded me how important it was to
stay calm to keep the baby and myself healthy.

Later that evening, I entered the hospital for my in-
duction and, on a hot day in July of 2039, I was lying on

242 ~ JENNIFER KASMAN

a bed with elastic bands strapped to my stomach that recorded our baby's heartbeat, writhing through over fourteen hours of labor while James held my hand and comforted me without missing a beat. Labor was some of the worst pain I had ever experienced in my life and, like all women in America who abided by the Party's national religious policies, I was not allowed to take pain medication. Since I had been on the inside of the White House when we worked with the CDC and Party to develop new guidelines for childbirth, I knew that the refusal to provide pain medication like epidurals was not only because the Party wanted to "debunk" various medical and scientific claims across the board but also because the Party considered the pain of childbirth a possible deterrent to unwanted pregnancies (and hopefully, in the Party's view, an additional way to prevent too much population growth).

Just as I thought I could not take the pain of labor any longer, the doctors told me it was "time to push." Years later I would tell a room of young women that, although you somehow forget the pain of childbirth, you never forget those brief moments right before the baby arrives. The moments right as you start to deliver a child seem to go in slow motion, although you know they are actually passing by with light speed. Right before the baby arrived, the doctors started to quickly dress in official blue scrubs and clear plastic glasses, their hasty change and attire reminding me of how serious, and possibly dangerous, giving birth was. The lights got so bright in the room that they felt almost metallic shining down on my body, and hurt my eyes. Silver trays were rolled out and the closet doors in the far corner of my room were flung open, revealing what I understood would be the spot where the baby would be checked out right away. I pushed into the light squeezing James's hand the entire time and, moments later, felt a release of primal power like nothing I could have ever imagined. My baby was born. The doctor held my son up so I could see him. And then a few minutes later, which felt like an eternity to me, James walked over from the closet area where they had rushed the baby to check him out right after deliver, and placed my son in my arms for the first time.

"Charlie. My baby, Charlie," were the only words I could muster as my son looked up at me, while I gently cradled him in my arms. We locked eyes. I had never seen anyone look into my eyes or into my insides so deeply and knowingly. And, all at once, I felt exactly as if Charlie knew not only that I was his mother, but that he also knew my soul and I knew his. I was breathless. The love that surged and flowed throughout my body was without parallel. I held him, whole, tender, and complete in a way I had never felt before, despite the pain that still racked my body from the experience. When they told me I should put him down and rest, I refused to place him in the clear plastic box of a crib next to my bed, because I was terrified he would feel alone. So I held him until I couldn't keep my eyes open any longer and, although I don't know for sure, I think James may have held him the entire time I was sleeping because that's how I found them when I woke up after sleeping for a few hours. Rapidly, in those still small but tremendous moments of early motherhood, I knew I never wanted Charlie to feel alone. The space felt different. I felt different. The energy force field of my life had changed, and I knew right away that the change was permanent.

Chapter Twenty

Once we left the cocoon of the hospital, the reality of returning to work in four weeks hit me like a ton of bricks. I tried as best I could to push the thought of going back to work out of my mind the second it would arise so I did not sully my time with Charlie, but it was hard to not feel depressed and angry at the thought of leaving him to return to the White House so soon. Despite the stress of the early days caring for my first child, I was also immersed in bliss and purpose. There was little sleep and constant feedings. I constantly worried about whether Charlie was still breathing when he slept, and my finger became a regular barometer under his nose as I would wait for the sensation of a little hot air to know he was still alright. I will never forget the first time James and I took the baby for a walk in his stroller on one of our favorite running trails, early in the morning to avoid the summer heat of the afternoon and before James had to go to work. We just kept smiling at each other, walking slowly, enjoying the thickness that was in the air around our newly configured family.

One morning, after an early walk, we stopped for pancakes and as the baby sat in his car seat positioned securely on a high chair next to me, it briefly occurred to me that one day I would sit next to a grown version of my son. It was impossible for me to imagine my tiny boy growing into a man one day.

"Do you think he will be tall like you?" I asked James in between syrupy bites of blueberry pancakes.

"I don't care what size he is as long as he stays healthy," James replied as he shoved another forkful of his whole wheat banana pancakes down.

"Do you think he will like cheese?" I asked.

"Are you worried about that?" James asked me, eyes smiling, prepared to break out in one of his typical fits of laughter when I went on a random tangent.

"No. I just wondered. Because I like cheese. I wonder if he will like cheese like I do," I replied without so much as a hint that I was joking, because I wasn't.

James smiled and shook his head in a little disbelief as he added more milk to his second cup of coffee.

"What do you think he will want to be when he grows up?" I asked, hopeful and with a determination in my voice to get a straight answer from James. For some reason, the insidious notion that baby Charlie would somehow be afforded the luxury to be whatever he wanted had entered my mind over the early days of his life as I would hold him and consider what he would be like, or what he might like to be, when he grew up. The notion of him having the freedom to choose was only insidious because of who James and I were.

James knew to respond to me carefully given the emotional state I was in, and I could tell he considered his next words cautiously. Over the past few days, James had witnessed my angry outbursts after I had received various communication from the White House, including one call when Peyton phoned to inform me that she would be sending nanny candidates for me to interview beginning the following Monday and another call informing me that the baby would have to be bottle fed to avoid the time and other inconveniences associated with breastfeeding and returning to work. James and I were both accustomed to any potential problem or obstacle we ran into being "handled" for us by the White House staff (or the Family) from plumbing leaks to doctors' appointments (it was how they assured we were always available for our work), but the notion that they had a say in how my child would be raised had rubbed me the wrong way.

"I'm not sure what he will want to be, but I know we will both do our best to help him become the best thing he can be," James replied.

"Oh," I said in a snarky tone. "Will that be what Laurel North decides or what we decide or what he decides? I am not clear since we don't seem to have too much of a say in things."

"Anna, don't. Please. This is our time and we don't have that much of it left with you home. I don't want to ruin it with fights. Lots of people don't even have the luxury of time off after having a baby and we should be grateful..." James could not continue because I cut him off having felt the rage creep back into my spine when the word luxury crept out of his mouth.

"Really? Grateful? Is that how I should feel?" I replied and I could hear the heat in my voice. Although I felt bad that it was being directed towards James, I had no idea how to stop myself from continuing to explode on him.

"Anna, he will have more than most people do if we are lucky enough to remain in the good graces of the Family. If we play our cards right, we can keep his future secure, or at least as secure as we can. Let's try to keep that in mind. Please, Anna. I love him as much as you do and I love you. I know this is hard on you, but you have to try to be ok with things, you have to try to look at the positive side of things," James pleaded quietly with me. I watched him nod to one passerby who had clearly noticed some drama occurring at our table.

And I did, try. I felt myself waffling between an acceptance of the truth and reality James kept reminding me of, which I knew existed, and my desire to protect Charlie. I did everything I possibly could, sometimes frantically, to make sure Charlie was "set up" for my return to work. I hated all of the nannies, but one of the younger ones seemed the most kind so I selected her. Three weeks after my argument with James over pancakes, in what felt like the blink of an eye, my leave was over and once we hit the Key Bridge on our way to work, I cried the entire time until we parked. James kissed my cheeks on top of my tears, told me to be strong, and reminded me that in a few hours I would be home with Charlie again. I knew the words James said were true, but I felt as though a part of my insides had been ripped away from me. Interestingly, the thought of getting dressed like a real person and taking a break from the baby to do something else with my mind was not the worst feeling. The worst feeling was that Charlie and my time away, although brief, felt like light and walking back into the White House felt dark.

I knew I could have worked harder to convince myself as I returned to work that I was doing what was best for my son. After all, everything he would experience would be a direct result of the life James and I led, but for some reason my soul wasn't buying the theory. There was something deep in my veins that knew, knowing the people that I worked for, that all I had done was given them more leverage over me by having Charlie. A child to these people, like any fortunate in life we might experience, was not a gift or a trump card for us. Instead, it was a bargaining chip and part of the carrot and stick game for them to use against us. I had seen them do it to others, and I knew James and I would be no different.

So I wandered back into my office on my first day back at the White House in an sullen daze, only stopping to politely and robotically accept the congratulations some colleagues offered me as I passed by them on the way to my office. On arrival at my desk, which looked nothing short of devastatingly sad at my first sight of it, a post it asked me to stop by Harper's office when I arrived. I didn't bother to sit down and headed straight for Harper's office.

"Hi, Anna. Welcome back," Harper said with zero emotion, as usual, "Sit down. I'd like to bring you up to speed on a few things."

I sunk into the chair across from her in front of her desk without saying a word.

"Anna, We need you to travel to Wyoming and Texas and a few other places. The trip has been arranged and you leave tomorrow morning," Harper informed me.

I felt like someone had slapped me across the face with a brick.

"What? Now? Tomorrow? I don't understand," I sputtered, "What do you possibly need me there for? Why? I just got here. I thought..." I was stammering as I sought answers. My mind was racing. I was panicked and by the look on Harper's face, I knew she could tell exactly how panicked I was. How could they expect me to leave Charlie so soon?

"Anna. I know you just got back, but you have to focus and stay calm. Your work is critical and this trip is critical. We have reason to believe the Network has gained more momentum and is more highly organized than we originally thought. We can't lose all of the progress we have made. We need you to make visits to some academies," Harper said plainly.

The Network was considered the enemy of the Party, it was the organization that people who resisted the Party affiliated with. We were required to regular training meetings at the White House where we learned how to detect possible Network affiliates who might be undercover. Network members were considered guilty of treason. Individuals were confirmed to be a member of the Network, and guilty of such treason, based on proof of at least two social media posts hostile to the Party during the time before the internet was restricted (since everything everyone had ever posted on the internet was kept for historical reference on government servers anyway) plus the Party's receipt of a sworn affidavit by at least two people who could confirm the individual in question had described the Network in a positive light or solicited participation from the person signing the affidavit in a Network event. I had heard plenty about the Network, it was a constant topic of communication at the White House. I had not, however, heard of anything called the academies.

"The academies?" I searched my brain and immediately wondered if in my lack of sleep haze I had forgotten something I was supposed to know.

"Yes. The academies. Phase II of our youth efforts. It is where we train the children," Harper replied.

"What children?" I asked.

Harper paused as if she was not sure how to respond for a second, "Well, most children Anna. It is where the majority of children that would have gone to public schools of the past go to a form of school now. Each academy is chartered to ensure that the youth thrive and have a stable path towards a future working for the Party."

I was bewildered. How had I not known about, or at least heard of, academies?

"Why do you need me to go? Can't someone else go? What would my visits have to do with the Network resistance anyway?" I asked with more than a hint of desperate pleading in my request.

"I'm sorry, Anna. It has to be you that goes. Look, since your image is so highly tied to our youth public service announcements, it has to be you. You are like our poster child at these places," Harper replied.

I was bewildered. "Your what?" I asked, totally confused.

"Anna, since you started at the White House you have been a part of the youth messaging, even before you joined us you were a major part of it when you worked with Maridel. You know that," Harper said flatly, "I can't imagine you are actually surprised to hear that your image has become synonymous with the Party's youth efforts. While you were out on leave, I suggested you take this trip in the highest-level meetings. Laurel agreed the trip is a good way to get you back in the correct mindset about work coming back from maternity leave."

I didn't know what to say. I was devastated at the thought of leaving Charlie, so the confusion I had about being called the poster child of these academies or the fact that she hadn't responded to my question about what my visit had to do with the Network resistance issues she mentioned took a back seat in the moment. The floor felt like it had dropped out from under me. I knew in the pit of my stomach that I could not say no. Plus, I had seen what happened to people who said no and, suddenly, the thought of Charlie in my mind prevented me from saying anything else combative to Harper.

I sat unmoved for a few more seconds until Harper dismissed me, but not before she reminded me to make sure I had enough camera ready outfits for the trip and, since I was only a few weeks post-childbirth, some good Spanx.

Chapter Twenty-One

Less than twenty-four hours later, I was devastated to leave Charlie, but packed in an oversized black suitcase nonetheless, waiting for the car that would drive me to the private plane that would take me and some other White House staff to Texas, the first stop on our trip. James had promised me everything would be ok. I could tell by the look in his eyes while I sobbed about being forced to leave that his heart was breaking for me. James seemed particularly unsettled about the fact that I was visiting academies. Although I did not know for sure, I got the sense that he had complained to Harper about the trip, which was an unusual step for him given his abiding caution about staying within the spoken, and unspoken, limits of our positions. James had even hinted that he knew a little about the academies given the funding of them and his role in finance and budget, but he was rather paralyzed when I asked him to tell me more about them.

I was slated to tour three national academies in Texas, first, followed by other academy tours in five states that had formerly been the largest coal producers in the U.S., Wyoming, West Virginia, Pennsylvania, Illinois, and Kentucky. I was told that I was scheduled to fly into Dallas the night before the morning of my first academy visit. Needless to say, I was not in my best condition when I woke up in Dallas the first morning, having barely slept. I was beyond anxious about being away from Charlie. I kept thinking of him in the little white and green sleeper pajamas he was wearing when I kissed his forehead goodbye, the smell of his formula breath on my nose.

Every motion I made on the first morning of my trip, forcing myself to get dressed in the freshly pressed outfit my assistant had hung on my closet door, felt heavy with sadness. I begrudgingly accepted the hair and makeup that had been arranged for me in my room, knowing that I really had no choice. Given that I was on official business representing the Party, we were required to be camera ready, a well-known travel and official engagement requirement. I had not been on the road for work with much intensity since the Maridel days, which I tried not to think about apart from an occasional pang of guilt for never returning to Veronica, but I had travelled a few times here and there for the Party with others from our unit in the White House. And if James and I occasionally wanted to grab a weekend away or when we "honeymooned", we were always "put up" at top notch hotels with security detail. Long gone were the days when the opulence of a five star hotel seemed shocking, although I still always felt a bit uneasy at the five star hotels, as if I was playing pretend. It occurred to me as my hair was getting let out of the large plastic rollers that had been pinned on the top of my head to ensure "volume and substance" (in the words of my hairdresser) that although the perks of traveling for the Party were far more palatable than the family meeting trips with Claire and Maridel, the feeling in the pit of my stomach before I would attend an official Party engagement felt eerily similar.

A few hours later, I stepped out of the black SUV that drove me to National Academy 372 and walked up to the massive tan brick building with black metal entry doors and no windows. The building reminded me of a typical public school, but without any windows. The chemical scents of industrial cleaning supplies somewhat overwhelmed me as I entered, the smell reminded me of the indoor pool that I learned to swim at. A group of children of various heights and ages, wearing military fatigues, were lined up in a perfect horizontal row in the lobby. One girl with long blond braided pigtails stepped forward to hand me a single daisy before returning to her row position. None of the children were smiling, their eyes staring straight ahead and their arms positioned straight by their sides, at attention. A burly man standing at the end of the row stepped forward as soon as the daisy girl had settled into her spot.

"Jude Thomas, principal," he barked sharply while shaking my hand with his firm grip. "It is an honor to have you visit us today, Mrs. York.

"Thank you," I replied noticing how uncertain I sounded, the atmosphere in the lobby feeling tense.

I turned to the row of children instinctively, "and thank you for the daisy ... and greeting, I fumbled over my words a bit realizing quickly that I was completely unprepared for whatever the hell this encounter was.

"Yes. Of course," Jude replied curtly, "shall we take your tour now?"

"Ok," I replied turning again to face the children. I could see that their jackets said Jr. Military Force on the left side of their jackets.

Jude quickly motioned for me to begin to walk towards the hallway. I hung back a few inches behind him as we entered a long hallway and he began his clearly rehearsed tour talk. I was baffled about why I had not been more prepared for what the purpose of this visit was. In all of the emotion of leaving Charlie, I supposed I hadn't asked too many questions. As I followed Jude, listening to bits and pieces he spouted off about when the building was constructed, I noticed he was made of muscles, his military fatigues stretching over his arms and backside, the dark spots on the fatigues matching his brown buzz cut.

"We are particularly proud of what we have been able to accomplish here," Jude said in his gruff voice as we continued down a pristine hallway made of white tile and cream-colored walls. I noticed various inspirational and patriotic quotes framed and hung on the walls at regular intervals.

"How many children attend school here?" I asked.

Jude looked confused for a moment. "I thought I shared that already, Ms. York, I apologize if I did not."

I could tell he was chiding me a bit for not listening closely to his earlier remarks.

"We top out at about five hundred on this campus. Since we are at capacity, we send overflow to our sister campuses but, as you probably heard before your visit, we are hopeful to receive funding to construct two duplicate campuses nearby given the demand."

I wasn't big on math, but the thought suddenly occurred to me that for five hundred students, things in the building seemed incredibly quiet. Given his mention of funding, I quickly surmised that I must be visiting to determine if the Party would provide such additional funding. James had mentioned that the academies were run by private organizations the government selected and paid.

"Demand for more campus space?" I questioned, clearly a bit confused about exactly what I was supposed to be asking.

"Well. Sure. I assumed you would have been briefed in more detail, but perhaps that is part of my job today," Jude said, sounding even more annoyed.

I motioned for him to continue with my hand.

"We are overwhelmed with children being enrolled. Joining our academies is the only way many of these children can eat and be sheltered and educated. We need more space. And I understand that we are slated to begin to receive children from out of state here in Texas very soon. As I am sure you know, this is often not only the best financial alternative for these parents, but our academy provides the students with the greatest chance of success in our economy in the future."

I stopped in my tracks for a minute noticing that I stopped so abruptly that my assistant bumped into my back.

"Out of state. You mean these children will move away from their parents?" I asked quizzically.

"Of course," Jude replied, "how else would they survive? All of the children who come here live here. We take charge of their care, and they become a tremendous opportunity for our United States military."

I started to feel as if sirens were going off in my head but, perfectly trained as I was, I remained composed. I knew from working for the Party long enough that my behavior and reactions were always being watched and reported back. Inside, the sirens were devolving into panic. I quickly thought of Charlie and took a measured breath.

"How old are the children when they come here?" I asked.

"We used to only take children eight years or older, but now we accept children as long as they are at least five years old," Jude reported with zero emotion in his voice.

"Babies," I uttered and on hearing my response out loud and seeing Jude and some of the others around me fidget, I realized I probably should have kept my response to myself. I suddenly knew I was entering dangerous territory. "Remember Charlie," I started to silently repeat to myself as Jude motioned for me to continue down another hallway to the right of where we started.

A few minutes later we were in an area that looked more like an obstacle course than a classroom. Jude explained that the goal was for every student to join some branch of public service for security, whether it was the military, national police, local police etc.

"So, the great thing is that we can modify this course to suit different ages," Jude explained as he motioned for some students in the room to begin demonstrating the obstacles for me. Our older children run drills clearing rooms, for example, with training from our special ops team, but our younger children can just play "get the bad guy" or other games we have created in the spirit of military style. Of course, we start weapons training around ten years old."

I nodded and did not offer any response words. The area felt more like a boot camp than a school and the thought of weapons training for children seemed horrifying. I had expected the academies were a form of school, it felt more like an institution and war training ground.

After the obstacle course, we visited an auditorium. Jude explained to me that several large lectures and patriotic performances took place there mostly, in his words, "focused on American values, military lessons, and God's word." A group of students who were introduced to me as third graders were standing on stage in uniform and repeated what Jude explained was the Junior Military Force pledge for me before singing God Bless America, stone faced and staring straight ahead. A few of the children glanced at me briefly, as if I looked familiar to them, but their face did not share any emotion, as if their souls were on mute.

As we left the auditorium, despite the fluorescence of the fixtures that lit the ceiling, the newness of the halls, and chemical scents of industrial cleaning supplies, I felt immersed in darkness. I thought of Charlie again and how much I desperately wanted to go home to his sweaty curled fingers that wrapped perfectly around my pinky.

As quickly as the thought of Charlie came to me, it disappeared as we stopped at the next spot on the tour, a hallway simply labeled, Solitary. Jude informed me that non-compliant children could spend time to cool off and come to a better understanding of the rules if they needed some extra reinforcement. He started to walk down the hallway and I felt a wave of terror wash over me as I started to walk by his side. Jude must have noticed my horrified look and began to reassure me that "the mental illness medication, and advances in diagnosis of various mental health conditions the national academy leaders prided themselves on, significantly helped to minimize the number of visits problem students made to solitary."

I nodded. I was well aware of the Party view that mental illness had become an epidemic, and had been reduced significantly given the Party's health guidelines for doctors requiring much more frequent prescribing of various anti-depressants and anti-anxiety medications to large swaths of the population. It had never occurred to me that children were included in those policies.

As Jude continued to tell me about the incredible technology that had been woven into the cells we walked by, each one with a single rectangular pane of glass that was too high for most small children to see out of, I noticed a touch screen built into the wall outside of each cell.

"What's this?" I asked quietly pointing to a screen.

"These are the master controls for each room," Jude explained factually , "it's how we can control what plays in each cell. We try to customize the messaging to the needs of the individual child. We can also control light, temperature, and humidity, as needed.

I gulped, trying to do my best not to react.

"I can demonstrate for you," Jude continued with pride and I felt his hot breath near my right shoulder as his fingers extended past it to start tapping on one of the screens. Within a few seconds, the bright light of a video in the now dark room to my left grabbed my attention. I walked over and peered through the pane of glass before letting out an audible gasp.

There was a video of a young woman playing on the back wall of the cell. She had long blond hair and I heard her screaming. Even more terrifying than what I heard her screaming in the cell at a child, was the fact that it was me on the screen.

Chapter Twenty-Two

It was past dinnertime when the SUV driving her home from the airport pulled up in front of our house. I had been waiting at the window with Charlie because the schedule she gave me, before she left for the trip, estimated the time she would be home. I made sure Charlie and I were at the window so she could see us right away. It would have been impossible to describe at that moment how much I longed to have her home and how much I longed to touch her and hold her in my arms.

If you had told me when I was informed by my boss that I was being "arranged" to marry a woman in the communications division of the White House that I would end up falling madly in love with her, I would not have believed you. And not because Anna wasn't beautiful. She was stunning. Even with mascara stains under her eyes the first night we were officially introduced at the staff holiday party, she took my breath away. She was the kind of woman that men were in awe of in terms of her physical appearance. But, I just didn't think that it was possible to wind up falling in love with someone you were forced to marry. That wasn't how things happened where I grew up. Moreover, I did not think it was possible that someone like her would fall in love with someone like me. Her physical beauty was only dwarfed by her incredible spirit. It was like she turned a light on in the universe every day she woke up.

As much as I had missed her over the past week, I was certain that my feelings could not compare to feelings she had over the last few days being separated from Charlie, likely nothing short of torture for her. We weren't allowed to communicate on the phone when we were on official Party travel, for security reasons, so I had no idea how things had gone on the trip. I was worried about what she might experience visiting the academies, but she had been so anxious before the trip that I didn't think it would be helpful to make her worry even more by telling her my worst fears about them. Being a "money guy," I understood how much funding was flowing to the academies, and I heard bits and pieces from others I worked with at the White House in hushed whispers about the goals of the academy programs.

Her car pulled up in front of our house, on schedule. I watched with anticipation as she stepped out of the back of the car, carefully putting one heel down before the other while the driver held her hand to help her out, the streetlights that lined the white picket fences on our street glowing soft orange around her. You would never know watching the grace Anna moved with that she grew up poor like me. I watched her express thanks to the driver and take her suitcase from him. She always thanked everyone around her, even people that she didn't have to. As she started to walk up the path across our front yard towards the front door, I jokingly made Charlie's hand wave at her through the living room window, but she didn't notice, her head down the entire time.

My gut immediately told me something was wrong. She wasn't ok. I left my perch at the window to hurry to the front door, throwing it open as she turned her key in the lock. I immediately grabbed her with my free arm that was not holding the baby right there on the threshold, the space between us making just enough room for my arm cradling Charlie to fit perfectly between our bellies.

"I'm so happy you're home," I whispered into her hair, "We have been looking out the window waiting for you. Charlie missed you. I missed you."

I backed away so I could offer her the baby. She stared back at me with a look I had never seen on her face before. She took a glance at Charlie, dropped her head into the palms of her hands and started to sob. I was stunned. I didn't know what was wrong, but I knew it was serious.

I felt a sense of panic creep up into my heart. I quickly ushered her into our foyer and took a quick look outside after she walked inside to make sure no one, including the driver, was watching her breakdown. There was no trace of anyone watching so I quickly shut the front door, before immediately embracing her again,

"Hey, hey, calm down, Anna. It's ok, you're here now, we're here...everything's alright, Charlie's ok and I'm ok....and your home, the trip is over now..." I found myself uttering various reassurances hoping one would work and calm her down.

"Nothing is over," she said as she pulled away from my embrace with mascara stains running down her face, "nothing is ok."

I had never seen her this upset.

"What do you mean? What is not over?" I asked, concerned.

"James, the academies, they aren't what you think. Where I went. These places. They aren't schools," she was stuttering a bit and struggling to get her words out through sobs.

I took a deep breath. The baby started to fuss in my arms.

"Come inside, sit down," I offered, as I motioned for her to head to the living room.

Anna plopped down on our living room sofa. She was still sobbing, wiping away snot from her nose with the sleeve of her dress coat. I closed the living room blinds, put Charlie down in the cradle that we kept in the corner of the living room and sat down next to her on the couch.

"What happened?" I asked as I grabbed her hand.

"It was awful," she started, "I don't know where to begin. There are kids, all of these kids, and they are taken away from their parents and their homes and put in these places...they are so little ... and they make them wear military uniforms, and they medicate them and teach them to use guns ... and I'm not even sure what the point is except that it appears we are raising another army ... and then they showed me how they punish them and I didn't realize, I didn't realize..." she couldn't finish because she had broken into sobs again. Before I could even try to calm her back down, she leapt off the couch with her hand over her mouth and ran to the kitchen. I got in the kitchen just in time to see her hurl in the garbage can she pulled out from under our kitchen sink.

I walked over and put my hand on her back while she heaved a few more times before slowly returning to an upright position and rinsing her mouth out with some water from the kitchen sink. My insides felt like they were on full alert, the adrenaline racing through my body faster than I could realize what was happening.

"Anna. I'm so sorry. I don't know what to say. I knew they would be tough places, but I didn't expect things to be so difficult..." I hadn't finished my sentence before she cut me off sharply.

"So you knew? You knew about these places and you didn't tell me?" she was screaming at me by the time she finished her question.

Charlie started to cry from his cradle.

"I knew it felt like there was something you didn't want to tell me before I left. I knew it. How could you?"

"Anna, Please. Calm down. I didn't know the extent of things, I just knew that these places seemed to be growing in scope by the day in terms of the number of kids there. I knew the government was spending a lot of money on the places. I don't know much else about them apart from what we see on budgets and what I hear in bits and pieces. You know better than anyone that the planning for this academy business has been kept pretty close to the vest in the West Wing," I offered.

"Right," she said sarcastically, "well, did your budgets include a line item for putting me on videos to brainwash these kids? Or did your friend Harper already explain to you what being the poster child for the academies involves?"

"What are you talking about, Anna?" I retorted, noticing that I had started to sound angry and defensive, more than I wish I had looking back on it, but feeling nothing short of sheer desperation for her to calm down. "I know you have made videos for all kinds of things at the White House for as long as I have known you. I don't know what you mean about videos for these kids. What do you mean by poster child and what does Harper have to do with this?"

"Oh, so you think I should have realized this, James? Is that what you are saying? How very Party line of you! I guess this is what I get for marrying one of them."

"Anna, stop, please. Why are you calling me one of them? You know I am no different than you in terms of our connection to these people. If you would calm down, maybe you could explain to me what happened. Maybe I can help? I don't even understand what is going on," I begged.

"I didn't make these videos, James," she screamed, sobbing at this point, "the videos they use to torture and brainwash and punish these kids – they use my face and my voice and my body in them, but it is me saying things I never said. They use something they told me is called face swapping. Apparently, James, I am the primary face of the academies and youth messaging all over the country. Apparently, I am also on other video messages broadcast to poor people persuading them to give up their kids to these places when they can't take care of them. I am helping the Party steal children, James."

It took me a minute to process what she had told me. I hadn't heard that her videos were being used by the Party at academies specifically, but I knew her face was well known in any number of propaganda videos. Laurel North seemed to have a real penchant for using Anna in Party propaganda videos and had since before I was even introduced to Anna.

"Anna, clearly I haven't seen what you are talking about, but I know you would never hurt anyone. You have to remember there is so much we are not privy to. Maybe it was just more economical to use some of your old videos. You know you have worked on so many over the years. Maybe it just made sense for the Party to handle it this way. This isn't your fault," I offered, hoping to reassure her. I desperately wanted to hold her and kiss her. I couldn't stand the feeling of being right in front of her without her wanting to love me back.

"Of course this isn't my fault, James! That isn't the point. We can't just be ok with this. Why are you ok with this and trying to blame this on funding issues?" she said sharply.

I quickly realized that nothing I said had made anything better for her. When I look back and think about how I handled the rest of that night, I can tell you with absolute certainty that I wish I had handled it differently. Because what I said and did that night didn't work, so I know that I should have tried something else. But, in that moment, hearing Anna scream at me and suggest that I was some kind of a traitor or a bad person triggered something in me. I wanted her back. I wanted her to love me. I was desperate and, in the moment, anger was easier.

"Anna," I said in the most patronizing voice I had ever used with her, "You need to calm down. I know you are upset and I am trying to be here for you. Don't treat me as if I am the one who created the system we have to live in. You must have expected something like this was going on somewhere. You filmed all sorts of videos for the Party over the years – all of the PSA's you would tell me about. You know how desperate things are for most people...you know most people don't live the life we do. Most people are dirt poor, Anna. You know that."

She looked like I had stunned her in response.

"So let me get this straight. You are ok with all of this. You are ok with rooms for kids that are like prison cells and torture chambers, where they throw little kids, James. Little kids they consider non-compliant when they ask the wrong question or say the wrong thing that is considered against the Party. Can you imagine that? Can you imagine our boy being treated like that? Would that be something you can ever imagine him deserving as a child?"

She was speaking to me in a tone of voice I had never heard her use with me, or anyone.

"No, Anna. No. I could not imagine Charlie ever deserving that," James bellowed, "and in case you didn't notice, I work damn hard every single day to make sure he doesn't fall out of the Party's good graces. You should do the same if you care about him, Anna. Don't play dumb about all of this, Anna. You know who we are. You know who we work for. You see how everyone arounds us stays in the good graces of wealth and power every day. You see it with your own eyes so don't pretend like all of this is actually a shock to you."

She inched back towards the kitchen counter, moving away from me as if she was suddenly scared of me.

"I am not playing dumb," she replied firmly, "I did not know that my image was being used to brainwash children. I did not know that the people we work for have been forming a militia made of kids, and drugging them, and doing god knows what else to force them into compliance. It was one thing for me to be shuttled off to a CEP. It was one thing to understand that my liberty evaporated during my lifetime, but this is too much, James. It's too much for me. I can't be a part of this."

"Anna, We are no different than anyone else around us with our lack of choices. You will make a mistake if you go down a path where you think we somehow deserve choies that most other people don't have. Or thinking that you or I or Charlie are somehow entitled for the world to give us other more pleasant choices. You don't think for everyone of "us" out there who has been fortunate to get a patron backed by wealth and power to bring us into the fold, that there aren't a million more people lined up looking for a patron or willing to take our patron? That is what most people do on earth and they always have. People fight and struggle and search for a patron one way or another. Whether the patron is a job, or a partner, or a god to believe in, or a community to belong to. Everyone is looking for patronage."

"I never wanted a patron, James. For as long as I can remember, I always felt like I did something to deserve my lot in life. I wondered what I had done wrong...what we had done wrong ... people like my family and the neighbors around me who struggled with the same realities of our day to day life. Hunger. Not Enough Money. Struggle. Exhaustion. Working around the clock just to stay poor. No recourses at school. No help. I did what I was told. I followed the rules. Then the people who make the rules found me and offered me a job. I have worked my ass off trying to take advantage of the opportunity to be something more, with more dignity than my birth and youth provided me. I have worked so hard at this job, listening and following the rules and trying to make my life better, but I never agreed to this. I am so ashamed of myself for thinking I was valued by these people when I was only being used. My body is just a resource for them, nothing more. I had no control over who I was born or the economic status I was born into, but I can control what I decide to do now. I deserve the right to at least control my own voice."

"No, Anna, you don't necessarily," I continued with frustration, "Not everyone has the luxury in life to protest what is dealt to them. If we are valued by anyone with power, most of us are valued because we can be used for something. I hate the system we live in, but I can tell you one thing for sure. We can't change it. We just can't. You know what happens to the person who tries! Those people get punished for speaking up or, at best, ostracized and labeled a freak, a crazy, or a nut bag, or the Party says that person has a problem with authority, or they say that person wasn't that great at their job to begin with. These are not the labels you want to receive, Anna, because they will ruin your life and end everything you have. And long before the Party won and the country became an authoritarian regime, ordinary American life for most people in the U.S. was like living in an authoritarian regime in one way or another, but people just answered to forces other than the President and the Party, like their job, or popular pressure, or a religious organization, or whatever else came their way that had more power than they did."

We stood in silence for a second, both of us breathing heavily from yelling. After a few moments as I stood watching tears fall from her eyes, she left the kitchen and walked into the living room and over to the bassinet. I followed her. I watched as she gently rubbed Charlie's stomach and gave him a pacifier while his eyes fought to stay open, exhausted from crying. I desperately wanted to hug her, but I was afraid to. I waited a few more minutes before whispering to her in the darkness of the living room.

"Anna, I want us to have the best life we can. I know it may not be a perfect situation, hell, far from it. But it's pretty damn good wouldn't you say? Food on the table, a beautiful home, and safety. You wear nice clothes. You have a job. Why throw it all away? We have a nice life don't we?"

I could hear the desperation in my voice.

"Right now, it feels like we have a nice life for all the wrong reasons. If you saw the faces of these kids, James. If you saw these places. What am I doing to stop the problem if I am becoming one of them? What does it mean if I buy into the life security they hold over my head, the money, the status, and the perception of safety in exchange for doing exactly what they did to me, and worse, to other children? I don't think I can live with myself if I don't fight back on this somehow."

She was crying again but this time it was a defeated whimper, not the hot angry tears that she had arrived home with. I walked over to her and put my arms around her, hugging her from behind. I kissed the back of her head.

"I love you. I love that you care. But you can't fight this. I know you have been through a lot. I know your life has not been easy. Neither has mine. I know this is another tough stop on the journey, but you have to also think about the fact that we have a good thing going. We should protect our family before we worry about anyone else's family."

I waited for her to respond while I held her, but she didn't say anything. She just stood, looking down at Charlie while I held her. I told myself it would just take time, but the truth is in that moment I knew that something between us had been torn. Anna was home alright, but it was as if she was still very far away.

PART THREE

The Treehouse

Chapter Twenty-Three

A few hours later, a little after 8:00 p.m. on the same day I had arrived at Mrs. Rhodes doorstep, I was rocking Charlie to sleep while pacing back and forth in front of the living room windows of the Rhodes's house, curtains now drawn shut since the sun had gone down. Kat was peeking through a small spot in one of the curtains, looking out a window for the truck that was arriving to take Charlie and me to what they told me was a Network "safe house." They also informed me that they could not share the location of the safe house with me in advance because, in case I was located by the Party on the way, it was best that I had as little information as possible about where I was going. I was warned that I would have to do everything in my power to keep Charlie quiet for parts of the journey. Despite the obvious risk involved in a plan to keep a baby quiet on command, it was concluded that the risk of me not getting into more secure hiding immediately was far greater. Apparently, the Rhodes were informed by whoever they had talked with while I was sleeping that people were already looking for me. This did not surprise any of us, but it did make me wince in pain thinking of what James was going through.

As I paced while feeding Charlie a bottle, I tried my best to contend with the feelings of sheer terror I was experiencing. I hoped that James would quickly consider me the enemy after he realized I was gone. After all, I figured he could truthfully say he had known nothing of my plan and his genuine shock would help his case. And, if I was caught, I figured he could insist that as a victim of my bad acts he deserved his son and, in that case, they would return Charlie to him no matter how they punished me. Knowing who he was and how much he loved me, I was worried he wouldn't despise me as fast as I hoped he would for his own sake. Charlie and I were the only family he had given that his parents had been deported when he was a child.

Mrs. Rhodes was sitting on the couch watching me pace as we waited for the van. The shock of my initial arrival had worn off and for the last two hours it had been replaced with a sensation between Mrs. Rhodes and me that was a mix of tenderness and awkwardness. Not only had I not seen her in years, but I had done my best to avoid seeing her following the Incident. I wanted to ask her about my mother and my sister, the fact that I was only a few doors down from the home I grew up in not being lost on me, but the air was so heavy, and I was so terrified of what was to come, that I was afraid too to ask much.

Eventually she spoke.

"I know this is a lot for you, Anna."

"He may be hurt or punished because of me. I took my son away from his father."

"It's complicated, Anna. The most important decisions we make usually are."

I nodded as I continued to pace.

"Anna, there are some things I want to say to you...that I have wished I could have said a long time ago and, frankly, blamed myself for not finding a way to say sooner."

"It's ok. You are helping me. You don't have to say anything else. The past can stay where it belongs."

"No. It's important. Listen, you must know that I have always thought of you like another daughter. It wasn't easy for me knowing you and your family for so long and watching the things you struggled with as a kid. You reminded me a lot of myself as a child. Despite the fact that we grew up in different decades, I grew up in a similar type of place with similar types of people who faced similar pressures. And I wanted to try to help you survive."

Mrs. Rhodes put her head down for a minute and I kept pacing in silence, holding Charlie. When she looked back up, I could see the tears in her eyes.

"I feel like I failed you, Anna, because of what happened that summer. I have felt regret every day for not being able to protect you and I hate myself for being partially complicit by keeping my mouth shut to keep my job. I mean, I invited you there. I didn't know what would happen when I invited you to work with me that summer, but maybe I should have known given the world we live in. Maybe I should have known that someone like you would so clearly be a target for a monster like him. When you pulled away and avoided me after that summer, I wanted to respect your space. But, I want you to know that I never once stopped caring for you. When I watched what you appeared to become over the last few years, as we saw you on television or read about you in the papers or realized that you were the Party's ..." she paused, and I could tell she had stopped herself from saying something else.

I stopped pacing and looked directly at her, immediately unsure if what she would say would make me feel better or more enraged about everything.

"Well, I felt like if it weren't for that summer, you would never have wound up involved with the Party. And, I am so sorry, Anna. I may not have been able to make it right then, but I will do everything I can to protect you and Charlie now," she whispered, finishing with a few nods of her head in affirmation.

I turned my head deeper into Charlie's curls and took a breath of his intoxicating baby scent, tears falling hot and fast out of my eyes.

Mrs. Rhodes got up and placed her arms around me and Charlie, embracing us.

"Mom, he's here." Kat's voice interrupted the embrace.

I pulled back from her embrace and looked at Mrs. Rhodes, saturated with fear.

"I'm scared," I said.

"I know, Anna. Be brave. You have to be. Life always throws us moments where being brave is not a choice. Plus, the best people are working on this tonight given who you are and where you ran from."

Mrs. Rhodes walked over to me and put her hand on Charlie's hair while she gave him a little kiss on his forehead. The moment was interrupted by Kat's stern voice speaking to me from her perch by the front door.

"Anna," Kat said firmly, "it's time, he's parking and will start to open up the back doors of the truck and pull the ramp down any second before he comes to get you."

Kat motioned for me to get into the brown wardrobe box they had explained to me earlier that I would be transported in.

Kat had told me that the Network relied on Amazon workers to transport people and other items to safe houses and other places. Despite the lack of open internet access in America, there remained an app for Amazon that allowed people to shop and ship only, Amazon having purchased most of the major parcel shipping companies and becoming the only shipping company in the U.S. by this point. E-commerce was a way of life since the wealth gap prevented many small businesses from opening and paying rent for a storefront. Plus, brick and mortar retail had started its slow march to death B.E. since the internet resulted in more online shopping and most people who were employed couldn't justify spending time shopping in person anyway. Even though citizens of the U.S. were banned from connecting with each other on the internet, they were still permitted to buy

things on the internet. Of course, data about all purchases could be monitored by the Party.

"Mrs. Rhodes?" I asked after I stepped in the box before I sat down in it.

"Yes, Anna."

"How's my mother? I asked, hopeful, not knowing if I
would hear she was alive or dead, that uncertainty also
being one of the other reasons I had not asked about my
family previously. "Does Lowe still live in the neighborhood?"

"Your mom is the same," Mrs. Rhodes quickly reported, "although she doesn't get out much. Lizzie does
a good job taking care of her and we make sure to send
meals over. For a long time, your notoriety didn't seem
to make anything better or worse for them since they
could, and do, honestly tell people they haven't seen
you in years. Your mother used to brag about how much
potential she always knew you had when you were on
Unity with Maridel at those rallies. Of course, things
changed quite a bit as your role at the White House expanded and parents started being forced to send their
kids away to academies. It's not safe for her or Lizzie to
go out much anymore. Your brothers left home a long
time ago, no one has heard from them in years."

I nodded, taking the information in. I immediately felt the, now quite familiar, nauseous feeling in my stomach grow. Anytime I thought about the academies or the fact that I left James, I felt the urge to vomit.

I noticed Mrs. Rhodes had not responded to my question about Lowe. But, before I could ask again if she knew how Lowe was, I heard three firm knocks on the front door, and a quick pause, followed by three more knocks. Kat motioned for me to sit down in the box. I sat down Indian style on the bottom of the wardrobe box, as Kat had instructed me to do, knees up towards the side of the box. I wrapped Charlie's legs around my sides towards my back as he napped in his baby carrier, facing me, full from the bottle he had devoured a few minutes earlier. I looked up at Kat one last time. I watched as the light of the living room become dim as Kat furiously taped the box shut. I heard the lock of the front door open and the sound of a man's voice.

A man asked, "I think we have a pick up here or is it three?"

"Hi Alex. Yes. That's right. Just some linens mom has been embroidering for the family she works for. Just one package, not three," Kat replied.

Kat had told me in advance that the question and her confirmation about one or three packages was specific language memorized in advance to confirm the transport of a human being.

It had become clear to me over the prior hours that this was not the first time Mrs. Rhodes and her family had shipped for the Network using Amazon. Since the Cov-19 Pandemic, large bags and anything that could further crowd mass transit were banned to maintain social distancing. So it was not unusual for people who only used mass transit to ship any number of things, from place to place, that they might have normally carried with them to and from work or any other place. There were regular daily pickups of packages in every neighborhood.

Kat had assured me that Alex was one of the best "cargo" carriers working for the Network. She also briefly explained that the entire Network movement had code language and "cargo" referred to people that were being moved to safe houses. She told me that Network members were a part of almost every industry. In all the training I had at the White House about the Network, I certainly had never heard about Amazon shipping people or supplies for the Network.

A few minutes after the last strip of tape had sealed our box shut, Kat issued her final thank you to Alex and I suddenly fell back onto what I expected was the dolly I had been told would wheel us out of the Rhodes's house and onto the truck. The box also had small squares in select places that enabled us to breathe through, what I was told, was enhanced Phifertex mesh in the same color of the box blended into the box to keep vents hidden that allowed us to breathe. On the inside, I found the box was also reinforced with a firm material so I could not bend the shape with my body at all. I felt very grateful for the long pillow behind my head that cushioned our fall onto the metal bars of the dolly. I felt us inch up the ramp onto the back of Alex's truck. I felt him gently set us down flat in the truck after we made it up the ramp. I saw Alex's fingertips inside the handle holes where the metal bar of the wardrobe box would have normally been located making sure he had a tight grip on us as he dragged the box off the dolly. It was dark in the box, but even darker once he finished rolling us into the back of the truck.

Although Kat told me not to expect Alex to say one word to us during the journey, I found myself nonetheless wishing that he would offer some reassuring words. There was only silence until I heard Alex turn on the radio as we pulled away. Although Charlie stirred a few times, I was able to hush him back to sleep on my chest with his pacifier. I was told that Alex would have to make a few stops to keep things looking normal on the journey. I had no idea if there were other people getting on the truck with us or not.

The longer we drove, making a few more stops, the more nervous I got. It began to sink in further that I had no control over where Alex was taking us, or whether he would follow through on what he had promised Kat or Mrs. Rhodes. Kat told me I was one of his last pickups of the day, but she did not know how long it would take us to arrive at the safe house. Feeling frighteningly alone, I watched as 20, 30, 40 and 50 minutes passed on my watch which, thankfully, had hands that glowed in the dark.

Eventually, I heard Alex open the back of the truck again, pull down the ramp, and walk up the ramp into the back of the truck. I again saw his gloved fingertips through the wardrobe bar holes. In an instant, we were tilted back on the dolly again. Charlie was out like a light, thankfully, and I had his pacifier in my hand wrapped around his back just in case he stirred. After a trip backwards down the truck ramp and a bumpy pull up over what I assumed was a curb, we were rolled for a few moments before gently being placed flat again. I noticed that Alex had turned on the small battery powered radio I was told, by Kat, that he wore on his belt and would turn on to play music if Charlie made noise, or he was worried our motion might cause Charlie to make noise. When I asked Kat if people passing by us might think a battery powered radio blasting music in public was suspicious, she had shrugged off my concern and informed me that weirdos in New York City had been blasting radios as they walked down the street for years, so it would seem perfectly ordinary. Plus, Alex would explain his lack of ear buds on not wanting to drown out traffic for safety as he made his stops.

"Evening, Alex. How are things?" I heard another man ask.

"Very well. Thanks. Did you hit up Gino's for pizza tonight?" Alex asked.

"Not yet. Taking my break in another hour. This for the penthouse?" I quickly surmised by this other man's mention of a penthouse that Alex was talking to some kind of guard or doorman.

"Yes. Ok to take it up?" Alex asked.

"Yup. Go for it. I will give a ring and let 'em know you are on the way," the man replied to Alex.

"Keep an eye on the truck, will you?" Alex asked, "that new officer working this corner has been a real jerk the last few times about my truck being double-parked too long. Some kid cop...looks like he is barely legal."

"You got it," the doorman said protectively, "and you're right, he pisses everyone off and I think he is only sixteen. Maybe I'll catch you at Gino's later?"

"You got it. Check you later. You da man," I heard Alex reply in his thick New York accent.

With that, we were tilted back again and on the move. Charlie wiggled a bit and I quickly put his pacifier up to his mouth, which he happily took. I heard Alex push a button and I assumed we were near an elevator. I heard the sound of what I assumed were elevator doors open and we moved again, this time only a little bit. I felt the familiar stomach drop of an elevator start to move us with a ping passing each floor, but I lost count after twenty-two and had no idea how many floors we were traveling.

When we stopped, we tilted back again onto the dolly and rolled a few feet until Alex gently placed us flat on the floor again. Alex knocked three times with a pause and three more times in the same unusually quick succession that he had knocked at the Rhodes. I heard the door open.

"Good Evening, Alex. Thank you," a woman's voice responded. Her voice sounded syrupy and oddly familiar to me, although I initially had no idea why.

"Of course. The pleasure is all mine, ma'am. Let me roll it in for you," Alex replied calmly. I felt us cross the lump of a threshold before we were plopped down flat again and slowly pushed off the dolly. I heard Alex wish the woman a good evening before I heard a door shut followed by the click of three locks. Within seconds, I heard the tape start to be ripped off the box and worried I might vomit or worse given the fear pulsing through my body. I took a few deep breaths as the flaps of the top of the box were ripped opened and I grabbed the hands extended to me over the side as I stood up, sweating and in tremendous pain as I unfolded my muscles from their curled up position in the box. As my head crossed the top of the box, I gasped audibly as I saw the woman standing in front of me holding my hands with a firm grip.

Laura Maack took in my stunned face, but did not waiver or let go of my hands.

"Hi, Anna. We're glad you're here. Now, let me help you get out."

Chapter Twenty-Four

A few hours later, a little after 8:00 p.m. on the same day I had arrived at Mrs. Rhodes doorstep, I was rocking Charlie to sleep while pacing back and forth in front of the living room windows of the Rhodes's house, curtains now drawn shut since the sun had gone down. Kat was peeking through a small spot in one of the curtains, looking out a window for the truck that was arriving to take Charlie and me to what they told me was a Network "safe house." They also informed me that they could not share the location of the safe house with me in advance because, in case I was located by the Party on the way, it was best that I had as little information as possible about where I was going. I was warned that I would have to do everything in my power to keep Charlie quiet for parts of the journey. Despite the obvious risk involved in a plan to keep a baby quiet on command, it was concluded that the risk of me not getting into more secure hiding immediately was far greater. Apparently, the Rhodes were informed by whoever they had talked with while I was sleeping that people were already looking for me. This did not surprise any of us, but it did make me wince in pain thinking of what James was going through.

As I paced while feeding Charlie a bottle, I tried my best to contend with the feelings of sheer terror I was experiencing. I hoped that James would quickly consider me the enemy after he realized I was gone. After all, I figured he could truthfully say he had known nothing of my plan and his genuine shock would help his case. And, if I was caught, I figured he could insist that as a victim of my bad acts he deserved his son and, in that case, they would return Charlie to him no matter how they punished me. Knowing who he was and how much he loved me, I was worried he wouldn't despise me as fast as I hoped he would for his own sake. Charlie and I were the only family he had given that his parents had been deported when he was a child.

Mrs. Rhodes was sitting on the couch watching me pace as we waited for the van. The shock of my initial arrival had worn off and for the last two hours it had been replaced with a sensation between Mrs. Rhodes and me that was a mix of tenderness and awkwardness. Not only had I not seen her in years, but I had done my best to avoid seeing her following the Incident. I wanted to ask her about my mother and my sister, the fact that I was only a few doors down from the home I grew up in not being lost on me, but the air was so heavy, and I was so terrified of what was to come, that I was afraid too to ask much.

Eventually she spoke.

"I know this is a lot for you, Anna."

"He may be hurt or punished because of me. I took my son away from his father."

"It's complicated, Anna. The most important decisions we make usually are."

I nodded as I continued to pace.

"Anna, there are some things I want to say to you...that I have wished I could have said a long time ago and, frankly, blamed myself for not finding a way to say sooner."

"It's ok. You are helping me. You don't have to say anything else. The past can stay where it belongs."

"No. It's important. Listen, you must know that I have always thought of you like another daughter. It wasn't easy for me knowing you and your family for so long and watching the things you struggled with as a kid. You reminded me a lot of myself as a child. Despite the fact that we grew up in different decades, I grew up in a similar type of place with similar types of people who faced similar pressures. And I wanted to try to help you survive."

Mrs. Rhodes put her head down for a minute and I kept pacing in silence, holding Charlie. When she looked back up, I could see the tears in her eyes.

"I feel like I failed you, Anna, because of what happened that summer. I have felt regret every day for not being able to protect you and I hate myself for being partially complicit by keeping my mouth shut to keep my job. I mean, I invited you there. I didn't know what would happen when I invited you to work with me that summer, but maybe I should have known given the world we live in. Maybe I should have known that someone like you would so clearly be a target for a monster like him. When you pulled away and avoided me after that summer, I wanted to respect your space. But, I want you to know that I never once stopped caring for you. When I watched what you appeared to become over the last few years, as we saw you on television or read about you in the papers or realized that you were the Party's ..." she paused, and I could tell she had stopped herself from saying something else.

I stopped pacing and looked directly at her, immediately unsure if what she would say would make me feel better or more enraged about everything.

"Well, I felt like if it weren't for that summer, you would never have wound up involved with the Party. And, I am so sorry, Anna. I may not have been able to make it right then, but I will do everything I can to protect you and Charlie now," she whispered, finishing with a few nods of her head in affirmation.

I turned my head deeper into Charlie's curls and took a breath of his intoxicating baby scent, tears falling hot and fast out of my eyes.

Mrs. Rhodes got up and placed her arms around me and Charlie, embracing us.

"Mom, he's here." Kat's voice interrupted the embrace.

I pulled back from her embrace and looked at Mrs. Rhodes, saturated with fear.

"I'm scared," I said.

"I know, Anna. Be brave. You have to be. Life always throws us moments where being brave is not a choice. Plus, the best people are working on this tonight given who you are and where you ran from."

Mrs. Rhodes walked over to me and put her hand on Charlie's hair while she gave him a little kiss on his forehead. The moment was interrupted by Kat's stern voice speaking to me from her perch by the front door.

"Anna," Kat said firmly, "it's time, he's parking and will start to open up the back doors of the truck and pull the ramp down any second before he comes to get you."

Kat motioned for me to get into the brown wardrobe box they had explained to me earlier that I would be transported in.

Kat had told me that the Network relied on Amazon workers to transport people and other items to safe houses and other places. Despite the lack of open internet access in America, there remained an app for Amazon that allowed people to shop and ship only, Amazon having purchased most of the major parcel shipping companies and becoming the only shipping company in the U.S. by this point. E-commerce was a way of life since the wealth gap prevented many small businesses from opening and paying rent for a storefront. Plus, brick and mortar retail had started its slow march to death B.E. since the internet resulted in more online shopping and most people who were employed couldn't justify spending time shopping in person anyway. Even though citizens of the U.S. were banned from connecting with each other on the internet, they were still permitted to buy things on the internet. Of course, data about all purchases could be monitored by the Party.

"Mrs. Rhodes?" I asked after I stepped in the box before I sat down in it.

"Yes, Anna."

"How's my mother? I asked, hopeful, not knowing if I would hear she was alive or dead, that uncertainty also being one of the other reasons I had not asked about my family previously. "Does Lowe still live in the neighborhood?"

"Your mom is the same," Mrs. Rhodes quickly reported, "although she doesn't get out much. Lizzie does a good job taking care of her and we make sure to send meals over. For a long time, your notoriety didn't seem to make anything better or worse for them since they could, and do, honestly tell people they haven't seen you in years. Your mother used to brag about how much potential she always knew you had when you were on Unity with Maridel at those rallies. Of course, things changed quite a bit as your role at the White House expanded and parents started being forced to send their kids away to academies. It's not safe for her or Lizzie to go out much anymore. Your brothers left home a long time ago, no one has heard from them in years."

I nodded, taking the information in. I immediately felt the, now quite familiar, nauseous feeling in my stomach grow. Anytime I thought about the academies or the fact that I left James, I felt the urge to vomit.

I noticed Mrs. Rhodes had not responded to my question about Lowe. But, before I could ask again if she knew how Lowe was, I heard three firm knocks on the front door, and a quick pause, followed by three more knocks. Kat motioned for me to sit down in the box. I sat down Indian style on the bottom of the wardrobe box, as Kat had instructed me to do, knees up towards the side of the box. I wrapped Charlie's legs around my sides towards my back as he napped in his baby carrier, facing me, full from the bottle he had devoured a few minutes earlier. I looked up at Kat one last time. I watched as the light of the living room become dim as Kat furiously taped the box shut. I heard the lock of the front door open and the sound of a man's voice.

A man asked, "I think we have a pick up here or is it three?"

"Hi Alex. Yes. That's right. Just some linens mom has been embroidering for the family she works for. Just one package, not three," Kat replied.

Kat had told me in advance that the question and her confirmation about one or three packages was specific language memorized in advance to confirm the transport of a human being.

It had become clear to me over the prior hours that this was not the first time Mrs. Rhodes and her family had shipped for the Network using Amazon. Since the Cov-19 Pandemic, large bags and anything that could further crowd mass transit were banned to maintain social distancing. So it was not unusual for people who only used mass transit to ship any number of things, from place to place, that they might have normally carried with them to and from work or any other place. There were regular daily pickups of packages in every neighborhood.

Kat had assured me that Alex was one of the best "cargo" carriers working for the Network. She also briefly explained that the entire Network movement had code language and "cargo" referred to people that were being moved to safe houses. She told me that Network members were a part of almost every industry. In all the training I had at the White House about the Network, I certainly had never heard about Amazon shipping people or supplies for the Network.

A few minutes after the last strip of tape had sealed our box shut, Kat issued her final thank you to Alex and I suddenly fell back onto what I expected was the dolly I had been told would wheel us out of the Rhodes's house and onto the truck. The box also had small squares in select places that enabled us to breathe through, what I was told, was enhanced Phifertex mesh in the same color of the box blended into the box to keep vents hidden that allowed us to breathe. On the inside, I found the box was also reinforced with a firm material so I could not bend the shape with my body at all. I felt very grateful for the long pillow behind my head that cushioned our fall onto the metal bars of the dolly. I felt us inch up the ramp onto the back of Alex's truck. I felt him gently set us down flat in the truck after we made it up the ramp. I saw Alex's fingertips inside the handle holes where the metal bar of the wardrobe box would have normally been located making sure he had a tight grip on us as he dragged the box off the dolly. It was dark in the box, but even darker once he finished rolling us into the back of the truck.

Although Kat told me not to expect Alex to say one word to us during the journey, I found myself nonetheless wishing that he would offer some reassuring words. There was only silence until I heard Alex turn on the radio as we pulled away. Although Charlie stirred a few times, I was able to hush him back to sleep on my chest with his pacifier. I was told that Alex would have to make a few stops to keep things looking normal on the journey. I had no idea if there were other people getting on the truck with us or not.

The longer we drove, making a few more stops, the more nervous I got. It began to sink in further that I had no control over where Alex was taking us, or whether he would follow through on what he had promised Kat or Mrs. Rhodes. Kat told me I was one of his last pickups of the day, but she did not know how long it would take us to arrive at the safe house. Feeling frighteningly alone, I watched as 20, 30, 40 and 50 minutes passed on my watch which, thankfully, had hands that glowed in the dark.

Eventually, I heard Alex open the back of the truck again, pull down the ramp, and walk up the ramp into the back of the truck. I again saw his gloved fingertips through the wardrobe bar holes. In an instant, we were tilted back on the dolly again. Charlie was out like a light, thankfully, and I had his pacifier in my hand wrapped around his back just in case he stirred. After a trip backwards down the truck ramp and a bumpy pull up over what I assumed was a curb, we were rolled for a few moments before gently being placed flat again. I noticed that Alex had turned on the small battery powered radio I was told, by Kat, that he wore on his belt and would turn on to play music if Charlie made noise, or he was worried our motion might cause Charlie to make noise. When I asked Kat if people passing by us might think a battery powered radio blasting music in public was suspicious, she had shrugged off my concern and informed me that weirdos in New York City had been blasting radios as they walked down the street for years, so it would seem perfectly ordinary. Plus, Alex would explain his lack of ear buds on not wanting to drown out traffic for safety as he made his stops.

"Evening, Alex. How are things?" I heard another man ask.

"Very well. Thanks. Did you hit up Gino's for pizza tonight?" Alex asked.

"Not yet. Taking my break in another hour. This for the penthouse?" I quickly surmised by this other man's mention of a penthouse that Alex was talking to some kind of guard or doorman.

"Yes. Ok to take it up?" Alex asked.

"Yup. Go for it. I will give a ring and let 'em know you are on the way," the man replied to Alex.

"Keep an eye on the truck, will you?" Alex asked, "that new officer working this corner has been a real jerk the last few times about my truck being double-parked too long. Some kid cop...looks like he is barely legal."

"You got it," the doorman said protectively, "and you're right, he pisses everyone off and I think he is only sixteen. Maybe I'll catch you at Gino's later?"

"You got it. Check you later. You da man," I heard Alex reply in his thick New York accent.

With that, we were tilted back again and on the move. Charlie wiggled a bit and I quickly put his pacifier up to his mouth, which he happily took. I heard Alex push a button and I assumed we were near an elevator. I heard the sound of what I assumed were elevator doors open and we moved again, this time only a little bit. I felt the familiar stomach drop of an elevator start to move us with a ping passing each floor, but I lost count after twenty-two and had no idea how many floors we were traveling.

When we stopped, we tilted back again onto the dolly and rolled a few feet until Alex gently placed us flat on the floor again. Alex knocked three times with a pause and three more times in the same unusually quick succession that he had knocked at the Rhodes. I heard the door open.

"Good Evening, Alex. Thank you," a woman's voice responded. Her voice sounded syrupy and oddly familiar to me, although I initially had no idea why.

"Of course. The pleasure is all mine, ma'am. Let me roll it in for you," Alex replied calmly. I felt us cross the lump of a threshold before we were plopped down flat again and slowly pushed off the dolly. I heard Alex wish the woman a good evening before I heard a door shut followed by the click of three locks. Within seconds, I heard the tape start to be ripped off the box and worried I might vomit or worse given the fear pulsing through my body. I took a few deep breaths as the flaps of the top of the box were ripped opened and I grabbed the hands extended to me over the side as I stood up, sweating and in tremendous pain as I unfolded my muscles from their curled up position in the box. As my head crossed the top of the box, I gasped audibly as I saw the woman standing in front of me holding my hands with a firm grip.

Laura Maack took in my stunned face, but did not waiver or let go of my hands.

"Hi, Anna. We're glad you're here. Now, let me help you get out."

Chapter Twenty-Five

I remained standing up in the box, frozen. I heard a plopping sound as Charlie spit the pacifier out of his mouth and it fell on the floor next to me. Being pulled up from the box had jarred him. He started to fuss.

"Please don't be scared. I know this is a shock. Mrs. Rhodes didn't want to tell you that I would receive you. She was afraid you wouldn't come. You are safe here, but we have to get you downstairs right away to make sure it stays that way," Laura said gently, "You should get out and stretch your legs. Is the baby ok?"

I nodded yes. My insides were still quivering at the realization that I was standing in front of Laura Maack. A moment later Kevin Maack, still tall and muscular as I remembered him, walked barefoot into the room across the pristine chocolate colored wood floors of the apartment wearing dark jeans and a black tee shirt. Kevin and Laura looked the same as they had that summer, but older (although not as much changed by time as Mrs. Rhodes had looked).

"Hi, Anna. Let me cut down the front of this box so you don't have to climb over it," Kevin said gingerly, as if he was afraid to frighten me. He took a box cutter to the front panel of the box, made a ripping motion towards the ground a few times and rolled down the front of the box. I stepped out, wincing in pain given how much my knees ached.

"Ok. Let's go. I'm going to take her down," Laura said firmly to Kevin. Kevin nodded in agreement.

"Down where?" I asked.

"The basement. We call it the Treehouse. It's our safe house here in the building. We have to move quickly. Although I am not expecting anyone, we can't be too careful, particularly given who you are," Laura instructed with a slight rise in her voice when she referenced "who" I was.

The mention of the importance of "who" I was became no less alarming each time I heard myself being described this way. I had heard similar descriptions about my identity a few times at Mrs. Rhodes's house including descriptions like "high value" and "high risk target." Although I clearly understood walking away from the

White House and my life was a "big deal," the notion of me having any real significance had not emotionally dawned on me while planning to leave, and certainly wasn't something I felt about myself.

"This way," Laura motioned pointing towards her foyer. I didn't want to follow Laura because I didn't trust her. But I knew I had no choice. So I followed Laura to the front door after placing the spare pacifier from my pocket into Charlie's mouth.

"Kevin and I occupy the entire floor so there is no risk of anyone seeing us get on the service elevator," Laura explained quietly, "Try your best to keep him quiet. Even if he cries, no one in the building should think anything of it since plenty of babies live here, but let's try to keep things quiet if we can."

I nodded again. I still hadn't uttered one word out loud to either of them.

We walked out the front door of the apartment and I caught a quick glance of the letters PH emblazoned in a gold plaque on her front door. The appearance of the hallway reminded me of a five-star hotel with the same huge painting that Harper had in her office adorning a wall above a console table next to the elevators. We rounded a corner into another doorway where another elevator was located. Laura ushered Charlie and I inside the elevator after quickly using a key to open the elevator doors. I learned later the elevator was one of two service elevators in the building, one being for residents to use moving in and out and the other being locked to only travel with a key that Laura and Kevin had, a benefit of living in the Penthouse encompassing the entire floor. I would also learn later that Laura owned the entire building and could impose whatever rules she wanted on the building, including many rules that allowed the Treehouse to thrive.

Laura pushed the elevator button marked B. The elevator was silver metal on the inside, and looked beat up, with large vinyl blue padded panels hanging on the walls. I noticed the light in the elevator ceiling was flickering. The buttons were old and yellowed. As we rumbled down, I looked down at Charlie and noticed that smaller wet curls had joined his chubbier curls as a result of being sweaty in the box. I kissed his head.

When the elevator landed in the basement, the doors opened and a man in military fatigues was standing across from us in the vestibule holding an assault rifle across his body at an angle. I gasped and immediately shrunk back into the corner of the elevator with my arms around Charlie.

"Don't worry, Anna. Gus is here for your protection and to keep you and Charlie safe," Laura explained.

Gus did not move. He stood as still a statute. By this point, my heart was beating out of my chest. Laura gently touched my elbow and tried to coax me out of the elevator. I shook her hand off of me, but complied with her instruction and stepped off the elevator as Kevin held his hand in front of the elevator doors to keep them open while I exited.

I entered a brightly lit hallway without any windows, clearly underground, the musty smell of a basement greeting my nose. The pipes running the lengths of the hallway ceilings were painted yellow, with the bottom half of the bumpy concrete walls painted chocolate brown and the top half of the walls painted white. The paint was thick, like it had been layered on for years and the floors were a light brown tile that looked like it belonged in a public space and not the kind of luxury building that Laura's penthouse floor suggested this building was.

We walked down one hallway passing a few doorways including one marked "boiler room", with a red bucket and fire extinguisher located outside of it, before turning right to head down another hallway until we reached a large laundry room on the right. We entered the laundry room and I followed Laura and Kevin down the narrow space where the dryers were contained until we all made a right into what appeared to be a small bathroom. The guard, Gus, was the last to enter and shut the bathroom door behind us. As we stood cramped in the tiny sterile room, Gus pulled a device out of his pocket that looked like an old flip phone I used to see pictures of when I was a child. He opened the top of the phone, punched in some numbers and suddenly the white tile wall in front of us opened to reveal another hallway. I gasped.

"See. Surprises everywhere, here," Laura said gently smiling at me and I could tell she was trying to ease my noticeable anxiety.

"Right," I whispered.

We walked through the doorway into the new hallway that had appeared and the wall that had opened shut just as quickly behind us. After making our way down a dimly lit and narrow corridor, we paused while the guard repeated the same procedure with the device and another wall opened. Suddenly I was in the middle of a room that looked more like the Starship Enterprise than a "treehouse." Computers were located in a circle in the middle of the floor and televisions and more computers surrounded the exterior of a dark gray room, people stationed at almost every seat, typing and talking, some standing in a few clusters around the room.

"Anna...." I heard in a breathless voice as I noticed a woman suddenly leave one of the groups near the wall and rush towards me with arms extended.

I couldn't believe it.

"Sophie?" I cried out. A moment later, Sophie was embracing me and Charlie.

I started to cry.

"Oh my god, Anna. I am so glad to see you. Are you ok?" she said pulling away to examine my face putting my chin in her cupped hands, "Oh my god. It's you and you have a baby, Anna!" she cried out emotionally as she embraced me.

Like everyone else from my past I had seen in the last several hours, Sophie had changed with time too, but I noticed that her eyes still sparkled in the exact same way they had when we were kids.

"How?" I asked, nothing short of overwhelmed with everything going on around me and full of questions.

"I know you have a lot of questions," Sophie replied, "and there is so much to tell you and so much I want to ask you. But I suspect you need some rest after the journey I understand you have had. And we have a number of procedures here to get you settled in, so I think we will have to save a detailed reunion for tomorrow."

I stood staring at her, still bewildered.

"I am exhausted," I replied.

"Yes. I'm sure. And we try to keep everyone rested and healthy down here given our close quarters, so let's get you to bed. We can catch up more in the morning," Sophie confirmed.

"I am sorry if this was too much of a surprise, Anna. I should have mentioned that Sophie was here when you arrived upstairs, but we moved so quickly I didn't have a chance," Laura said from behind me.

I turned around to look at Laura.

"No. It's ok. It is a good surprise," I said quietly uttering words to Laura for the first time since I arrived. I noticed Laura breathe a small sigh of appreciation when I spoke to her.

"Sophie, Will you get Anna settled in her room? Fiona is going to help with her intake process," Laura instructed.

A woman stood up from a computer and walked over to where we were standing, arm outstretched for a handshake. I had been so immersed in the shock of seeing Sophie that it wasn't until the woman, Fiona, stood up that I noticed most people in the room were frozen in silence, staring at me.

"Anna, I'm Fiona," the woman said, "I am going to get you settled in and explain a few rules, but we will go over most things you need to know tomorrow since I am sure you must be tired."

I shook her hand and nodded in response as I continued to look around the room, starting to feel uncomfortable at how intensely people were starting at me, various expressions on their face but not many warm ones. Fiona glanced at Sophie, both women clearly noticing my discomfort.

"Don't worry, Anna. It is just a bit shocking for people to see you here given ..." Sophie paused before continuing, "... who you were involved with before you got here. Just give it some time, the shock will wear off."

I nodded at Sophie feeling sick to my stomach again. In the process of planning to leave, I suppose I had not considered what people, in general, would think when they saw me given what I had learned about my image and the academies.

I put my head down and focused on Charlie as Fiona and Sophie led me to a bookcase at the far end of the room where the guard who had brought us down was standing. I watched as he repeated the procedure with the flip phone. I marveled momentarily as I watched the bookcase full of books leave the floor and enter the air so we could walk under it into another hallway.

At the end of the next hallway, on the other side of the wall that had just opened, I entered a dimly lit room that looked to be about three times the size of the large laundry room we had started our journey in, with rows of bunk beds full of people sleeping. Sophie put a finger up in front of her lips motioning for me to be quiet. As we got to the far side of the room, we entered another small and narrow hallway where Sophie opened a door on the right. We walked into a larger square room that appeared to be a private bedroom with a double bed, crib, light blue simple bedding and a brass floor lamp with tweed shade standing next to a red and gold plaid chair.

"Here we are," Sophie said, "you have your own shower in here and we put an infant bath in the shower for the baby. We figured it would be safer and more comfortable for you to have your own room given everything. Gus and another guard will take turns being stationed outside 24/7."

She opened another door inside the room to show me the bathroom.

"Everything you need to clean up should be in there. I made sure it was well stocked and there is a little set of plastic drawers next to the crib with formula, bottles diapers and wipes ... and diaper cream if you need it for the baby. The mini fridge is stocked with waters and fruit and there are snacks in the plastic drawer as well. Mrs. Rhodes sent some instructions to Laura in advance of your arrival and Laura made sure we got things ready for you."

"Thank you," I replied still shocked but grateful. Hearing Mrs. Rhodes name reminded me that I had just been at her house only a few hours ago, although it felt like weeks at this point.

"Listen, Anna. You have been through a lot and, not just today," Sophie said tenderly.

I nodded.

"So...here is the thing. You need sleep. I can come help with Charlie in the morning if you want. I will stop by early and I'll bring my little ones by so you can meet them."

"Little ones?" I questioned, eyes lifting with surprise and voice raised as if she were telling me this years ago while we were still kids hanging out in my bedroom.

"Yes! I am so excited for you to meet them. Girls. 6 and 7," Sophie said joyfully, "Of course, you will meet Larry too."

"Your husband?"

"Yup."

"And you all live down here?"

"Yes. For just over two years now."

"And you never go outside?" I asked, the uncertainty in my voice apparent.

I could see Sophie consider her words before responding.

"No. We do. But not exactly like people on the outside roam the streets. Look, there is a lot for you to learn and I will explain it all, but tonight you need to sleep. I don't want to overwhelm you too much right now. There are about seventy-five of us underground in this location which is made up of the basement levels of several adjacent buildings, all connected and secure thanks to Laura's wise planning. We have a location across the street as well made up of a few building basements that houses about fifty people and, of course, more locations like ours all across New York and the country. Some are in high rises and others are in places you would never imagine."

"Wow." I whispered, stunned. I had never heard anyone at the White House mention being aware that the Network had underground bunkers, much less in Manhattan.

"I know. It's a lot to take in. It will all make more sense when I give you the background, but I think you should rest up right now."

"They have no idea," I blurted out.

"Who? The Party?" Sophie laughed, "well that may be true in one sense, but not others. In any case, let's talk more tomorrow after some breakfast."

"Ok."

Sophie hugged me again and smiled at me one last time as she gently shut the door to my room. I laid Charlie down in the crib while I made him a bottle, amazed at how he had managed to get through our journey. I sat down on the edge of the quilted bed next to the crib.

The bed and the crib were placed so close together given how tiny the room was that I basically took two steps back from the crib before being able to plop down on the bed. I laid down halfway, my back flat on the bed but legs still hanging down, feet on the ground, and stared at the ceiling for a while. I thought of James and started to cry again. Eventually, I pulled my legs up onto the bed, rolling over onto my left side facing the crib so I could see Charlie while he slept. One of my favorite things in the world was watching Charlie sleep in peace at night. The feeling of watching him rest always made my heart full beyond words. I allowed the feeling to wash over me, noticed my eyelids getting heavier and, eventually, drifted off to sleep.

Chapter Twenty-Six

I woke up to Charlie crying in his crib.

"Little peanut..." I clucked hopping out of the bed. I quickly made a bottle for Charlie from the supplies in the room and, a few moments later, I was seated on the corner of my bed as he looked up at me and drank the bottle. I loved the glugging sound he made while he drank his bottles, equal parts sweet and needy. As Charlie finished and I put him up on my shoulder to burp, I heard a gentle knock on my door.

I opened the door to find a smiling Sophie, along with two little girls holding each of her hands.

"Good Morning. We figured you would be up. Anna, I would like you to meet my girls, Blair and Stephanie, we call her Steph for short," she said, rubbing the hair of the shorter girl who was smiling at me.

"Hi there," I replied smiling at the two girls. It was still hard for me to believe that Sophie had children.

"I'm your cousin, Anna, and this is my son, Charlie," I turned Charlie around to face the girls. The girls beamed as they started to coo at Charlie.

"This room is a bit small to catch up in," Sophie suggested, "Why don't we go grab some breakfast down the hall after you shower up and I can give you a better tour than you got last night. There is a children's room a few doors down where the kids here play. Ok if we take Charlie down there while you clean up? There are some little play lounge chair things for the infants and the caregivers there can keep an eye on him and the girls."

I felt a pang of nervous energy at the thought of being separated from Charlie, but I agreed.

"Where should I meet you?" I asked, as Sophie offered her arms to take Charlie.

"When you leave head down the hallway to the right and you will see a glass door marked Classroom 1, the first classroom on the right. You can't miss it. You will see us in there through the door. I'll hang there while you shower and wait for you to make sure Charlie gets adjusted ok."

I nodded, gently handed Charlie to Sophie, and expressed my gratitude for the help as they departed my room, Blair and Steph practically bouncing out of my room with excitement. After everyone left the room, I shut the door and turned to lean my back against it. It was the first moment I had been alone without Charlie since we left home. Almost immediately, James entered my mind and the sobs started to come again. I let the sobs consume me for a few minutes without moving before heading into the bathroom to shower.

I showered and dressed in the clothes Sophie had mentioned were in the dresser for me, black leggings and a loose long sleeve black cotton scoop next shirt with tan flip-flops. There was even a little sample mascara and a new Chapstick for me to use. I still felt shock every time I looked in a mirror and saw my new jet black hair. I pulled my hair back in a low bun and blew out my bangs using the hair dryer from the bathroom. I almost looked normal. After leaving my room and following Sophie's instructions, I found what appeared to be a collection of classrooms with signs above each one indicating their classroom numbers. I looked in Classroom 1, from the outside through the rectangular glass window built into the door and, without going in, I found myself breaking out into a huge smile watching Charlie sit in a little chair low to the ground while his cousins dangled toys in front of him.

I gently opened the door to the classroom.

"Hey there!" Sophie was beaming as she watched the girls play with Charlie, "you look more refreshed! Did you find everything you needed?"

I nodded.

"Great. Let's go get some food. Girls, can you put Charlie in the umbrella stroller by the door and push him to breakfast with us?"

"I can carry him," I offered.

"Don't worry about it. The stroller has some toys that dangle. Charlie will like them and we have a bit of a walk to get to the cafeteria, so it will be easier to use the stroller. I know you are still exhausted. It will be fun for the girls to push him in the stroller and we can catch up a little more on the walk."

A few moments later, after strapping Charlie into the stroller, we were ready to leave the classroom. Sophie swung the classroom door opened and I immediately gasped. The guard from the prior night, Gus, was standing right outside the door, weapon in place, posed like the statue he appeared to be the first time I saw him. I hadn't noticed him when I left my room to walk towards the classrooms, so seeing him startled me.

"Anna, Don't be alarmed. Gus is only here for your protection. Laura insisted that you stay safe. It is for the best that he is with us, especially given your past work with the Party."

It made me nervous, to say the least, to be so close to a gun. Despite having been around any number of Secret Service agents, having Gus as security felt much different. The thought that people inside of the Treehouse might actually want to hurt me or think I was the enemy scared me tremendously.

We started to walk to the cafeteria. Sophie was right that it took a while to get to the cafeteria. It turned out the cafeteria was located three full basement buildings away connected to the building I had arrived at with more tunnels similar to those I had walked through the night before. Sophie explained to me that the safe house we were in was made up of five high rise buildings on the block we were located on, connected underground in the basements. Laura owned four of the buildings and another Network member owned one in the middle.

"Anna, We have a daily bulletin that is issued three times a day (morning, noon and evening) on the television screens you will see everywhere. It fills us in on information we need to know on a day to day basis or added security decisions that are being made, meetings,

and that sort of thing. Yesterday, we got the announce-
ment on the bulletin that you were arriving and some
of the people here expressed concern, so I want you to
be prepared for that. They don't know your story, yet.
In some of their eyes, they just know you were with the
Party. They have seen you giving speeches and..." Sophie
paused, "they know about you and the academies."

If the way my face looked when she mentioned my
image and the academies conveyed any portion of the
shame I felt on my insides, my look must have displayed
one thousand synonyms for shame.

"I didn't know about my image being used in academies until recently. I didn't really understand what the
academies were until recently."

"You aren't the only person who has been digitally
manipulated. We have some pretty good tech down here
and the technology team can tell when the videos are
the actual person speaking, most of the time. But the
technology does get better and better and confirming
perfectly in all cases can be difficult. The Party has certainly used digital face swapping and other technology
to their advantage," Sophie explained, "and, although
most people down here know about this type of video
tech being used to manipulate faces and voices, they
also have such a distrust of anyone in the Party that it is

hard for them to always be certain of what the truth is when people like you defect."

I nodded. Everything Sophie was sharing was a lot to take in. I certainly had no idea during my training on the Network at the White House that the group was so highly organized. A question about something Sophie had mentioned was suddenly burning a hole in my pocket.

"I'm not the only one who has left? I can't recall hearing about anyone leaving the White House and being suspected of joining the Network when I was there."

"Well, I doubt you would have. But I am sure people have "disappeared" here and there. You probably just got a different story about where they went. After all, the Party would never want to seem like they were losing control of anyone."

I quickly racked my brain. I was aware of a handful of people who had suddenly disappeared during my time at the White House. I remember being told one man had to suddenly take care of his seriously ill mother.

"Are we safe here?" I asked, "Should we leave?"

"No, leaving is not an option, as I'm sure Sheila explained to you, particularly given your profile. You have to trust us. Sheila and I will make sure you stay safe ... and Laura will too."

Sheila was Mrs. Rhodes first name. It was odd hearing Sophie call her by her first name. Sophie must have noticed the somewhat skeptical look on my face when she mentioned Laura. I couldn't help it. Although Laura had done nothing since my arrival to lend to any notion that I shouldn't trust her, the fact remained that she was still the same Laura Maack from that summer, something I had not yet reached resolution on in the few hours I had been hidden in a basement. I had also not completely processed that Mrs. Rhodes and Laura were working together, as if they were equals in some way.

"I totally get why you might not feel comfortable trusting Laura, but there is a lot you don't know about her. She is part of a group that organized in secret A.E., made up of various people who were leaders in different industries B.E. You might be shocked to learn who some of our members are. We have former CEO's, journalists, bankers, former politicians, and even some pop culture celebrities, among others. Once term limits for the President were eliminated, I think more people saw the writing on the wall and took more aggressive action to get involved in resisting. In Laura's case, she worked up plans with other commercial real estate owners to take existing buildings they owned and buy more buildings to turn them into safety and shelter for Network leaders and those labeled enemies of the Party. The Treehouse is the oldest and most established Network safe house and has been around the longest."

I was practically breathless at the thought of how intense and wide scale the Network was. I knew the Party considered the Network a real threat, but I had never heard any detail about the level of Network organization and locations Sophie was describing to me during my time at the White House. Sophie must have noticed the look of sheer astonishment on my face.

"It's a lot to take in and there will be more to take in," Sophie continued as we walked, "there are ways we get everything we need taken care of down here, even getting sunlight, but secrecy and safety is the number one priority."

A few moments later, Sophie and I were at a set of double doors labeled cafeteria. Sophie paused before opening the door.

"Listen, Anna. People may stare at you. Try to be open to people who do speak to you, but don't feel pressure to answer too many questions about your past. You can say that you have been instructed to wait to respond to questions until you go through full orientation. Plus, you can always answer questions at your welcome Q&A session. There is a Q&A session for all new arrivals where you get a chance to share more about your background and other residents can ask you questions. I think the Q&A session will be particularly important for you to start the process of adjusting here."

"Because I am not trusted," I stated matter-of-factly.

"Anna, I wouldn't think of it exactly like that. You need to respect that everyone here has been at this for years and there is a lot at stake. And, like I said, many of the people here will only know what they have seen about you in the media, which sounds like it was more than even you knew until recently. Try to be patient and just sink in and pitch in, as we say around here."

Sophie smiled at me reassuringly as she pushed the cafeteria doors open, the setup I observed inside reminding me of a school cafeteria. I noticed a long buffet of food on one side of the room with large metal gates rolled up to the ceiling. The tables were fairly full. Immediately, I noticed the room got quiet when I entered. Most people were staring at me as I walked in.

"C'mon. Follow me," Sophie instructed leading us to the buffet area. As I walked closer I heard a familiar voice barking orders. It was Mrs. Rhodes! She turned around suddenly with a crate full of oranges and broke out into a smile.

"Well. Good Morning. I see you arrived alright," Mrs. Rhodes said, smiling.

I started to tear up and I didn't even let her put the oranges down before throwing myself at her with a bear hug.

"I had no idea you would be here," I exclaimed as I hugged her.

"I know. One more surprise right?" she said embracing me in return. "Unfortunately, I couldn't tell you any of this until we made sure you arrived here safely for security reasons. I enter as an employee of Laura's penthouse every day and head right down here on the service elevator. Laura's team has figured out a way to block the Party common area cameras so they don't see anyone going downstairs. Kat comes along with me and acts as the housekeeper in the PH so the work upstairs still gets done. How are you? Did you settle in all right? How is Charlie?"

"He's fine. We're fine. I mean, I am totally overwhelmed, but extremely grateful for your help and Sophie has been so kind to help me settle in," I said.

"Oh. Yes," Mrs. Rhodes nodded glancing over at Gus, "well, I am sure some of this is overwhelming. But, I think the security is necessary for a bit while you get settled in. You have a lot of good people here vouching for you, including Laura too." I noticed Mrs. Rhodes said Laura's name gently, as if she were afraid of my response.

I nodded, accepting her instructions, but still not ready to touch the topic of Laura.

"Now," she continued as she dropped the oranges down on the buffet, "let me wash my hands so I can get some of that fresh baby love from that little man of yours. Grab a tray, Anna. Take whatever you want. We are not on rations right now as far as anything fresh or prepared goes. We do limit the dry goods, like cereal, to one dry good per person per meal for now, since that stuff will keep longer if the fresh foods runs low or we can't get any."

It was a stark reality check to hear that food was rationed. I had not thought about rations or limitations on food since before the point that I entered the CEP. For a moment, I thought about the kitchen where James and I lived and the always full refrigerator. I immediately felt nauseous again.

Mrs. Rhodes picked up Charlie from his stroller while Sophie, her girls, and I made trays of food before sitting at a table in the front of the room near the buffet. I had forgotten how hungry I was and had just torn into the flesh of an orange when a woman with mousy brown hair walked towards our table. She appeared to be around my age and as she approached G walked towards me from his perch on the wall as if he had to intervene. My stomach dropped with fear and his movement must have startled her because she froze in her tracks.

"I..." she stammered, "I just wanted to offer the high-chair ... for the baby. It's in the closet in the corner."

"Thank you," I replied softly and stood up extending my hand to her, noticing that the entire room seemed to be watching our interaction in silence.

She did not extend her hand back as I stood there with my hand out.

"I'm Christina," the woman said coldly. Christina stared at me for another second before brushing past me towards the corner of the room. I felt red and flushed, embarrassed, and inched back down into my seat, looking down at my half-eaten orange. A few moments later, she returned with the highchair and placed it at the end of the table briskly before walking back to her table. Mrs. Rhodes and Sophie looked at me with concern. The room remained quiet, except for some hushed whispers and the sound of utensils scraping plates. I felt Mrs. Rhodes hand on my back a few moments later.

"Give it time, Anna," she whispered, "I know this is a lot. Hang in there. I promise these people with thaw out a bit. It will just take time."

I half nodded without looking up.

"Once we get you busy, I have a feeling things will get a bit easier too. I need an extra set of hands in the cafeteria so the leadership has agreed you can work in here with me, if that is ok with you?" Mrs. Rhodes asked tenderly.

I nodded my agreement, this time looking up with a slight smile to meet her eyes, grateful that she was still trying to look out for me.

"What about Charlie? Can I bring him here?" I asked.

"Charlie will go to the nursery every day. It will be good for him and you can visit and check on him as much as you like while he transitions to the new routine. They sing and play – we have a number of teachers and other early childhood specialists here. It is really lovely and Michelle, the lead teacher, does a wonderful job."

"Sounds good," I replied, the sadness in my voice apparent. The interaction with Christina had quickly reminded me, again, how I may be perceived underground.

"Eat something," Mrs. Rhodes coaxed me picking up my orange and motioning for me to take it, "You need some strength. There is a lot to learn about your new home and Charlie needs you to be at your best. After breakfast, I'll give you a tour of the kitchen and explain your job to you."

"What will my job be?" I asked as I took the orange from her hand. I wasn't hungry anymore, but I complied with her request to try to eat something.

"You are going to make the coffee. It is a constant revolving door in here all day. You are going to run our version of a coffee shop at the other end of the cafeteria down there," she said pointing to the opposite end of the cafeteria where I saw some kind of makeshift installation in a corner of the long rectangular room. "Several people have been taking turns running it," she continued, "but I have recommended that you run it every day. With the exception of a few people that I could count on one hand, pretty much everyone here drinks coffee and those who don't drink coffee drink the tea. Everyone wants a paper cup of something every day, or multiple times a day. It never ceases to amaze me what an important role coffee plays in humanity."

Sophie giggled in response to Mrs. Rhodes observation about the amount of coffee that was consumed in the Treehouse and, somehow, despite my sadness, I felt a small smile appear on my face too.

Chapter Twenty-Seven

Over the next several weeks I worked the coffee bar, every single day, starting before 5:00 every morning when I would begin making the coffee and finishing late in the evening. Charlie would sit in various baby apparatus next to me for part of the day and spend the rest of the day in the nursery. Running the coffee shop was active, to say the least. Mrs. Rhodes was right when she joked about a potential coffee supply issue. It wasn't such a shock that coffee was popular but, while working behind the counter every day, I was surprised to gain a different perspective on just how much coffee people drink, how people rely on it, and how it seemingly plays such an important role, daily, in so many lives.

The coffee bar was located in the back corner of the cafeteria. It was constructed from three restaurant style rectangular trash cans that we placed horizontally and had covered with a long piece of wood to create the "counter." A long and tall table in the back supported the coffee pot, espresso machine, and supplies. A few weeks into my gig serving coffee, I asked Mrs. Rhodes if I could set up a few small round tables and chairs in front of the bar so people could sit with coffee if they wanted to. She agreed. I added some string lights from the supply closet to the front of the bar and had Mrs. Rhodes ask Laura for some fresh flowers, weekly, to put on top of the refrigerator we had in the back next to the coffee machines.

People would stop by the shop for coffee as a form of comfort, as part of a daily ritual, when they were sad, to celebrate a good moment, or when they wanted to chat with a friend. The rainbow of human life and emotion was displayed on a revolving stream of the people coming to pick up coffee. In a single day, I could encounter the full range of human emotions as people approached my counter - tears, anger, fear, joy, anxiety, love, stress, exhaustion, and more. Although a soothing drink for many, there was never any amount of coffee a person could drink to permanently soothe away their problems. Ironically, the distraction of working at the coffee bar allowed me to avoid my own feelings while encountering everyone else's feelings on a daily basis. Since the visit to the academies and everything that came after it, you could have filled a river with the flood of shame and guilt that filled me.

I got to know almost everyone living in the Treehouse while working at the coffee bar. Even those people who

342 ~ JENNIFER KASMAN

didn't drink coffee would stop by to grab a tea or a sweet treat from time to time, when we had sweets. During the first few weeks, I made sure to introduce or reintroduce myself to anyone who stopped by the shop that I didn't know. Not everyone was kind. There were a number of people who would not speak to me or spoke in a cruel tone. A few more asked me invasive questions or things like "Had I tortured children in the academies? Was my marriage real? Was I actually Charlie's mom?" I may have marveled more at the emotional brutality of the questioning had it not been for the fact that rejection felt familiar to me. And I had been treated similarly after the Incident so it didn't take much for me to remember how to feel unworthy of respect or kindness – to feel that familiar sense of being a broken person. Although I had not been the designer of my life, I knew by now that the way the world worked required that I take responsibility for any identity my journey inflicted on me.

I learned more during my interactions with customers at the shop about what they knew about me from seeing me on posters, videos, and commercials in their daily life. I learned things about my "impact" beyond what I learned at the academies. My face was, in fact, synonymous with the move to send children to academies. I was the face of the program to steal children from their parents. I started to slowly remember who everyone was and what they looked like. I asked questions about their lives. I came to understand why Mrs. Rhodes had insisted that I work at the coffee shop. She wanted me to meet everyone there. She was trying to help me build community. Mrs. Rhodes would always say to us as children that there was something sacred about the act of serving people food or drinks, and she described doing so as an unparalleled level of care and tenderness you could provide with a seemingly routine gesture. I started to understand why she would say that as I worked the shop.

As time passed, some of the iciness I had encountered in my interactions with people at the Treehouse when I had first arrived started to thaw a bit. As I got to know more people, in addition to learning more about what people "knew" about my role with the Party, I also got to know more about the Network. Sophie may have accurately reported that people with resources had started the Network in the time period A.E., but the day to day workers of the Network were a much more diverse story, not a group of only those with power and wealth, but also of a range of what you might consider ordinary people devoting themselves to an extraordinary, and risky, undertaking.

I learned more about how the Network communicated when the communications team members would stop by the shop. Given the restrictions on cell and internet usage, the Network communications team had tapped into old unused land line copper fiber to create a private communication network. The Network had telephone workers, who had been largely phased out of jobs by advances in technology B.E., that used their skills to set up the secret system using the old land line fiber. To gain internet access, the Network had to dial into the internet and somehow rigged a system to keep the Network internet activity secret in this way. Records were kept on discs, a relic from past computer use, instead of a cloud that could be hacked.

By chatting with the Network media team that would stop by the shop, I learned that since television was restricted too, the media team, made up of some former magazine and newspaper writers and editors, would print paper newspapers (which had largely gone out of business) to spread by hand. Stacks of papers would be left in places frequently travelled. I learned from security team members that the security team was made up of former Secret Service and military leaders.

But of all of the people I met, the best new friend I made at the Treehouse was John, a former sanitation worker who was also responsible for managing sanitation in the Treehouse. John had used his trash trucks to transport large numbers of children and their families into hiding when children began to be identified for transport to academies. As a result, he had been listed on a most wanted target list by the Party before Laura invited him and his family into the Treehouse. While underground, I learned that when families applied for food assistance or other social services, the Party began to deem families unfit to care for their children, offering them the option to enroll their children in academies. If parents declined the offer to enroll, the Party would assign a "social worker" to manage the case. If the social worker determined after four weeks that the family was, in fact, unable to pay for the proper care of their child, or children, the parents could be forced to send their children to academies.

John liked to linger and chat at the coffee bar. Chatting with him reminded me of how all of us Brooklynites would chat with the proprietors of different stores in our neighborhood on a daily basis, like the bagel place or drycleaners. He was one of the people who was most kind to me early on during my time at the Treehouse. When I asked him one day why he had been so nice to me from the start, he told me that there were more people than he could count that looked down on him for being a "trashman" when he was on the outside, so he refused to look down on anyone without getting to know them first.

One Wednesday, about six months into my time in the Treehouse, John seemed especially agitated when he stopped by the coffee shop. I had noticed many of my regulars at the shop seemed more stressed too.

"What's up, John? You want the usual today?" I asked.

"Morning. Actually, I am going to need a red eye today. Not much sleep last night," John replied softly.

"Late meetings?"

"Some. I've been going over back-up plans with the person who would take over my job if ... well, the thing is, it's almost time for things to go to the next level with our work here, in the Network, and any of us who are going to participate in things on the outside have to make plans in case ..."

I realized quickly that John was talking about something happening to him.

"What is happening?" I asked, "Everyone around here seems like they are on high alert. I don't want you to get in trouble for telling me anything. I know the leadership meetings are classified, but I'll hear what is going on at some point right?"

"Well, we're going to march. There's a massive protest planned. And if it works out as we have planned it, we think the number of people taking to the streets in the city and all over the country in other cities at the same time will be massive, like nothing seen before. It's scheduled for the end of the month and we have been working on plans for over a year. Since I will be out there at the March, I am required to start making some contingency plans in case something happens to me. Just not an easy few days discussing this with Eva."

Eva was John's wife. I had also become friends with her since she worked in the childcare center where Charlie spent part of this days. She had invited me to do yoga with her on the weekends and it had become a part of my weekly ritual I never missed. John looked like he might cry as he was sharing the information with me.

"I just worry about Eva and the kids," John continued, "we have been through a lot and I think we all just got to this place where we started to feel safe here at the Treehouse, despite how different our lives are living underground. I know it was probably a false sense of security and you can't avoid reality forever, particularly when reality needs to change. I just wish what is necessary didn't have to be so hard. I know Eva values the importance of one of us joining the March, but it is just hard to think of the potential consequences, that's all. It is going to be really dangerous out there."

"I'm sure it is," I replied quietly, "If anyone understands what the Party is capable of, I do. What is the plan for this thing? Do we have weapons? Are we doing that kind of thing? I assume everyone knows they have plenty of weapons and are not afraid to use them," I asked. I'm sure John could tell by the tone of my voice that I doubted the Network's ability to battle the Party.

"Look, you've seen Gus and the other security team members. You know we have some weapons for security purposes but the goal is non-violence as it always has been for any legitimate movement. So we mainly have bodies, and since bodies will be used, bodies will be lost," John replied bluntly.

"I don't understand. What is the point if everyone ends up dead or in prison? How do we actually plan to succeed at this?"

I noticed a snap of anger start to appear in my voice.

"The same way good guys in the past have succeeded, Anna. Non-violence, not backing down, and a whole hell of a lot of caring and spirited people who think there is something bigger than themselves to protect. But, I'll tell you, Anna..." John said as he started to choke up again, "I love the hell out of my family. My wife and my kids are the best thing to ever happen to me. I never even knew the kind of love I feel for them existed in the universe until I built a family. I am devastated to know what I have to do to try to protect them, and to protect all of our families. I don't want to die and I don't want to lose anyone else down here either. And, I know we will. I know that is inevitable."

I didn't know what to say. I quietly slipped the sleeve on John's coffee and gently placed in down in front of him, both of us deep in thought. And then, rather instinctively, I walked out from behind the coffee bar and gave him a hug. It was the first time I remembered offering a hug to a friend since I hugged Veronica the day I left the CEP, not knowing when I hugged her that I would never see her again. As I hugged John, I knew exactly what I had to do next. And, although hidden underground, I finally felt free for the first time ever.

Chapter Twenty-Eight

The next morning before I opened up the coffee bar, I stopped by the kitchen to talk to Mrs. Rhodes. I found her packing up small bags of snack foods.

"Why didn't you tell me that all of this March stuff was going to happen?" I asked as I entered the kitchen.

I noticed I sounded heated as soon as I started speaking, but I didn't pull back.

"What happens to Charlie and I? What is going to happen to everyone here? These people have families you know. We can't just treat people as dispensable like the Party does. And, by the way, they will beat us. Trust me. I know how much power they have. They will beat us one by one to a pulp and they won't stop until all of us are gone. This is just going to end up getting more people killed. Why can't we just build more bunkers? I mean life isn't so bad this way, at least compared to getting all of us killed."

Mrs. Rhodes eyes were wide. She sat down at a stool at the counter and motioned for me to sit down. I declined, continuing to pace back and forth in the kitchen, my arms crossed.

"Anna. If things become more complicated in terms of this location not being safe, Laura is planning to move you and the others to another safe house. I know she will do everything in her power to keep you and Charlie safe," Mrs. Rhodes said calmly.

"I don't want to move. And it is not only me and Charlie that I am worried about. What about the other families here? They don't love their kids any less than I do. Don't they deserve peace and safety too? I just think this whole concept seems like a fool's errand, like you all are unaware of the reality of the Party."

"Well, there's no other way. Bodies on the line, hip to hip and arm to arm, resisting is all we have left, Anna. Many movements before you and I suffered through this phase of the cycle of history and this time will be no different. I wish history were easier on those who power treads on, but it never has been and I'm afraid it won't be now. Ultimately, the armor that protects a good society is only ever as good or bad as the heart of the person next to us.

"But these are ordinary people, not fighters."

"Oh really, that's what you think?" I noticed Mrs. Rhodes voice rising as much as mine. "And do you actually think the American soldiers we expected to fight to protect us for years ... our boys and girls, mostly poor, signing up to defend our freedom were something other than ordinary people? It is only ordinary people who have fought our most important battles, Anna."

I finally sat down across from her on a stool exasperated. And we just sat there in silence that way for a while.

"What happens to the children if something happens to a parent?" I asked.

"Well, we are only allowing one parent from a set of parents to go, so one parent would be left behind."

"What would happen if a single parent went?"

Mrs. Rhodes started to shake her head.

"Oh no, Anna. That is not happening. Not after everything you have been through. That wouldn't be fair to Charlie. You are too high risk to go out there anyway."

"It's not your choice," I replied bluntly.

Mrs. Rhodes didn't say anything. At first, she looked exasperated but then I noticed her face soften.

"Would you take care of Charlie?" I asked.

Mrs. Rhodes looked at me, stunned.

"Anna, as you said earlier, it's going to be bad out there. The Party and their "army of God" as they call it will use you as an example possibly worse than anyone else if you are caught. As you said yourself, it's a big army they have."

"Well," I replied with certainty before standing up to leave, "then I guess our army needs to be bigger. And now our army has one more."

I turned on my heel and left the kitchen.

Later that day, Mrs. Rhodes stopped by the coffee bar to tell me that she had talked with Laura and explained that I wanted to be involved. Laura insisted that I be included in the top-level planning meetings at the Treehouse once I decided to participate in the March. Mrs. Rhodes told me that starting the following morning, I should plan to be in the main conference room at 8am. Mrs. Rhodes had arranged with Christina, the woman who had refused to shake my hand on the first day at the

Treehouse, to take over my coffee bar duties so I could attend leadership meetings going forward.

There was some resistance to my participation in the March, and I knew this because I heard the resistance expressed by some people in leadership to my face during the meetings I attended. Ultimately, most of those who disagreed with me being involved were persuaded of the potentially positive impact my participation might have as a meaningful statement about rejecting the Party. Laura pointed out in one meeting that people on the outside would not know my real story, which could be problematic for the Network if I did appear visible at the March since most citizens had nothing short of a terrible view of my Party persona. I suggested that I do what I had been trained to do best and tape a series of video public service announcements telling my story. I was reminded that the problem would be disseminating any videos I filmed, since the only way to do so would involve hacking Party controls over broadcasting and the internet. Despite years of internal Network tech teams trying to complete a hack, it required assistance from within the Party and the Network had never found a reliable path in. Laura decided it would be a good idea to film the videos in case she could figure out a solution to get them broadcast. She mentioned there was one favor she was owed by someone in the Party that she hadn't yet called in yet.

During my participation in the final planning meetings, I offered any additional information I had from my time in the White House in case it was helpful. I learned that the Network already knew most of what I had to share. As I learned more about it during our leadership meetings, I was honestly blown away at the sophistication of the Network, not only in New York City, but also across the entire country. Even old abandoned manufacturing plants in the U.S. had been turned into bunkers in the Midwestern United States, not to mention countless other apartment buildings, abandoned malls, and vacant office buildings across the nation too. Part of the reason the Party had suspected the Network was gaining more traction was because of the number of citizens that were just disappearing without a trace.

About two days before the March was scheduled, I was reading to Charlie after dinner when an emergency notification came across the television in my room. PC 1, the planning committee group I was on, was asked to report to the central conference room immediately. I ran to Eva's room and asked her to watch Charlie. After planting a kiss on Charlie's head and handing him off to Eva, I raced to central. As I walked into the room, I noticed the White House briefing room on the television screen and got the chills.

"What's going on?" I asked.

Sophie's husband, Larry, was standing near the television with his arms crossed.

"As far as we understand, news of the March has made its way to Washington and the President has scheduled an emergency news conference to address the rumors," Larry replied flatly.

A second later, the White House communications team filed in to the briefing room on the left side of the screen. I felt my skin start to tingle. I had not seen so many of the faces on the television screen in so long. My insides felt as if I was afraid they would see me through the screen and I found myself leaning against a wall as if I could disappear into it. I saw Harper in a chair next to the podium along with Peyton and the other interns and assistants I had worked closely with, faces stone cold. Tears started to gather in my eyes as a I scanned the briefing room on screen, wondering if I would catch a glimpse of James. Although he wasn't part of the communications team, for some reason I thought I would see him there along with everyone else from my former life. I had asked Mrs. Rhodes and Laura several times if they could get me information on James and whether he was safe. They never told me anything in response to my questions, and I never pushed to understand if it was because they couldn't find out or if they were scared to tell me.

Sophie walked over to where I was standing and grabbed my hand. The central conference room was full, not only with PC 1 members, but everyone else in the chain of leadership, including Laura. With all of our eyes fixed on the television, the group of us waited for what felt like hours but, in reality, was probably only a few minutes for something to happen on the screen. A few seconds later, the blue door in the back of the briefing room slid open and the President walked in and approached the podium.

The President took a deep breath that could be heard loudly on the microphone before starting to speak.

"Good Evening. Rumors and detail about a potential protest in several major cities has made its way to the White House. The detail is so specific and the information we have received is so credible, that we are of the belief that some citizens will attempt to take some type of protest action against our government this weekend. Let me be clear. It has long been settled that the act of protest is against the law. Any people who decide to participate in these events will face the strictest consequences our government has at its disposal in recognition of the fact that they have not only broken a law and put others at risk of danger by their acts, but also because they have defied a direct order from the President of the United States. And I also want to say to those of you who have supported this act of treason, we know who you are, we know where we will find you, and soon you will be reminded of who we are. Thank you for your time and attention. God Bless America."

With that, the President turned to his right and walked off stage, hands in fists by his side. Harper and the communications team followed him out the door. Our room was silent for a few minutes, but soon started to buzz with whispers of opinions and commentary on what we had just seen. Sophie whispered she wanted to talk to Larry and would come back to check on me in a few minutes. The air was somber and tense. I found a chair along the corner of the room right next to the television and slunk down. For some reason, seeing the conference had not only made me more frightened than ever before about our next steps, but it had also caused me to feel a pang of missing James and my old life. I knew better than to admit that to anyone in the room out loud and I was ashamed for having the feelings. My face must have revealed my struggle because Mila and Terrance, two of our high level IT workers, were standing nearby and walked over to sit down next to me.

"You ok, Anna?" Mila asked gently.

I nodded yes but didn't say anything, afraid I would start to cry.

"I'm sure it's hard, to see those people on screen. I'm grateful you are here now, Anna," Mila said kindly.

I offered a teary smile of gratitude in response.

"Have you been able to get any information about your husband?" Terrance asked.

"Nope. Not a thing. I asked Laura for updates from the outside but it is like he became a ghost. I have no idea where he is ... or if he is ok," I replied.

Mila and Terrance nodded in understanding.

"Are you having second thoughts about participating?" Terrance asked curiously and I noticed him glance at Mila with concern as he asked the question.

I closed my eyes for a second and did what I had over the last several weeks each time I got scared. I thought of some of the faces in the academies. I opened my eyes before responding.

"No. No. I don't have second thoughts," I confirmed.

Mila nodded, glancing back at Terrance, and I noticed she rolled her eyes a bit at Terrance as if she was annoyed at what he had asked me. I glanced back to the television where the special report had ended. No one had turned the screen off and the station picked back up in the middle of an old interview with Laurel North on the Unity Media television station. It has been a long time since I heard Laurel's nasal and shrill voice. Terrance and Mila turned to the screen as well as we heard the host ask Laurel about her father.

"Well you know", Laurel responded to the question she had been asked, "My daddy was a product of a farming family and, being forever the farmer, he always used to remind me "Laurel, being rich is not enough, you have to know how to manipulate the soil."

I noticed Mila roll her eyes again, but this time at the screen, before she sharply said out loud, "So I guess we're her soil?"

"Nope," Terrance replied confidently with a smirk, "I think she and her friends are about to learn that we're the grassroots. After all, things tend to grow when you manipulate the soil enough."

Chapter Twenty-Nine

On the night of March 30th, the night before the March, I was the most nervous I had ever been. I knew that we would be traveling to the west side of Manhattan somewhere near Central Park in the morning. I also knew what some of the overall goals of the protest were from the planning meetings. We planned to storm different facilities and spread more pamphlets of information to the masses that were expected to come, pushing for further coordinated protests and organization. The primary goal was motivating even more people to protest going forward. The March was scheduled to be the first of several Marches, almost a nonstop schedule, as long as bodies would hold out. Sophie had informed me that the other details of my specific participation would be relayed to me on our way to the March. Apparently there had been some continued internal disagreement about how "public" of a role I should play that day.

Among the many things I was thinking about as I laid in my bed the night before, I thought about the fact that

I would see Manhattan for the first time since the day before I was taken to the CEP. The last time I had been in Manhattan, at least above ground, was the night before my high school graduation. Lowe and I had gone into the city together to celebrate by walking around Times Square, snacking on our favorite street foods while we looked at the signs and the lights. We had wanted to do something special and Manhattan was always special. It was even special A.E., although it was so drastically changed A.E. The electronic billboards of Times Square at the time we were graduating from high school advertised very different things than they had when I was a younger kid. Given Party Guidelines, there were more military recruitment ads versus clothing ads with scantily clad models. Some of the large retail establishments had been filled with churches or other Party related establishments. Despite all of the changes, there was still something magical about being in the shine of Times Square

If you grew up in New York City, it didn't matter what borough you grew up in, you were a city kid. Brooklyn was home and I loved my neighborhood, but there was always something seductive about Manhattan. It smelled different and felt different, the energy in the air was magnetic. When I was small, we would travel into Manhattan for some doctors' appointments or occasional social gatherings with family friends, like birthday parties for cousins, including Sophie who lived downtown near the Village. We would meet up with family friends who had kids for occasional holiday picnics in Central Park or to celebrate birthdays, where we would literally run in the grass of places like the East Meadow as the sun would beat down on us for hours, before we would collapse on a picnic blanket and enjoy a hot dog or soft ice cream from the carts and trucks that would station themselves at the park border.

On special occasions, we would travel into Manhattan to get the best smoked salmon from our favorite shop on the Upper East Side. Of course, as life changed A.E., we travelled less and less frequently into Manhattan not only because my mother had to work more, especially after my father walked out, but because we had less money to enjoy the treats we would get there. As I laid in bed, I remembered telling my mother than I missed Manhattan when we hadn't been there in a while. She looked sad for a moment but, as with most moments where she started to show sadness, she quickly turned stoic before replying "that's the benefit and burden of Manhattan, it gets in your bones."

I fell asleep, eventually, but it must not have been until the wee hours of the morning. I woke up exhausted when my alarm went off, before the sun came up, but full of even more adrenaline than I felt the night I left James. I got dressed in the protest clothes that were suggested for all of us, put on the bullet proof vest I was told was necessary for me to wear, and grabbed the mask I had been given to carry with me in the event we were gassed or sprayed. I walked over to the crib and looked down at Charlie. I thought about waking him, but decided against it because I wanted the motivation to see him awake again to remain in the back of my mind. All safe houses, including the Treehouse, were going on full lockdown after we left for the protest and I had been informed that I would be returned to a different safe house after the March until I could be safely returned to the Treehouse.

I quietly opened the door to my room and expected to find Eva waiting to watch Charlie as we had planned. Instead of seeing Eva, Mrs. Rhodes and Gus were leaning against the wall across the hallway from my door. My lip started to quiver and Mrs. Rhodes immediately rushed towards me and we embraced.

"Of course, I will take care of him, Anna," Mrs. Rhodes said tenderly as she hugged me.

"Tell him I love him so much," I replied.

Mrs. Rhodes backed away, visibly upset. I nodded at Gus and started to walk to the central conference room as he trailed me. Although central and most of the hallways Gus ushered me through were packed with people in various states of dress getting ready to leave, all with masks either in their hand or tied to their pants, there was almost no one talking – no sound. The air was thick with the enormity of what was about to happen.

Sophie and Larry walked towards me as Sophie was pulling her hair off her face and into a ponytail.

"Ready?" she asked me.

I nodded.

Larry and Sophie embraced quickly, but intensely. Sophie backed away, blew Larry a kiss with her fingers touching her lips, and nodded at Gus and the group of two additional security guards that had joined our small group. I followed Gus out of the Treehouse traveling the same basement corridors I had travelled to arrive at the Treehouse the first night. I couldn't believe I was going outside.

When we got to the lobby, a temporary hallway (like those at construction sites) had been set up between the service elevator vestibule and the front door of the building. Gus got on a radio as we walked down the hidden hallway and uttered "motion." As we walked out the glass front door of the building, outside air hit my nasal passages and I took a deep breath like I hadn't in a long time. Over the past several months, I had participated in the minimal outdoor time we were allowed for health reasons under a canopy in an alley that had small cracks for some sun and air, but there was no view of anything other than alley bricks when we did that. In an instant, a van pulled up, the side door flung open and a guard in the van motioned for us to get inside. Gus practically shoved me down the last few feet of the hallway and threw me across the middle seat of the van.

We slowly pulled away and I couldn't help but be glued to the window, taking in what I saw in the city. It looked like a different place. Most things were boarded up. The residential awnings still lined the streets like I remembered, but most storefronts were boarded up. Party slogans and ads were on every bus stop at every corner. My gawking was interrupted by Sophie.

"Ok, Anna. Here is the deal," Sophie started to explain,
the goal is to walk all the way from 68th on the west side up to 86th and then cross 86th to the east and head to the Mayor's mansion. Since the Party has had control of the mayor's mansion since they ordered that there would no longer be any mayors or local leaders apart from governors and local Party leaders, we are going to try to take it back today. It's going to require rushing it and we want as many people inside as possible while we try to build a broader perimeter around it, if we make it that far.

I gulped at her mention of "making it that far."

There is a park next to the Mayor's mansion and if we get you into the park, there is a sewer top on the ground that we plan to open up. You will have a detail surrounding you while Gus drops you in and no one will see you disappear into the ground. Another detail will be waiting for you underground and will get you to the new safe house. The underground paths have been planned and tested for months," Sophie informed me calmly.

I nodded.

"We want you to be noticed at the mayor's house before we get you out of there. We think it will be extremely motivating for so many people to see you in person there and spread the word so they know the PSA's that have been running where you explain why you defected are real and not fake video.

"The PSA's...," I asked in a bit of shock, "they've been running. I thought we couldn't figure out how..."

"Oh yes, they've been running for sure, a hell of a lot more than we ever expected to accomplish. It turns out Laura was able to call in that favor after all. And I think you'll be shocked at the difference you made, Anna. I think your story and honesty has inspired even more people than we ever expected to take to the streets today based on the initial intelligence we have. If our hunch is right, I'm not sure the Party will know what to do with the numbers that are expected to take to the streets today across the country."

I had filmed a series of ten short videos over the prior weeks at the Treehouse. I told my story in short bursts describing how my childhood had changed A.E, that I ended up in a CEP, and how I wound up working at the White House. In the last video, I shared why I left the White House after visiting the academies. Each video started the same way.

"Hi, I'm Anna. I know you think you know me, but I'm here to tell you my real story. If anyone knows what we are up against when it comes to the Party, it is me..."

The process of filming the videos had been difficult and emotional for me, but when the camera turned on, I was clear and did the job at hand, like I was well trained to do. My shock at hearing from Sophie that the videos had aired was interrupted when the van came to an abrupt stop.

"Time to move," Gus said plainly, "put your mask on until we read the air." With that command, Gus pulled his mask on and took out what appeared to be some kind of a sensor that Sophie had informed me he would use to register any chemicals that the Party might release into the crowd.

My stomach jumped into my throat. I nodded, quickly put my mask on inched down the middle seat behind Gus and got out of the van. In an instant, I was surrounded by the security guards, basically blocking my body in a circle so almost no one could see my five foot six frame inside of them. I looked up and saw the street sign for 68th Street. We proceeded to move, in a tight circle, walking down the block, two of the guards with hands my back and shoulders, Gus in front. The first thing I noticed as we approached Central Park West were the huge crowds already there. All I saw were heads for what felt like miles, tightly packed together and wearing masks. Although we had gas masks, I noticed most people were only wearing the national Party issued standardized cloth masks that citizens were only legally allowed to wear while carrying a doctor's note with them. Following the Cov-19 Pandemic, sick people were encouraged to mask with any kind of virus symptoms, but only for a temporary period of time while symptomatic with a doctor's note to prove the need for masking, so they couldn't avoid being identified on the Party's national facial recognition technology by wearing a mask.

A human path had been formed to allow us to walk straight down 68th to Central Park West. Sophie was in front of Gus leading the way. It was clear the entire human chain making a path for us had been planned meticulously. I knew from attending planning meetings that the detail with which the March had been planned was impressive. However, I had not been privy to all of the plans related to my role. As for the people forming the human chain, it suddenly occurred to me how odd it was that I would never know who they were, despite all they were doing to protect me, their backs turned to me and most wearing all black and masks that prevented me from seeing their faces.

I heard Sophie shout, "This way...the next spot for her is over here."

The hum and noise of the people packed on Central Park West was loud. Many had pots and pans they were banging. I could feel the body heat from all of the people, despite the cool temperature outside. The path of backs was tighter around us as we got onto Central Park West, as if it was tougher for the human chain around me to maintain a boundary given the press of the crowd.

"On it," Gus shouted to Sophie.

Rather suddenly, I was rushed down the rest of the path to another waiting group where I was slipped inside a larger circle of people with their backs to me. I'm not sure in all my life I had ever experienced more of a nervous adrenaline rush. The nerves in my stomach soared out of control and pulsed through my veins, dwarfing any butterflies I had ever experienced in my life.

"What now?" I screamed over the roar of the crowd.

"Wait for it, Anna. We start marching soon. We have a plan," Sophie shouted over the noise, "hang in there for a few more, it's ok. We've got you."

Sophie's words were not much comfort to my nerves, although my heart heard them loud and clear. I looked up to the sky, the only place I could see anything other than bodies near me and I noticed how gray and smoky it seemed, it must have rained a lot the day before. As my eyes scanned the trees next, I couldn't believe what I saw. People were peeking out from every tree, the branches of the trees above us full of bodies. I saw one man with his feet on a branch and his back propped against a nearby lamppost pointing out where Party police were running to and screaming the information to the crowd.

"We're on the move," I heard Gus say. I was somewhat smashed at this point given the security blanketed around me, in the middle of the masses. The larger circle that had insulated me on the sidelines tightened up around Gus and the rest so I had two layers of protection.

As we continued moving towards the Mayor's house, I remember everything that followed after in slow motion. There were screams, cries, chants, horns, and even more banging noises. I saw signs and messages on posters that I could sometimes read in passing. There were pictures of children on posters, and I knew that they must be kids that had been taken away to academies. I could feel the heat of the people around me. I could see sticks coming down from the sky only a few bodies away from me as we pressed uptown. I could hear thuds and I knew it was likely the sticks of Party police making contact with body parts. I heard screams for help. It was hard to breathe given how crowded it was. Sweat drenched every ounce of my body. I just kept moving forward, one step, after another step, after another. In that moment, I was just one body, dust from the street at my feet, present to be counted.

Eventually, we made it into the former Mayor's house. I was asked to stand up and talk. So with help from Gus and some others, I stood up on a chair and I spoke on a megaphone to a group of more battered protestors that I could count, all of us crammed into a room with walls colored robin's egg blue. And, with those words on that day, from that moment on in my life, I started nodding a lot less, and spoke a lot more.

Chapter Thirty

We lost a lot of people on March 31st and during the two years of nonstop protest and fighting after the first March. I now liken the "blurriness" of my memories of those two years to how women forget the exact pain of childbirth, although the intensity of the experience permanently changes you forever and never fades. I guess comparing what happened in the years after the March to a birth is appropriate in more ways than one because, following those years, a new America was born. Over the next several decades, American was rebuilt into a more perfect democracy because while the nation was rebuilt, for the first time in human history, *democratic technology* was created. Our new markets were truth and equitably sharing resources, with the assistance of this new form of technology. And even though technology wasn't restricted anymore as it had been during my early life, people respected using it in a different and more profound way.

Like so many others, I was weary from the horrors and brutality of the process we had been through. The experience had required the level of adrenaline someone needs to run from a predator for several years straight, no days off. Of course, this level of intensity was completely unnatural, but it was necessary. I knew my scars, and the scars of so many others who suffered in the process we had to go through, would never disappear.

After that first March I attended and the many other Marches that took place after it, our ranks multiplied in numbers we did not expect. As it turned out, the sight of so many of us being brutalized, but continuing to stand arm in arm in disobedience was enough to cause more and more people, some even strongly affiliated with the Party, to step out and fight with us. Some of our biggest supporters, including benefactors like Laura, remained hidden for longer so they could help even more behind the scenes once the real leadership transition began that got the Party out of the White House, and fully out of power. Three former living Presidents formed a tribunal to lead the country until a new free and fair election took place. I learned later that former Presidents and high-level government intelligence officials had begun planning, almost immediately A.E., how they would help restore democracy if their worst fears about the Party and the President wound up to be true. It didn't hurt that there were also many people in the Party and the White House that secretly worked with the Network. As it turns out, the fact that the same painting appeared in Laura's hallway and outside of Harper's office was not an accident.

There were spans of time I had to go into hiding during the two years following the first March and Charlie and I moved to different safe houses a few times. Eventually, when the Presidential Tribunal helped put a temporary congress and judiciary in place, I was back out in the sunlight (with my actual hair color) and with G still by my side for a while until things felt more secure. I was fortunate to be involved in liberation day at several academies, but it wasn't a quick or easy process. For starters, scant records had been kept on the identity of the children shipped to academies which made reuniting families extremely difficult. And, of course, the children were not returning home in the same condition they had left having been so traumatized, tortured, and medicated. We had an entire generation of broken kids, and the process of unwinding what had been done would turn out to be a major challenge for the next several generations of citizens.

A number of individuals who had done some of the most heinous work for the Party, including many of my former colleagues at the White House as well as ordinary people who had become local leaders in various jurisdictions, were imprisoned for their crimes against humanity. Both Laurel North and the President were among those imprisoned. On one Tuesday afternoon, at my request, I was transported to a New York City prison and buzzed in through several gates to visit someone who I had learned had become a high level local leader in Brooklyn, New York for the Party. As I walked through the last gate and she came into view, it occurred to me that she did not look as changed by years as so many others from my past had.

"Anna?" she whispered and immediately started to sob as she walked towards me. "I can't believe it's you."

A second later, I was being embraced by Lowe in the same way she had hugged me so often when we were kids. I let her hold me for a second before gently backing away from her embrace.

"Let's sit down." I suggested pointing to the long plastic folding table that was in the center of the room with a few chairs on each side. She nodded, wiping away snot and tears on each side of her face with her forearms.

We stared at each other for a few moments. She offered me a hopeful and tiny smile at one point during our silence, while I sat stone faced with sadness. Eventually, I found one word.

"Why?"

She fidgeted and waited a few minutes before responding.

"Do you think I really had a choice, Anna? Is it really so hard for you to imagine that I didn't really have any choice in order to survive? I mean considering some of the things you went through, I would think that you would understand, but I guess the fact that I am in here is proof that understanding only flows in a one way direction, right?"

I noticed the anger and indignation in her voice continuing to rise as she continued to respond to me.

"I mean, it was kill or be killed. That's it. Not complicated. I certainly ended up in a position I did not expect. But I did what had to be done. You are not the only one with a child and a family. And once River took on a big role with the local Party leadership, our fate working for them was sealed. What was I supposed to do, leave my family? Go hungry? Walk away from my entire support network? Not all of us were lucky enough to have the Network rescue us," she said putting up air quotes when she referenced the Network.

Hearing her mention River brought me back to the day when she tried to get his dad to rehire me that summer. The memory of that moment made me instantly remember all of the love I had for my best friend and I choked up. I stood up from the table and walked to a corner in the room with my arms crossed and faced the wall so she wouldn't see me cry, unsure of what to say next.

"It's complicated, Anna. You know that," Lowe begged in a whisper from where she was still seated at the table, "I watched you on television and saw you in the papers and the ads you appeared in. I saw the glamorous pictures of your wedding and saw so many pictures of you while you worked in the White House in the perfect clothes, with the expensive shoes, and blown out hair. I saw the picture of you and your husband and baby splashed across the news when he was born. I know if your life was half as cushy on the inside as it looked on the outside, you must have had pretty strong reasons for leaving the White House when I heard you became a "fugitive." But making decisions like you did to get out and walk away is a luxury that is not afforded to all of us."

I looked back over towards where she was sitting, orange jumpsuit and tears staining her face and all I could feel was sorrow. For a second, it felt like we were back in my room, as kids, figuring something out together. The truth was, nothing she said surprised me.

"Did you ever have the chance to change? Any chance, at all? Was there ever a fork where you could have chosen to act in another way? Was there any moment, Lowe? Any?"

The tone in my voice as I asked her the question was nothing short of pleading with her.

And almost as quickly as I asked the question, I knew the answer. Lowe looked down at her hands and didn't respond. And I knew enough to know that her answer was that there had been at least one moment where she had a choice to do something better, and had not. Like so many others, she could pinpoint at least one point where the opportunity presented itself to reject the Party and she hadn't. And it's not that rejecting darkness just once makes the end of a story different, but in some way doing so, at least once, proves goodness. Little packets of energy create light and, similarly, it is the individual decisions we make that have the capacity to create the greatest glow of good.

I stood there for a minute more while she remained silent, looking at the top of her head sitting at the table. We were two girls from the same neighborhood with completely different endings --- this fact being both completely understandable and making no sense at the same time. The two of us, and so many others, all pieces of the same American puzzle.

Epilogue

I have been thinking about what to write in this letter for a while. I always knew the job was temporary and so, I suppose, I always knew I would need to come up with some parting words. Deciding what to write in this letter as I finally put pen to paper took me through a series of flashbacks over the last eight years. In these flashbacks, I see glimpses and pictures in my mind of many moments, each moment important, even the small ones. In some, I am on planes high above the ground traveling from place to place in the wide and still varied world. In others, I am on the ground shaking hands and offering an embrace when I sense one is needed, without hesitation. In my most cherished memories, I am speaking to some of our smallest citizens that visit the White House — reminded by their presence that at some point the "game" stops being about us and starts only being about them, our primary purpose being to leave behind a better world for those who we are trustees of it for.

You won't be able to manufacture these moments in any way during your time as President, they happen upon you. As a protector, the needs of everyone around you, many stretching out their hand as you drive by them in a motorcade, will impress upon you the true weight of all you have been asked to do, and of all the people you have been asked to lead. So, you put one foot in front of the other every day knowing that you were called to do this job by important forces. You become a vessel of goodness and light and your day to day routine becomes formulaic in that sense. After all, becoming a vessel of goodness and light is the only approach any person with the privilege of doing this job should take to the only position of leadership that has ever mattered in this world to the entire world, the leader of the United States of America, a country that is finally back to being, although permanently changed and scarred, freer.

I can't imagine what my mother would say, if she were still here, witnessing a woman be elected President of the United States. I would not have predicted that I would wind up sitting in this office. I certainly never could have predicted the awakening that led me here or what happened in my life following that first March. I hope she would be proud of me and the work that I have done. I still grieve for the relationship we never had that simply wasn't possible in the world she was born into. I hope that the work I have done as President honors the obstacles of poverty and lack of choice that she, and so many like her, could never overcome.

Like me, I know you will continue to reflect on the process that brought you to this office as you lead. Understanding how and why you got here, and what led you here, is the key to doing the job properly, and respectfully. It is most importantly your charge to instill the principle in every citizen that not one of us willed ourselves to be, or had any control over who, what, and where we were born. This charge has even more added weight and meaning now after what our country has overcome, and this principle is why we must always fight for equality. History tells us that we will face other grave challenges to our democracy in the future – that fact is certain -- for that is the cycle of light and dark that we live in. Do everything in your power to make us stronger so, as a country, we are better prepared for the future moments when those challenges arise.

So, in conclusion, I wish you wind under your wings and I leave this letter for you, our second female President. I hope you are pleased to find it on top of this desk, ever resolute.

Anna, Number ____.

CPSIA information can be obtained
at www.ICGtesting.com
Printed in the USA
BVHW030904051220
594961BV00023B/198